11 WA

11
WARTEN WAY

BY T W PETTET

To Chris
Glad you enjoyed
the book

Conies Pettet

11 Warten Way
© Tania Pettet, 2025

Published by Tania Pettet
ISBN: 978-1-0369-0554-5

Book design by Barış Şehri
https://sehribookdesign.com

This book is dedicated to and inspired by my grandparent's stories. Bill and Ersilia, who, despite the harsh times of war, found love, laughter and hope.

We are the D-Day Dodgers,
Out in Italy,
Always on the vino,
Always on the spree.
Eighth Army skivers and their tanks,
We go to war in ties like swanks.
For we are the D-Day Dodgers,
In sunny Italy.

Hamish Henderson, 8th Army
soldier, Italian front, 1944

Chapters

1

Without Mamma

"*Octavia Ma che staje faccen'? O ppane?*"

Her father's shadow cast across the door of the crypt. He spoke to her in Neapolitan dialect. Picking out one of his favoured proverbs.

"No, I am not making bread," Ottie muttered.

The crypt's air cloaked itself around her, seeping its dampness into her bones. She had no cause to repine her pain, it was beyond physical. She traced each letter engraved into the simple stone: *Nella Matanti*. In time, Mamma's bones would be dug from the crypt's earth, cleaned and placed with her lineage overlooking the mountains. Ottie picked up her brother's photograph, illuminated by the candle placed on their mother's grave. His strong, handsome face, framed by thick blond hair—a rare colour for their kin—stared back at her. She kissed the picture. *We will find you, brother. I promise, Mamma, we will find Marcello.*

The letter Mamma had written to the Pope remained unanswered. His family knew only that his ship was hit en route to Montenegro. He was assumed dead, a casualty of war. By fate, Marcello had sailed a week later than intended after taking leave to marry Anna, his teenage sweet-heart. That was nine months ago. Three months later, Mamma was dead.

Poor Mamma, Marcello was the fifth of her eleven children she had outlived. He was her firstborn son, the only one of her dead brood to reach adulthood before death visited him. The only one she hadn't held at the moment of passing. Ottie had been a spectator when her baby brother Angelo had died. Angelic as his namesake, the little toddler cradled in Mamma's arms let go serenely. The relentless fever left him weak, and he fell into a slumber from which he never emerged. In the warm glow of the fire, his face appeared peaceful, almost as if he were sleeping, but the sharp cessation of his breath, the sudden stillness of his chest, betrayed the reality of his passing. His cherubic face, encased by dark ringlets, remained as beautiful in death as it had been in life.

"Octavia! Tavi! Andiamo! Vai!" Papa's voice echoed into the crypt, more insistent now.

There was an undeniable authority in Signore Renzo Matanti's voice, demanding attention that could not be dismissed. He had been unusually patient, and Ottie didn't dare to overstretch his goodwill. She hastily brushed out the grit that had embedded in her knees and ascended the uneven stone steps into the day's heat. Ottie shielded her eyes from the sun's glare and the disapproval in her father's eyes. He clasped at her elbow in a bid for her to quicken her step. His voice was as powerful as his stride.

"Your brother has waited long enough."

Papa half dragged her across the dusty cemetery path, quickening his pace as they neared the ornate arches of its entrance. Ottie noticed her brother, Geno, through the railings, his legs stretched across the horse cart's carriage, a cigarette idly hanging from his lips, his face hidden by the battered fedora angled on his head in a bid to obscure the sun's rays. His posture quickly changed when he noticed their fast approach. He sat upright, removed his cigarette, straightened his hat and took the horse's reins, ready for action.

"Make sure, Gennaro. You watch her get on the army truck," Papa commanded, lifting Ottie onto the back of the cart.

He slapped his hand hard onto the horse's rear, and the cart sprung forward. Ottie watched her father's stocky frame disappear as the horse bolted away. The cart's wooden wheels made for a bumpy, tumultuous ride. Conversation with her brother over the din was impossible as they descended the winding, tree-dappled road close to the mountain's edge. Not that she could persuade Geno to go against her father's orders. No one went against Papa. She touched her lip—it still felt tender from the backhand slap he'd given her when she questioned his decision to send her to work for the British Army. Papa thought Ottie mourned excessively, spending hours in her mother's crypt. It wasn't healthy, he'd decided. Sending her to work would fix it and bring in much-needed money.

They reached Vietri, the old fishing port where the truck was due to arrive, sooner than Ottie would have liked. She had already resigned herself to her fate and jumped from the cart before Geno had time to help. He had been delayed, fussing with his hair and then replacing his hat for the benefit of two passing signorinas, their appreciative smiles momentarily distracting him. Ottie caught him staring at the women. She rolled her eyes at him, and he reciprocated.

"How does Carlotta put up with you?" Ottie questioned.

Geno lowered his head until his eyes met Ottie's. His warm brown eyes glinted with mischief.

"She is lucky to have me." His words paused, his tone turning serious. "Sometimes, Tavi, you need to appreciate what you have in your life instead of what you have lost."

The moment of seriousness that replaced Geno's typical merriment was fleeting.

"Our country will get through this war, and Fatty," Ottie smirked at the nickname for Mussolini, the pompous dictator tightening his grip on their homeland - "will step down, we'll rebuild this beautiful part of Italy. Then, I promise, then, I will make a wife out of Carlotta. But right now, you need to get on that."

Geno gestured to the harbour's edge, where the khaki truck haloed by the sun's haze had shuddered to a halt. An ensemble of workers had descended ant-like into its opened door. From the cart, he retrieved a neatly wrapped parcel and handed it to her. It was her lunch, made by their eldest sister, Rufina, the matriarch of the family. As he did so, Geno noticed another British Army truck pull up nearby. Weary from their travels, the soldiers disembarked. The young men stretched their stiff muscles and set their sights on the nearest bar. Their desires were simple: a cold beer, women's company, and a haircut, before returning to their duties.

Soldiers needing haircuts equalled money to Geno. He was a skilled barber and could swiftly cut his way through this group. His wallet felt unusually light, a consequence of his bad luck at the card table the night before. By late morning, he hoped to get his hands on some illicit coffee, or perhaps even chocolate, from the British. He should visit Carlotta to make amends for once again breaking his promise of a romantic evening with her. He believed his gifts, acquired on the black market, would sway her. Pushing aside the fleeting pang of guilt, he headed towards his shop.

Ottie jumped onto the truck as its engine revved, and the doors closed. The wooden bench seats were crowded with workers, mostly women. A kind face moved aside to accommodate her. Ottie staggered across towards the available space, using heads and shoulders as props to prevent her from falling as the vehicle sped away.

The camp was near Positano, about an hour's ride along the coast. The shorter routes were bomb-damaged, the land scarred by war. Southern Italy had taken the lion's share of the damage as the Allies marched from the beaches and pushed the Nazis back into Europe.

A cordial and, at times, unruly mix of Brits, Americans, Canadians, Australians, and New Zealanders had replaced the German soldiers - who were on the whole polite and orderly individuals. Ottie's territory remained untouched by the feared Moroccan and Russian soldiers who fought on the Allied side. The partisans concealed in the mountains had reported harrowing stories about how these soldiers had mistreated women, and she remained thankful that she had not encountered them. Soldiers were always best avoided. Given respect but kept at a distance. Father had drummed such advice into her, yet here he was, sending her into the midst of the British Army camp. The shift in his scruples had not escaped her.

Italy felt more settled now, and for that, she was grateful. Ottie's thoughts drifted to the nights they'd hidden in the mountains during the bombings, waiting for the signal that it was safe. She and her sisters huddled in makeshift shelters, praying for the attacks to end. Towards the end, Ottie had stopped seeking cover, resigned to whatever fate awaited. Instead, she sat with her siblings in a crescent-shaped formation around their dying mother's bed. Her mother was too ill to be moved. The alabaster Jesus on the crucifix above Mamma's bed stood out against the dark wood of the cross. The bedroom window was draped with blackout curtains, creating a dark refuge, and the family huddled together, their faces illuminated by the flickering candlelight, electricity a luxury they rarely enjoyed.

One bomb fell so close to the house that it shattered glass from the windows and shook the pictures off the walls. Ornaments crashed to the floor, and the bomb shunted Mamma's bed to the centre of the room. The family coughed and spluttered while the dust settled, a linear fog slowly dropping towards the floor until they had sight of each other again. Mamma, amongst the chaos, covered in a fine layer of dust and glass shards, remained motionless, bar the gentle rise and fall of her abdomen that disturbed the fallen debris on her bed with each shallow breath.

Mamma passed away that week as Italy's liberation peeked its head around the corner. War did not claim her life; it was life itself that dealt the final blow. Her body succumbed to the many pregnancies and miscarriages. She had worked herself to the bone and suffered under the oppressive hand of her husband. Surrounded by her loving family amidst the usual chaos, Mamma peacefully passed away that night. The house fell silent as the undertaker came and took Mamma away, leaving a void that felt impossible to fill. Papa at once moved Ottie and her two sisters, Rufina and Naria, into Mamma's still-warm bed, where the imprint from her body remained on the mattress. They had been sleeping in the bakery's back room, taking turns to be near her as she lay dying. The brothers shared the only other room in the cramped attic space.

Papa would often return home in the early hours and fall asleep on the chair or wherever he fell after another drinking session. To attend to Mamma, the girls would have to creep from the back room past him in his deep slumber, not wanting to be the one to catch his eye flick open. His capricious demeanour and reaction to being woken depended on the previous night's events. Nights without luck in betting or boxing were more ominous than returning from a night with a mistress. Papa never forgot a promised beating. Sometimes Mamma hid them, and other times Fina, with her determined, bespectacled, elfin face, would step in his path, always acting as a protector. Papa respected her resilient spirit and would never harm his children in such a circumstance.

Instead, he muttered, "*Non dimenticherò*, give it time."

And, on that day or the next, he would deliver his punishment when the opportunity presented itself. He always kept his word.

The truck bumped along the uneven road towards Positano. Ottie pressed her forehead against the cool glass, gazing out at the patchwork of vineyards. Workers with large wicker baskets strapped to their backs looked like giant snails in the distance. She thought of Alberto on his farm.

Her father had betrothed her to Alberto Orsini when she was sixteen. He admired the Orsini family, seeing mutual benefits in the union. The Orsinis, a farming family, had supplied the Matanti bakery for years. The businesses, previously successful, were now barely surviving. Papa had noticed the attraction between Ottie and Alberto and had encouraged it. He allowed Ottie, Octavia, his eighth child named by him, to go out for an evening's *passeggiata* with Alberto, accompanied by one of her brothers.

Papa had been relieved when Mussolini's grip on Italy weakened, and the Allies arrived. With sagacity, he wisely remained silent, evading attention and the control of the Blackshirts. He understood the greater forces and chose his battles with care. The Fascist Party ruled with an iron fist and expected complete subservience from its people. He had witnessed the punishment inflicted upon the townsfolk who publicly expressed their dissatisfaction with the state. The Blackshirts brought these mutineers in line through public humiliation, by forcing them to drink an entire bottle of castor oil so they would suffer from chronic diarrhoea or forcing them to eat a live toad. Castor oil, the most popular choice of torture, was now scarce and required for military planes. With that option removed, the punishments had become more brutal, no doubt influenced by Mussolini's restoration of the death penalty.

Papa kept his resistance low-key. On one occasion, the Blackshirts paid him an unannounced visit after being informed that his children had not been seen at the Fascist Balilla and Vanguard youth group meetings. Papa had calmly welcomed them into his home. The soldiers had been polite and removed their fezzes on entering the Matanti home. One of the trio, the eldest of the group, had shown a keen interest in Mina with her long auburn hair and lofty elegance. Papa quickly sent her into the kitchen with an invented chore. He had woefully informed the young men how impoverished he had become, how he could ill afford the uniforms required for his many children to attend the youth meetings and that they were needed to work in his bakery as he had no money to employ any help. He showed them his meagre stores and let the men greedily take the few warm loaves Mamma had baked that day. They had left in good spirits, having drunk the family's supply of homemade limoncello, now comrades-in-arms offering to find second-hand uniforms for the family. They returned Papa's Roman salute in a tipsy fashion as they sauntered down the road. Fortunately, they failed to keep their promise to return, and they did not discover the partisan seeking refuge in the basement.

The serpentine road threaded along the Amalfi coast with hairpin bends dipping into tunnels carved out from the mountains, speckled with the pastel hues of bougainvillaea blooms and the scent of citrus trees. The air in the truck was stuffy and not so sweet. Ottie felt alone, and she missed her younger sister.

Naria was always a fun distraction. Ottie recalled the time they had escaped from the house, squeezing their slight frames out via the little pantry window. They ran, not stopping until they reached the land at the mountain's edge. There, the modest little church of Santa Maria

Maddalena stood with an oversized cross at its apex facing out towards the ocean. They jumped and whooped and shouted up towards the twilight sky at the planes heading towards them. From the sienna-hued skyline, the plane's gentle hum grew into a roar as the formation approached. "*La libertà!*" they shouted up to their allies.

The reaction returned from the skies was not an expected one: bullets flew as the girls stumbled and crashed to the ground for shelter. Ottie found refuge behind a boulder. She heard a sharp whistle pierce the air and, seconds later, an explosion as the bomb hit the ground. The explosion propelled parts of the ancient church across the sky. The planes passed into the distance and left behind a moment's silence before the little church crumbled and rolled down the mountainside towards the sea.

"*Nari, dove sei!*" Ottie yelled as she scrambled to her knees, shaking the debris from her hair.

She desperately tried to call out, but fear had stolen her voice, leaving only a hollow silence in its wake. Her hands formed the sign of the *malocchio* to ward away the evil spirits' presence she felt surrounding her in the headwind that was forcing her back from the falling church. Ottie caught the redness of Naria's dress speckled through the foliage a few yards away. She ran across the rugged terrain and fell onto the prone figure.

"Nari, wake up," Ottie pleaded.

Naria groaned, pushing against her sister's grip as she regained consciousness. They stared at each other in shock before breaking into raucous laughter. Their hearts hammered in their chests, the adrenaline surging through their veins as they breathed a sigh of relief at their near escape. The sisters looked a pitiful sight covered in the mountain's underbelly. They could not conceal their clandestine activities when they returned home. They were thankful to be alive and didn't mind what punishment their parents gave them.

Ottie slipped back from her daydreams into reality, realising the truck was at a standstill, waiting to cross the army base's checkpoint. She recognised that the fight was far from over, this was merely the beginning of a new kind of battle.

2

The End

How does that happen? How can years of history be wiped in a moment?

The house had been stripped back to its bare bones. Fi wandered from room to room, her footsteps echoing into the cold emptiness, competing with the rhythmic sound of her heart in her ears. In each room, she paused, lightly placing a hand on the wall. A gentle "thank you" trailed from her lips as she closed her eyes, letting memories flood back. She inhaled the room's dormant air and familiar smell, sweet with the essence of old carpets. Dust particles danced in a stream of sunlight, jolted into action by her movement.

Memories overwhelmed Fi's aching head, too many to count. A wave of emotion drew her towards the heart of the home: the kitchen. The house seemed to reverberate, emitting its familiar creaks and groans. The kitchen, devoid of clutter, looked austere and silent. Everyday utensils were long gone, yet their silhouettes remained imprinted against the yellowing walls. The enamel stove, once the nucleus of domesticity, now stood alone, its surface worn by years of vigorous cleaning. Fi idly traced a blackened chipped scar on the hob, recalling how her grandmother, Ottie, had once tiptoed on a stool, reaching for pans on the top shelf. The pans had clattered down, scratching her prized stove. Ottie blamed Hal for putting them in the wrong order — meddling where he shouldn't have. Gentle Hal: damned if he did, damned if he didn't. A smile entered Fi's soul, recalling her grandfather.

Fi sifted through layers of memory, visualising the meals, the laughter, the arguments, the people, and the years that had passed. The heady scents of cooking had once permeated the house from six every morning when Ottie started her day. The noisy clanging of pots and pans had irritated Fi in her youth, making her burrow deeper under the duvet, savouring the clean linen smell. Lie-ins were impossible with Ottie around. As a teenager, frantic vacuuming outside her bedroom door thwarted her wish to sleep in.

The tiny galley kitchen stood at the back of the house, a typical layout for semi-detached homes built in the thirties. Most of the day, it remained dark, overshadowed by its neighbour. In other homes, newcomers had knocked down the wall to the dining room, creating airy, Scandinavian-style kitchens with granite countertops and bi-folding doors leading out to flagstone patios. They made the most of the long, narrow gardens sloping down towards the train tracks. The gentle rolling of trains had always been a comforting background noise: the crowded commuter trains bound for London and those heading in the opposite direction, carrying day-trippers to the coast.

Fi moved from room to room, past events flickering through her mind, resembling old cine film. Now it had ended. The era had ended, and her world had shattered.

A hollow knock at the front door rebounded through the house. She returned to reality with a stark awareness of her surroundings in the dusty, empty house. She turned the front door's handle, well accustomed to its quirks. The door lock required specific clicks and a counter-intuitive handle turn. The door obliged and opened. Her gaze met the rotund youth behind the door. He gave his fringe a self-conscious flick.

"Alright, this is eleven, right?" Impatient for a response, he continued, "Eleven Warten Way, yeah?"

"Oh, yes, sorry. I know it says one, the other one fell off, and we... well, I... I never got round to fixing it."

Fi cast an ashamed eye over the door's flaky mint-green paintwork. The youth stepped in uninvited.

"Well, love, ain't your problem no more." He chewed gum through his words, attempting a cheeky grin.

The gap his frame left from vacating the front door enabled her to take in the removal van parking outside the house. Her heart sank further. She returned her attention to the intruder, who had let out a sharp whistle and stood with his arms folded in a wide-legged stance, staring at the hallway's walls covered in indelible artwork.

"Blimey, that's some painting," he remarked.

"Yes, indeed. It was painted by my grandfather. There's plenty more throughout the house; he covered pretty much every wall."

Fi, acquainted with the paintings, contemplated the experience of viewing them for the first time. The bright colours, the thick van Gogh swirls, and the scenes and characters that were contained within them. The patterns and colours shifted with the changing light and different angles from which they were viewed. The youth swayed further along the hall, cowboy-style, his tool belt swaying with him. His gaze travelled from wall to ceiling, and he continued staring upward as if viewing the Sistine Chapel's ceiling.

"Bit of a bohemian, your grandad," he gave a wolf whistle as he glanced up the stairs and spotted Hal's magnum opus: a nude painting of a young Ottie, her long, raven-black hair draped across her breasts.

Fi called the youth back before he could intrude further. "I guess you will want these," she said, dangling the house keys in the air.

"Nah, not me. You wanna give them to Ryan from the estate agent? He's doing the exchange. Buyers are coming from France. That's where we went yesterday to pick up their gear."

He fell back on his heels to peer into the front room before returning his attention to Fi. She was conscious of the redness around her eyes, but if he noticed it, he was unaffected by her emotions.

He sniffed and said, "Right, you done, then? Best get this van backed up."

He pushed past her, swaggering off to help his mate.

"Yeah, I am done," she muttered.

As she stood in the empty hallway, she noticed the sudden aroma of aftershave cut through the dusty air. The assault on her nostrils was followed by a weak tap on the door and a polite throat clearing. Fi put her emotions away and raised her head to meet the noise, the clipboard, and then the suit that she assumed was Ryan.

"Good afternoon... Ms Bennett?" simpered Ryan.

Fi nodded and took his outstretched hand. A limp, light handshake was exchanged.

Ryan spoke speedily, a man with a mission. "Congratulations on the house sale. I'm here to collect the keys on the new buyer's behalf. They're coming from France, you know. I believe you've had word from the solicitors. The contracts were exchanged this morning."

He held his hand out, pushing for receipt of the house keys. Fi accommodated the gesture and brought the keys forward but felt compelled to hold on to them for a little longer.

"You say they are returning home from France?"

"Not quite. The buyer retired out there and wants a bolthole back in England. A bit of an investment, I believe. Trades start tomorrow, she is keen to modernise the old place."

"And rip out its soul." Fi spat out her words, unable to contain her bitterness.

Ryan, uncomfortable, busied himself with his clipboard, clearly reluctant to continue the exchange. Fi finally handed over the keys and turned away before he could respond. She couldn't fake any more pleasantries.

Keep going, don't look back. Her steps quickened as she fled from her past. Crossing the road to put distance between herself and the commotion, she glanced back once at the familiar street. Memories of the Queen's silver jubilee, when the street was decorated with balloons and bunting, flooded back as she passed the neat semi-detached houses with spring flowers raising their heads in the front gardens. Back then, the road was a community, and the people joined in celebration around pasting tables filled with typical seventies fare, fluorescent blancmanges, filled vol-au-vents and party rings. She'd worn a fairy costume, hand-made by her aunt, complete with tinfoil wings and a tinsel halo perched on her head by a proud Ottie. Her photo had made it into the local gazette, pinned to the pantry door until the sun bleached the image away. Turning onto the main road, Fi was met with the cacophony of traffic. She glanced at her phone: 12:10. She still had time to go home before starting work. She decided she needed a strong espresso.

3

The Orange Seller

Ottie emerged from the truck with the other workers. She felt sick with apprehension. This place was unlike anything she had ever seen – so many soldiers, so many vehicles. The hustle and bustle. Dark grey, industrial-looking military buildings of varying sizes surrounded the square. The ground hummed with the rumble of activity. The kind-faced lady she had sat next to on the truck touched her elbow, jolting her back into reality.

"Your first day?"

"Is it that obvious?" Ottie replied with a timorous smile.

"Come on, let's hurry up and get going. I think I know you. You're a Matanti, right? I am Annamaria, Valentina's sister. This way, I will show you where to go. The soldiers here don't take too kindly to lateness. We can get you some overalls at the stores. You'd best tie your hair up. Do you have a scarf?"

Ottie nodded her affirmation as she rolled her thick curly hair up into a polka dot headscarf, tucking her hair in at the front as they scurried across the busy square. It wasn't long before Ottie stood in front of her allocated bench, dressed in an oversized navy overall rolled up at her arms and legs—petite sizes were unavailable. Ottie was grateful for Annamaria's help. She was older than Ottie and had worked at the base for a couple of months to support her young family. Annamaria's husband had never returned from army duty in Russia. She found herself widowed with little financial aid. The job was her lifeline, and she worked as many hours as she could.

"Octavia, pack this box with the items on this list. Then package up the box and place it here to be distributed," Annamaria explained as she handed her one of the small cardboard boxes.

She pointed to the stores around the sides of the building that contained rows of shelves with different components stacked in open boxes. Ottie noted that most appeared to be metal nuts and bolts of various shapes and sizes. The building was large and functional, with a high ceiling and industrial pipes, wires, and lighting running across it. Small, grimy windows ran along each side of the building, letting in the crepuscular light. The building's structure amplified the continuous noise within, making conversation difficult. Due to its temporary nature, the building quickly became overheated or too cold, depending on the time of year.

"Whatever you do, don't make a mistake," advised Annamaria, filling up her box with just a cursory glance at her list. "Make sure you get the correct items. You'll soon get to know them. You'll be a bit slow at first, but they will expect you to speed up. If you can't work quickly, the British won't keep you on. We work until half-past twelve. Then you will hear the siren go off three times. If it's a continuous siren, this means we are under attack. But either way we down tools. We start again at one when the siren goes off, and we finish at four-thirty when the siren goes off again. You have ten minutes to get on the truck; it won't wait. Make sure you get on the right one, they all look the same, but they're not all going to Vietri."

"Thank you, Annamaria," Ottie replied, feeling overwhelmed.

"If you need to be excused, you must ask permission. The toilets—they call them latrines—are across the square. You ask one of the soldiers. They take turns supervising us." Annamaria pointed towards the open door. "That tall one is all right, and he speaks pretty good Italian. Some of the others aren't so friendly and don't understand Italian. Do you speak English?"

Ottie watched the tall soldier duck through the doorway, barely missing the frame as he removed his cap. She noticed Annamaria waiting for an answer.

"Not a word," Ottie replied.

The soldier's extraordinary height captivated her, causing her to lose track of everything around her.

***

Hal replaced his cap, allowing himself a minute for his eyes to adjust to the low light in the room. Everything seemed to be ticking over nicely. The Italians were working well. He was pleased to be on a shift in munitions today. Having just had three days' leave with his friends, he felt a little hungover. Some of his unit were heading out to Cassino today. Well, what remained of the place. He had seen it firsthand a few months before and never knew when he might be called back. Since arriving in Italy via Salerno's beaches, Hal's division had experienced several changes and re-groupings, often joining forces with the Americans. The Italian campaign wasn't proving straightforward, and Monty had left and moved on. No more bonhomie and doling out fags to the troops as he did in Africa.

Hal was glad to be away from the fighting in North Africa. Stationed there sometimes felt like being on the surface of the moon with its arenose landscape. The days were unbearably hot, and the nights ridiculously cold. At least at night, Jerry stopped dropping Stukas and firing Messerschmitt 109s on them. He didn't miss constantly listening out for tanks or aircraft approaching, the banging out of his desert boots every morning to remove any scorpions, coping with the delights of dust flies, desert sores and scabies, or the meagre diet of bully beef and tack biscuits. He soon became desert-wise, sympathetic to white-kneed newcomers unaware of the harsh conditions they would soon be facing. Lack of water, food, and intense heat, combined with the constant threat of attack, wears a man down. Reading, sketching, and the companionship of his unit were his only sources of sanity. They had become like family. Luckily, he and Stan, his best mate, had got through it, although not without a few close shaves. Seeing Stan head off to Cassino this morning had given him a pang of guilt. Being separated didn't feel right, they were part of a good team. Sadly, Jock hadn't made it back. The flashback of Jock's head being blown off whilst driving close to the salt marshes near El Alamein still haunted him in his dreams. He recalled pushing Jock's body aside so that he could drive away from the attack. It had happened so quickly: one minute, Jock was mid-sentence, and the next, he was gone.

Hal had been close to danger several times, leaving him deeply scarred. In this, he wasn't alone. Battle fatigue was not uncommon among the men, who spent months in harsh, demanding conditions. Hal endured months in the desert, with no bed, no water for washing, and barely any to drink. He had resorted to drinking contaminated water from the truck's radiator. No bathroom, not even a toilet, just a shovel and a short walk from your mates. Every day brought the threat of death and the never-ending remoteness whichever way you turned. The desert held only the certainty of space and deathly silence.

A loud bang jolted Hal, and he instinctively reached for his weapon. He gave a cursory scan of the factory floor, already knowing all was well. He noted the slight tremor in his hand and chastised himself for being jumpy. His tangled thoughts continued to unwind and flash through his mind.

Cairo had been much more vibrant and interesting. He had picked up enough Arabic whilst stationed there to get by. It proved useful in the desert, with passing traders and nomadic tribes like the Bedouin. He recalled marching along on the main desert road heading back to Tripoli where, on arrival, he had to endure a hell of a long wait before being transported to Salerno. Not enough ships to get across, typical bad planning, a balls-up, in his opinion.

On that lonely desert road, Hal noticed a hazy image on the horizon shimmering in the midday sun. The image gained clarity as Hal and his men approached. It was a man dressed in a Bedouin-style thobe of white cotton cascading to his ankles and a kufiya wrapped around his head, covering his face. Next to him was a basket full of fresh oranges for sale. The men, desperate for fresh fruit after months without tasting anything like it, eagerly ran towards the glorious sight. Hal picked up speed to keep pace. It didn't seem right. He hesitated.

"Wait up, Stan, it seems odd to me," he shouted.

"Oh, come on," Stan replied. "It's our first sight of civilisation, that's all. Tell him, Taffy, to lighten up."

Taffy faced his two mates. Being the smallest, he had to crane his neck to gaze up at Hal.

"Well, boyo. Has our Lofty gone windy?" Taffy grinned and walked towards the orange seller.

"*Kam hi alburtuqal alkhasu bik?*" shouted Hal over Taffy's head, aiming his gun at the orange seller, he repeated the question, louder this time. "How much are your oranges?"

"Hal, what are you playing at?" Stan spoke, his voice edged with impatience.

"Look at his feet, Stan, army boots. What Bedouin wears them? Get down, Taff!"

Hal fired his gun. Taffy fell to the floor as the Nazi soldier rose and started to fire, but not before Hal got his fatal shot in. Drawn by the noise, Hal's unit emerged from behind. They ran past the trio, who were catching their breath. One of the newer recruits got to the dead soldier.

"Get back!" shouted Stan. "It's a trap."

Stan dropped to the floor, clutching his head in his hands. The young lad gave a full-on smile and grabbed hungrily at the oranges. As the men dived for cover, the hidden mine tripped and blew him to pieces. The explosion from the mine projected oranges and human flesh in a rain of destruction over the prostrate soldiers. A couple of the soldiers suffered minor injuries; they were the fortunate ones. Private Russell's body was non-existent except for one booted foot that landed near Hal. As Hal pulled himself out of his shallow grave, the image of

Private Russell's smile was still imprinted on his retina—such a waste for a momentary blunder.

Despite heavy losses, they pushed Rommel's army back. The Battle of El Alamein was a success. Then Churchill ordered the Eighth Army to Italy. The men were stepping back into the fray, taking their battered minds and bodies with them. Hal received the all-clear to fight again. Not that he relished it—there was no glamour in looking into another soldier's eyes and making that split-second decision between them or him. The African infantry had reverted to trenches and bayonet combat at times, and Italy was proving to be no different. The only difference was the Italian terrain, consisting of rugged, snow-topped mountainous ranges, ravines, and fast-flowing rivers. The winter had made conditions more treacherous, and many roads towards the Gustav line had become impassable. The few remaining roads had turned into a quagmire of sodden earth, in which vehicles soon became stranded. Only local mules succeeded as a means of transport during this time.

Hal missed his old life. It was much simpler back at home. Farm work was a far cry from army life. He made a mental note to write to his mother and enclose one of his sketches. She sent him a letter last week. The weight of her worry lifted as she wrote, knowing that her only child had survived being stationed in Africa. In her letter, she described the church bells' celebratory peal throughout the country for the African victory, and added a photograph of Bonnie, their beloved Lakeland terrier.

"Scusi," Ottie's voice interrupted his thoughts. Hal leaned down towards her. "Lutrine. Voglio andare," she said nervously. Hal looked puzzled. Ottie huffed. "Il bagno voglio andare." Hal's expression softened. "Ah, the toilet. You mean latrine in English."

Ottie stumbled over the words. "La... t... rine. Toi... let, sì." The words felt strange in her mouth.

"Yes, you may go."

Hal watched her scurry across the factory floor, her polka dot headscarf moving faster as she approached the exit. She had obviously ignored the call of nature for a bit too long.

Ottie ran across the square, desperate to go. She found the outbuilding for the latrines. Struggling with her oversized overalls, her bladder aching by this time. Ottie started to go, relief washed over her, followed by the sound of the siren blaring three times.

4

Quin

In the flat, the percolator rudely spat out its dark contents. Fi poured herself a steamy cup and sat at the kitchen table, taking in the sea view and the comforting coffee aroma. She idly twirled the little espresso cup, deep in thought. The vibration of her phone interrupted her. It had spilled out of her bag along with her medication. She gave the phone a cursory look: *Dad Mob*. Fi paused, sighed heavily, and answered the call.

"Hi, Ed."

On paper: Dad. In reality: Ed. Always Ed.

"Fibell, how are you?"

The background crackle revealed this was a car phone conversation, a between-journey filler.

Ed continued speaking, leaving her no time to reply. "Are you in on Friday? I want to get the gas man in for the boiler service. You know, ready for when you move on, and I can sell it."

At the not-so-subtle hint, Fi made a face. Ed was always the businessman.

"Suzy, can be there if you're busy?" Ed offered.

Fi stuck her tongue out at the phone and rolled her eyes. Ed's wife was not on her list of favourite people.

"I can be here," she replied, not knowing if it was true.

"No work today?" Ed inquired.

She knew he asked as a cursory comment, and that he had hoped just to leave a voice message. His time was precious.

"No, Nonna's house sold today. I felt I needed to..."

Ed cut her off. " Ah, I see." He paused, and the crackles of interference dampened the silence. "Fi, honey, you understand why I couldn't invest in it, right? Ottie's home was a bit of a big project. Suzy had a point: we couldn't keep it as it was. I mean, it's a museum of sorts."

"Yeah, I know," answered Fi, eager to move the conversation forward.

"Well, I am away for the next two weeks. My Mexico holiday, remember? Let's meet for lunch when I get back, okay?"

Fi murmured her agreement, nodding to the phone. Ed had stopped the car, she could hear him unclipping his seat belt and opening the car door, already disengaging from their conversation. She heard him greet a client in the distance with his vendible charm. Fi ended the call, feeling the familiar sting of being dismissed.

Fi cast her eyes around the neat little studio flat. The beige and pale blue décor was complemented by tasteful ornaments and seascape paintings. Suzy had a real talent for decorating - image and taste were her priorities. Fi stepped onto the narrow Juliet balcony, the sea breeze brushing her cheeks, and breathed in the salty air. The smell of chips and candyfloss mingled with café conversations floated up from the strand three floors below. She gripped the balcony rail, raised her chin and squinted at the horizon to see if France was visible today. How did you do it, Ottie? Fi wondered. How did you cross that bit of water all that time ago? With nothing but faith in another person and the clothes on your back.

A pang of shame hit her. Here she was, relying on medication to keep her mood stable, when her family had faced far greater challenges. What gave her the right to wallow in self-pity? Fi thought about her life's downturn and how losing Ottie had been the final blow. She was living in one of her father's rentals—not for much longer, by the sound of it. At least the twins were independent now.

Everything will be fine when Quin returns. It has to be. Fi smiled, thinking of him. Their second anniversary was approaching, and she hoped he would be back to celebrate. She wished she could have gone with him. They had planned for her to join him once he settled into his job in Macau. This was his last big assignment, managing and setting up casinos worldwide—his last hurrah before early retirement. But a slither of doubt crept in. Does he feel the same urgency I do? She wondered, her heart tightening at the thought.

Quin had climbed his way up in the casino world, seeing life at its best and worst: dealing cards at exclusive London clubs, surviving Russian underworld casinos, taking private jets to meet Arabian princes, and sitting naked and handcuffed in an Israeli prison cell for gambling charges. He had lived through both highs and lows, charming everyone along the way. But Fi couldn't help but wonder if she knew all of him—or just the parts he revealed.

They met during a research study Fi was managing. The drug company she worked for was recruiting participants from within the local hospital. Fi replaced the research nurse, who withdrew at the last minute, for the interview. The participant was waiting at the hospital, having volunteered that morning. It was crucial to see volunteers at once, particularly this one who had a flight booked for that afternoon. The study was low on numbers, so any participants were vital.

Fi grabbed the study information pack and consent forms and rushed to the busy outpatient department to meet the participant. Sister Glenis was on the phone at the nurse's station, looking snowed under, as usual. She mouthed "Room two" and gestured right. Fi gave her the thumbs up. She entered the room and caught the silhouette of Quin at the window, his hands deep in his pockets. He turned, gave her a broad smile, and threw out his hand. The handshake was firm, his palm warm against hers.

Fi introduced herself and ran through the consent process. Quin listened intently, leaning forward with his chin resting on his hand. She felt flustered but maintained her professionalism, sliding the consent form and pen towards him.

"So, are you happy to sign up? Any questions?" Fi asked.

Quin crossed his legs and leaned back in his chair. Stretching slowly, he finished by crossing his hands behind his head.

"So, I just need to give two interviews, a year apart, and let you access my medical notes?"

"Exactly," Fi confirmed, noticing a flicker of something unreadable in his eyes.

Quin paused, his pen hovering over the dotted line. He held Fi's gaze. "Having one kidney certainly makes me popular."

Fi's smile faltered. She realised this was new information for him and felt a flicker of unease. Perhaps this wasn't the most professional approach. She hesitated to push him to take part, but there was something more - an undeniable attraction to him she couldn't shake.

"I'm sorry if it feels like you're being singled out," she offered

Quin's disarming grin reappeared. The intense green of his eyes, like emeralds, struck her.

"Ah well, it's not the best news I've ever had, but the upside is I get six months paid doing light duties in the UK, whilst the NHS repair Roger, of sorts." He noticed Fi's confusion. "Roger's the lazy kidney," he clarified with a playful eyebrow raise. "You with me?"

Fi laughed despite herself. Quin picked up her business card.

"Lucky for me, I've got no one tying me down. You got ties, Ms Bennett?"

"No, not really," she replied, suddenly aware of her rapid heartbeat.

Quin pushed the consent form back slowly, making a point of the action. Fi admired his flamboyant signature, the large, elegant Q crossing over the line with a flourish. An asterisk was placed at the bottom of the page, and he had written: *I only wish to be interviewed by Fiamma (if she has a coffee with me :-))*

"Hey, you can't write that," Fi objected. "This is a formal consent form." Quin shrugged. "I just did."

"But it can skew the data within the study. If you are familiar with your interviewer, you may change your answers accordingly."

Quin covered his mouth and whispered downwards, "Well, Roge, what do you think? Is she willing to take a risk?"

Fi focused on organising the study papers, trying to distract herself. "This is insane. You're wasting my time, Mr Potts." Quin remained composed, leaning back in his chair.

"I believe, Ms Bennett, as I am the volunteer and you are the paid employee doing her job—very well, I might add—it is my time that is being wasted."

He leant forward, devilment raising the corners of his mouth. Then he flashed her a winning smile and rose to leave. He held up her business card.

"I am away for a few days. I can give you a call when I get back. It's just a coffee, you know. I'm a nice guy. Maybe if you give me a chance, you'll see that. And if you don't, well, I walk away, and we both move on."

Fi softened. "I'm very flattered, but it's just not appropriate. You're a patient in the hospital, and erm, well, I just can't take personal calls on my work phone."

"My number is on that piece of paper." Quin pointed out with a smirk." I could write it out again if you want me to."

He stepped close enough to Fi for her to smell his soft citrus aftershave. She was attracted to him and felt her breathing shift down a level. This was out of her comfort zone. He was playing a cat-and-mouse game, and it made her restive. Fi stepped back from the space that Quin had encroached.

"I tend to lose bits of paper," she replied, feeling foolish.

"Oh, I see. Maybe that can be overcome." Quin smiled; a softness entering his voice. "Well, it's been marvellous," he said with a comfortable boldness.

He waved his hand and exited the room, akin to a ringmaster departing the circus ring. Fi caught her breath and jolted at the loud tap he landed on the frosted glass as she saw his shadow dance across the window and disappear. She had three missed calls on her work phone to deal with before she left to return to the office.

Sister Glenis bustled towards her, pushing back the hair escaping from her bun.

"Fi, Fi, I was asked to give this to you."

Sister Glenis reached into her bulging uniform pocket and produced a thick wad of paper. Giving Fi a cheeky wink before walking away, muttering about pharmacy issues. Left alone, Fi unfolded the paper, which had grown into an A2-size piece. In flamboyant writing, a mobile number followed by an elegant Q was on it.

Three days later, twenty-four red roses arrived at Fi's desk, the card signed with a simple Q. As she tried to hide them under her desk, Garth, her work colleague, entered the office.

"Woah, what have you been up to in your spare time?" he teased, lowering himself into the chair opposite her and peeking under the desk.

"Shh, this isn't funny." Fi said, pointing a finger at him as they both straightened up. "Not a word."

Garth zipped his lips in a gesture of mock secrecy, his freckled face breaking into a smile.

"No worries, I can save it until Sunday. You're still coming, right? Lil and the kids want to see you."

"Yes, yes, of course I am," Fi assured him.

"No bailing out last minute, you weirdo," Garth said, making his signature cross-eyed face that never failed to make her laugh.

Three more days passed. This time, twenty-four white roses arrived. A grumpy delivery woman handed them over, muttering complaints about future deliveries and the two flights of stairs worsening her sciatica. Garth set his coffee mug down to avoid spilling it, his body shaking with laughter as he snatched up the flowers.

"Well, well." He glanced at the card. "Q... Hmm, interesting."

The door swung open with a jolt, announcing the arrival of Carter, their anally retentive boss.

"Garth, where are those stats? I need them ASAP," Carter barked. His eyes shifted to the flowers. "Where did those come from?"

Garth shot a quick look at Fi before replying, "I ordered them for my wife. It's a surprise for our anniversary."

Carter looked unimpressed. "Get them out of here. They're terrible for my hay fever. And bring me those stats!" he ordered as he left the room.

"What's going on, Fi?" Garth asked once they were alone.

Fi let out a sigh. "I haven't done anything. It's a study participant. He... sort of asked me out."

She handed Garth the consent form Quin had signed.

"Bloody hell, Fi. Carter will have your arse for breaching study ethics." Garth scanned Quin's details and burst into a deep, throaty laugh. "Oh, my days! I know this guy. We grew up in the same neighbourhood. I see him down at the King's Head sometimes. He's in the casino business, I think. This is totally his style. Fi, he's a gem. But if you're not interested, at least tell him to stop with the flowers. Hay fever man is going to lose it."

Fi nodded. "Okay, I'll sort it out. Take the roses for Lil, would you?"

"No chance. She'd have my balls in a vice if I brought her flowers for no reason."

Fi snorted, then managed a smile. "Thank you."

Garth gave her a playful nudge. "No worries, kidda. Just don't leave Quin hanging. He's a good bloke."

Later that evening, Fi snuggled into her duvet, studying the large piece of paper on her lap. She couldn't help but smile at the red and white roses crammed into her small bedroom. She picked up her phone and typed a message: *Hello, could you please stop sending the roses? It's causing issues with my boss.*

The reply was almost instant: *Would they prefer gladioli?*

They ended up texting each other late into the night. The very next day, Fi sat with Quin in a quaint little coffee shop under the low brick arches overlooking the harbour, once the haunt of local fishermen. Coffee turned into lunch, lunch into drinks at a bar, and the day ended with a slow, meandering walk back to Fi's flat.

Nearly two years after that fateful day, Fi sat spinning the engagement ring Quin had spontaneously bought her during a whirlwind weekend in Florence. On bended knee, that sleepy afternoon by a fountain in a small piazza, he had proposed, cheered on by a few locals playing cards under a canopy of trees, sheltered from the Italian sun. Warm tears welled up as she recalled the scene. Lovely, bold Quin, who now felt too far away to help her after she had lost her rock, her Ottie. It was all becoming too much. They had both been her strength, and now she missed them terribly.

Fi thought of Ottie, and how she always knew how to make things better. Ottie had been the first to arrive at the hospital after Fi's car accident, bringing her home and nursing her back to health with an abundance of love and food. Ottie was always the nurturer. During those hospital visits, to pass the time, Ottie had shared stories of her life—how she survived war-torn Italy and journeyed across Europe's scarred landscape to reach England during the winter of 1946, where she saw snow for the first time.

Fi's thoughts turned to Ottie's last remaining sister, Zia Nari. Yet she couldn't summon the courage to call and break the news of Ottie's passing. How could she inflict such pain on Zia Nari, now in her nineties, a widow, and the last of her generation. Fi rummaged in her bag and pulled out the dented gold locket. It dangled from its delicate chain as she lifted it to have a closer look. It was the only personal item she had taken from Ottie's dressing table. Opening the locket, she studied the tiny black-and-white photograph. She recognised the familiar features of a young Zia Nari: thick black hair framing her delicate face. The stern young man beside her, with his deep-set stare and strong eyebrows, was unfamiliar. She wondered who he was. The answer lay in Zia's memories. It was time to return the locket to its rightful owner.

Fi longed to go back to Ottie's homeland and see the family again. There were few of them left now. Sure, there were plenty of cousins, but her childhood memories were tied to the aunts and uncles—the Zias and Zios—whose faces were now immortalised on little oval photos on the Matani family monument, entombed in the cemetery's walls, surrounded by the Campania mountains. She felt absurd, unable to summon the courage to tell her great-aunt she had lost her sister. Zia Nari, who used to pinch Fi's cheeks hard with affection, imprinting fuchsia lipstick kisses on her forehead, and always calling her *topolina schiva*. Fi wondered why she wasn't as brave as that generation. Why couldn't she just hop on a train and go, like her grandmother had done decades earlier. Was it really so hard to retrace Ottie's journey in reverse and travel by train to Italy? Quin would be impressed when he came back. If he could travel the world solo, why shouldn't she catch a train across Europe?

She texted Garth: *Sorry, Matey, I'm not coming in. Please cover for me today.*

5

Fish In Crazy Water

Ottie chewed on her panini while sitting on the grassy bank that ran adjacent to the munitions factory. She preferred to sit alone, away from the noise of the factory. From this position, she had a view of the walnut grove, which had been transformed into an army camp overspill for the regiment, with khaki tents visible among the trees. The troops were stationed in Nissen huts, their curved roofs visible to her on the far right of the walnut grove as the land sloped down. From her vantage point on higher ground, Ottie could observe without being seen.

To her left, Ottie noticed a larger, square building. Its double doors were flung open, and two men in civilian clothes were carrying sacks on their shoulders into the building. The black lettering sprayed onto the hessian sacks formed words in English that she didn't understand—except for one: *TEA* - she knew that word. The English drank lots of tea, although she couldn't see the appeal. They ruined it by adding milk—it was much better with a slice of lemon. Then again, she'd heard they also ate a lot of potatoes. Before the war, she used to feed potatoes to the pigs. How times had changed. If she brought home potatoes now, Fina would be delighted. They could even use the peelings. Only last week, they had eaten the last of the peas her eldest brother, Salvo, had grown. They used the empty pods the next day, painstakingly removing the fibrous inner skin. Nothing went to waste; rations were meagre, and prices had risen sharply. The civilian men finished unloading and closed the doors to the food store. She noticed they didn't lock it. The siren blared three times, and Ottie rose, her bones wearily, to return to her workbench. The rest of Ottie's working day went quickly; she felt she was getting the hang of her job. The journey home on the crowded truck was tedious. At Vietri, Ottie waved goodbye to Annamaria and set off up the hillside towards home, enjoying the coolness of the shade that the pine trees' umbrella canopies provided.

***

That evening, the Matani family gathered around the kitchen table for dinner. Geno had brought home a bucket of dubious white fish pieces from the harbour at Vietri. Fina and Nari had prepared a version of *pesce all'acqua pazza*, the traditional "fish in crazy water." The legendary story of the dish had been passed down through generations. Neapolitan fishermen originally created it onboard their boats, using freshly caught fish mixed with seawater and whatever ingredients they had on hand to flavour the stew. Geno arrived with his bucket of fish soaked in seawater. Everything was tossed into the pot, including the rare "crazy water," used as a salty seasoning. Despite containing more water than ingredients, the fish stew was warm and tasty. The stale bread soaked up the broth, filling their hungry bellies. Fina watched her family eat eagerly as she sipped from her spoon, the steam fogging up her spectacles. She missed cooking with Mamma, she missed having good food to prepare, and she missed taking meals to the partisans hiding in their basement.

Fina frequently thought about the day the partisan vanished, wondering if the pain in her heart would ever go away. She found it difficult sometimes to recall the exact details of his face. Bringing food to the Jewish partisan whom Papa had sheltered during the harsh winter months had soon become Fina's daily task. At first, she was wary of the quiet, bespectacled intellectual who had taken refuge in her basement. He wasn't how she expected a partisan to look or behave. He stood out from

41

the former partisans that Papa had concealed, this one seemed different. His requests were simple: the tools for writing and some books to read. When he received his sparse meal, he was always polite and humble, apologising as he turned away with compunctious shame when Fina collected his bucket, which was used as a makeshift toilet.

The partisan's name was Matteo. Before the war, he had been a law student in Naples. He was an Italian national, the son of a Catholic father and a Jewish mother. Matteo took pride in his heritage and believed that every Italian deserved freedom and the chance to contribute to society. He was a gentle, educated soul, and Fina grew to care for him deeply.

After finishing her chores each day, Fina would spend the long winter evenings sitting on the basement floor with Matteo. Leaning against the flour sacks, she loved listening to his stories about growing up in Naples. He often spoke of his dreams to help overthrow the Nazi and Fascist regimes. Fina and Matteo shared a deep love of literature, and as their bond grew, they spoke about their hopes for the future. Matteo dreamed of practicing law in a liberated Italy. Fina confided she had once wanted to become a teacher, but she had left school at fourteen to help Mamma raise her siblings. Holding her hands, Matteo shared his vision of a future Italy where women could achieve their aspirations. He explained that if the Allies hadn't advised retreat during the winter, he would have remained in the mountains, despite the harsh conditions.

The plan to increase rebel resistance in a bid to reduce the Nazi onslaught had backfired. The attacks had only spurred the Nazis on; their actions intensified, and their tolerance diminished. Partisans and their supporters suffered death or torture at the hands of the Nazis. News filtered through of plans developing in Naples for a counterattack. Neapolitans, disbanded soldiers, and the resistance groups were to be involved, along with the *scugnizzi*—the notorious street urchins who knew every alleyway, drain system, and hideout. He felt like a trapped rabbit and prayed for spring to come soon so that he could resume the fight. At least it was warm and dry in the basement, and he got to spend time with Fina.

Signore Matanti occasionally allowed him to bathe or stroll in the hidden courtyard at the back of the house—a rare chance to glimpse daylight and see Fina, which was always a bonus. He hoped one day to return as a free man and take her away from a life of endless struggle. When she visited, resisting the urge to be anything other than a gentleman became increasingly difficult. As she read to him or discussed world events, he would drift off, wondering if she felt the same. He found himself fixated on her moving lips, imagining the sensation of cupping her delicate face in his hands and kissing her. He feared his thoughts might betray him.

Then, news reached the Matanti household that a couple of partisans had been discovered nearby. The families' homes were burnt to the ground, and the men were shot. The captured partisans were extradited from Italy via trucks and then transported by train to detention camps. Signore Matanti made plans to move Matteo deeper south, awaiting further instructions from *La Resistenza*. Matteo wanted to leave to reduce any further risk to the Matanti family. Fina could hear their raised voices beneath her feet. She barely had time to hide away as Papa flung the basement hatch open and stormed out of the house.

Dust in the basement scattered from the low ceiling as the floorboards vibrated with the force of Signore Matanti's departure above. Matteo clasped his head in his hands, frustration building up inside him. He understood the sentiment behind Signore Matanti's words: alive and free, he held greater value. He was a threat to them. Fina—beautiful, gentle Fina—he had to protect her. He heard her light steps strike on the wooden rungs of the ladder. Her timid face peered cautiously around the corner. Fina did not move closer, she watched from a distance, as if the space between them became too agonising to cross.

"Rufina,"–Matteo's voice was laboured–"I guess you heard. I have to leave." He paused, but Fina did not fill the silence. "It's not safe for you if I stay."

Fina couldn't ease the tightness in her throat. She couldn't speak, fearing she might lose control—she was used to holding back her emotions.

Matteo stepped forward into the void between them. Her resolve crumbled, and the tears came in silence. He gently removed her spectacles, cupping his hands around her delicate features. Caught in the moment, they felt the love between them. Matteo tasted her warm mouth and pulled her against him, his body trembling with anticipation. Fina pushed him back by his shoulders. Her hair, now freed from its usual tight bun, fell in thick black waves framing her face. She unfastened her dress and let it drop to the floor.

"Fina, please, no, not like this."

Despite his reticence, he couldn't hold back; he grabbed and caressed her body. Fina felt the hunger in his touch. They fell onto the flour sacks.

He whispered into her hair, "You are so beautiful."

"No man has ever said that. You are the only one I've ever wanted to say it," Fina replied between his kisses.

She wrapped herself around him, willing the moment to last forever. Matteo became lost in the moment, his desire overriding his morals. It took every ounce of his willpower to push her away. Fina sensed his body pulling back.

"What's wrong?" she asked, her breathing ragged.

"My love, we can't—not like this. I can't taint you. It…"

Fina interrupted, kissing the words away. "Matteo," she murmured between kisses, "I want you for the rest of my life."

Matteo stood up, revealing the long, white scars that crisscrossed his torso.

He smiled shyly. "What?"

"I even love your scars," Fina replied. "They are signs you've overcome great trauma and survived."

He leaned over her, kissing each part of her body as he covered it with her dress. Then he moved upwards, lying above her. Placing his elbows on either side of her head, he felt them sink into the flour sacks. He looked into her endless eyes and kissed her nose.

"After this foolish war, I'll come back." He kissed her nose again. "I will make you my wife." He kissed her mouth hard. "I'll take you to bed every single night."

Fina chuckled and gently bit his lip. "Every night!"

They lay entwined among the disturbed flour sacks, contemplating their futile future until sleep overcame them.

Fina jolted awake, hearing her mother's voice in the depths of her dreams.

"Wake up! Fina, wake up!"

She roused herself from sleep to find Mamma leaning over her and Matteo, who was just beginning to shake off his slumber.

"Oh, Mamma, this isn't what you think. I—"

"I'm not thinking anything," Mamma interrupted. "We have no time!"

"Where is Papa? Is he here? Is he angry?"

"No, he never came home last night. You need to hurry! Germans are in the street, checking houses for stowaways. Quick, we have no time. Matteo, you must go! Get out, hide!" Mamma's voice was rushed and frantic as she pulled at Fina to get up.

Matteo quickly gathered his few possessions. Mamma recounted in a hurried whisper what she had seen when she rose early to prepare the first batch of bread. She had noticed Fina wasn't sleeping with her sisters, and Renzo wasn't on the settee. The events of the previous day were not overlooked by the household. She guessed where Fina was—it was obvious. She had decided just to nip across to their land to feed the chickens before dealing with Fina and Matteo. As she crossed the road, she heard a gunshot. Turning towards the sound, she saw the victim—a young man—drop to his knees and fall face down onto the pavement. Her gaze rose to the soldier holding the gun. An open-backed truck was nearby with armed soldiers, stood guarding the people huddled together in the rear. She rushed back in to warn Matteo.

The sound of metal scraping against wood at the front door echoed through the house. Mamma pushed Fina towards the ladder. There was no time for goodbyes.

Mamma called over her shoulder, "God be with you, Matteo."

***

Matteo checked around before leaving; no sign of his presence remained in the basement. He pushed his coat and small backpack out through the basement window, then squeezed himself through the frame, angling his shoulders into the corners. He replaced the grating, checked for footprints, and took one last look at the house. He could hear the blood pumping deep in his ears.

The Matanti house backed up against the mountainside, with an upward slope visible from the road. He couldn't risk scaling the hill, as he might be spotted from ground level, making his escape route obvious. Across the road, houses clung to the mountainside, dropping off steeply. The ground there offered protection amongst the many trees clinging to the sloping land. If he could cross the street, he may have a chance of rolling down the slope, his fall broken by the trees. If he survived the drop, he could escape. It was his only chance. He would have to walk along the street for a few yards before it would be safe to try and cross.

As Matteo slipped away, he could hear the commotion through the open kitchen window, but he dared not look back. He kept his head down and aimed up the street, away from the Germans. It took all his self-restraint not to run. He had to appear as inconspicuous as possible. Pulling his cap low over his head, he hunched his shoulders and moved at a steady pace. Just a few more steps to get around the corner, then he could cross the road and descend the mountainside. As he approached the turn, his step quickened, passing houses with front doors opening onto the pavement, one door flung open, nearly knocking him over. Matteo came face-to-face with a Nazi soldier. His heart sank into his boots. For a moment, he considered making a break for it until he spotted more soldiers across the road, running would be fruitless.

"Papers, me see," the soldier demanded in broken Italian.

Matteo held his arms open wide, trying to look as though he posed no threat.

"Yes, at my house. In the next village, I can get them. I bring," he said.

The soldier's colleague, dressed in the uniform of the Italian military police, appeared at his shoulder.

"If you have no papers to identify yourself, then you must accompany us," he said, waving his gun to indicate the direction Matteo needed to follow.

Fina saw Matteo walk past the kitchen window, sandwiched between the two men. She felt Mamma's grip tighten on her shoulder—a silent plea to hold it together.

"More espresso, gentlemen?" Mamma offered, glancing at the young soldiers, who she guessed to be close in age to her own sons.

Her remaining offspring had been roused from their beds and assembled in the front room, half-awake in their nightclothes, grateful for Mamma's hot coffee.

"No, thank you, Signora Matanti. It's unusual to find someone awake so early. All seems clear here. We must continue with our searches, unless you have any information for us. Have you seen anything suspicious in the neighbourhood?" The soldier with a squint spoke, studying her face for any reaction.

"You're welcome. My daughter and I wake early every morning to prepare the first batch of bread. Please feel free to come back later for some—a gift from the Matanti house." Mamma's voice was calm, her response measured. "I didn't see anything. I'm too busy working." She held the soldier's gaze as she finished speaking.

"And you?" The other soldier chipped in, aiming his words at Fina's back with a flick of his chin.

Fina, busying herself at the kitchen sink facing out towards the window, could see Matteo climbing onto the truck. She watched as it drove off, disappearing from view.

"Fina has been here with me," Mamma interjected. "She hasn't seen or heard anything."

Fina bit the inside of her mouth and nodded her response vigorously into the washing-up bowl, feeling the soldier's eyes boring into her back. She heard the scrape of a chair against the tile floor as he rose from the table. She turned to face the source of her pain.

Fina forced a smile. "I, sir, have seen nothing."

The soldier scrutinised her face. He was fair, with an angular jaw. To regain her composure and quell the tremor in her lower lip, Fina focused on the straight, silver scar etched across his cheek.

"Mmmm, very well." The soldier winked at her; his gaze traced the line of her body as he spoke. A long pause hung heavy in the air before he finished. "You make excellent coffee, Signorina Fina."

Once the soldiers departed, Fina's resolve folded. She collapsed to the floor, weeping in Mamma's arms until her soul felt numb and her body grew torpid from the exertion. Papa, with lipstick marks visible on his collar, looking tired and unshaven, returned home later that day to the news. His temper flared with frustration, and Mamma bore the brunt of it.

6

Courtship Rituals

The men sat and talked as the women cleared the table. Salvo had brought several red wine vats home and siphoned off a bottle to share with Papa and his brother, Geno.

"Ahh, it's young. Needs apricots to sweeten it," Papa commented ever the critic.

Salvo pinched his fingers together to gesture the *Mano a borso* sign, expressing his disbelief as he spoke. "*Ma che vuoi?* What do you expect? At least we have wine."

Papa snorted out a laugh and leant forward to ruffle his eldest son's hair.

He held the back of Salvo's head as he spoke. "Poor wine, mah. At least we have each other, eh? One day, you'll be head of this family."

Salvo ensnared the thought in his mind, feeling its burden weigh heavily. He wished the family chalice had remained in Marcello's hands. He missed his brother's dauntless ease, his warmth. Marcello had been the anchor of the family, the one who could silence a room with just a look or bring everyone to laughter with a single word. Salvo remembered the way his brother would toss him a lemon from the tree, saying life was too short to be soured by bitterness. Without him, everything felt unbalanced, like the earth had shifted under his feet. Now, the burden of their father's expectations was his alone to carry.

He considered Anna, Marcello's widow, feeling a duty towards her, a need to protect her welfare.

Salvo worked three jobs to support his family. He delivered goods between the surrounding towns and villages, hence the wine vats stacked in the kitchen corner, ready for the early-morning delivery to Coco's restaurant. He helped in the family bakery, assisting with chores and deliveries. He made a mental note to take the batch of bread to Coco's in the morning. If he had time, he wanted to visit and deliver a complimentary loaf to Signora Fragopane. He had heard rumours of an incident involving her daughter and wanted to make sure the widow was okay.

Most of his evenings were occupied by his third job at Bar Recci in Vietri. The job as barman involved pouring drinks and watching soldiers knock them back, becoming more debauched with each glass he served. The Brits, he noticed, were the ones who knocked back the booze the most. He kept serving and watching, always wary.

A rhythmic knock at the front door reminded Salvo that, as instigated by Papa, Alberto was visiting Octavia today. Salvo had to chaperone his sister tonight, a task he could do without, as it was his first evening off in a long time. Nari entered the room with Alberto in tow.

"I'll let Tavi know you're here." Nari swayed her hips from side to side, mirth rolling off her tongue as she finished the sentence: "Alberto." She smirked, purposely drawing out his name.

"Thank you, Naria. Evening, gents," answered Alberto as he turned away, trying to block her playfulness.

Papa gestured for Alberto to take a seat at the table. Geno poured him a glass of wine without seeking permission first.

***

Ottie applied a further coat of ruby red lipstick and smacked her lips together. She studied her reflection, deciding her nose was too flat before pressing her hands down on her hair, trying to reduce its volume. It hung in thick, inky black waves down to her waist. She loosely rolled it up at the nape of her neck and began securing it with pins. Nari appeared at the bedroom door, still wearing her apron, damp from washing up.

"Your boyfriend's here." She winked at Ottie through the mirror.

Ottie pulled a face back at her as best she could with a mouth full of hair grips, continuing to style her hair.

"Oh, Tavi, why must you wear that dowdy green dress? Why not wear my pretty red one? You look gorgeous in it."

"Why would I want to do that?" Ottie replied, inserting the last hair grip. "Anyway, I prefer blue. I keep my blue dress for best only."

She stood in front of the mirror and smoothed down her dress. Turning around, she took one last look at her reflection over her shoulder. She picked up her clutch bag on the bed next to where Nari had sat down and popped her lipstick in it before snapping it shut to confirm her preparation was complete. Nari flung herself back onto the bed in a swoon-like fashion. It rocked gently under her weight as she let out a sigh.

"Huh, I wish I had a boyfriend who would take me out." Nari closed her eyes as she spoke, a trace of a smile on her lips.

"Really? Hmm, perhaps you should find one?" Ottie paused at the bedroom door. "It's more trouble than it's worth, you know. It leads to... what? Marriage? Living on Alberto's farm just up the road until the day I die."

Nari opened one eye to look at her sister before opening the other and sitting up on her elbows.

"Tavi! What's got into you ever since..." Nari hesitated, choosing her words carefully, "you know, well..." She faltered for a moment under her sister's glare. "We've all lost Mamma. You do have Alberto. He *is* a good man."

"Yes," Ottie replied, her hand on the door handle, ready to leave, "Nari, he is that." Her words did not reach her eyes.

Ottie headed towards the kitchen, where she could hear the male voices coming from the open door. Alberto noticed Ottie first and stood up from the table, clearly pleased at the sight of her. Her brothers turned towards her. Geno gave his signature artful wink. Papa sat at the head of the table with his arms folded, his features steely—the resting face he was born with.

"Well, have a nice time." Papa lifted his eyes deliberately slow before adding sternly, "but not too nice."

***

The trio walked down the hill towards the centre of Carva. The night sky held onto a full moon. Its rays cast grey swirls through the branches of the trees. Salvo hung back to light his cigarette. Alberto felt for Ottie's hand.

"It feels like ages since I've seen you. I missed you." He squeezed her hand tighter.

"Well, you're busy with the farm, and I am working now."

"Yes, so I hear: your father got you a job at the British base up near Positano. I was surprised that he let you work with those men. Perhaps he will change his mind after what has happened."

"I like my job." Ottie answered, defiantly jutting out her chin.

She caught Alberto smiling at her, and she reciprocated.

They reached the Piazza Duomo, with its octagonal fountain prominent in the square. Four imposing dolphin statues rose from the water, each spouting a stream from its mouth. The fountain's centrepiece, a three-tiered structure of scalloped stone, babbled softly as water cascaded down. The lights no longer illuminated the fountain at night—it was an easy target for aircraft. Yet in the bright moonlight, the rippling water gave the fountain an enchanted quality. The grey stone, combined with its craftsmanship, granted the dolphins a lifelike appearance. The dolphin felt surprisingly real under her touch, almost as if it were mortal. She sat down and reached out, skimming her fingers through the cool water. Salvo caught them up by the fountain.

"Hey, listen, I'm going into Bar Tabacchi." He pointed to the bar overlooking the piazza. "Meet you there in about an hour. I'm all eyes and ears, remember." Salvo touched his ears as he skipped backwards before turning away.

Ottie rolled her eyes and watched her brother leave. She shuffled along the fountain wall to create space between herself and Alberto.

"So, tell me, what has happened that would change my father's mind?" Alberto leaned closer, eager to explain. "I'm surprised you haven't heard. I was just talking about it with your brothers before we left. It happened here at the fountain. You know the Fragopane sisters? One of them was waiting for her brother when a drunken soldier dragged her off. He beat her and raped her. Her brother found her; she was in a terrible state. The police were called. The local boys are after the soldier now—they're looking for a tall Englishman, but that doesn't narrow it down much."

"That's awful. I do know them. I wonder if it was Rosa or Elena."

"Not only do these soldiers take our willing women," said Alberto, "but they also see fit to take them by force, and an Englishman at that."

"Soldiers–English or whoever–it doesn't matter where they are from or what they do. They've all got one thing in common: they're men."

Alberto held Ottie's hand in his.

"Not all men are bad, Octavia. This one has good intentions. You know I do. You know how much you mean to me," emotion caught in his throat.

Ottie couldn't reciprocate. A sense of duress rose within her as she gently pulled her hand away. Alberto sucked in the air to control his rising frustration.

He chose his words carefully. "I'm a patient man. I know how hard losing your mother has been, especially with your brother still missing. I've given you time and space. It's not all soldiers or men, you know. My brothers and yours, we've all fought across Europe and Africa. Most of us made it back. I fought for our country, for our King, and I'd do it again for a free Italy—a place for us to grow old together, where our children will be safe. That's what kept me going. I need to know if things have changed between us."

Ottie recalled the intensity of the affection she once felt for Alberto. It seemed a lifetime ago, when he turned up in uniform for a last good-bye before going to war. She had feared she might never see him again. That night, when the house was quiet, she had given herself to him, driven by a mix of compassion, duty, and conflicting emotions—only to regret it immediately.

Since his return, she had felt trapped in a life planned for her. Not with her. She knew Alberto was kind and generous, but truth be told, he never fired her soul. She had distanced herself, longing for the independence she found in her work. The job at the British base had given her a taste of freedom—*a glimpse of what her life could be if she had the chance to make her own choices, to carve out her own path away from the expectations of marriage and family.* Things had changed now: Mussolini's regime was weakening, and Italy had a semblance of hope.

Alberto knelt on the floor in front of her and peered up at her downcast face, trying to catch her eyes, vying for her full attention. He spoke with a softness he reserved only for her.

"I know, Octavia, that this is not you. It's not the woman I left to fight for. I understand you're grieving. I have spoken with your father, and we both think it would be best if you and I got married soon. We can start a family. It will give you a new focus, a new life, a good life with me. I have your father's blessing."

Ottie's reaction was instant. She stood up abruptly, causing Alberto to stumble back on his heels. Her voice shook with emotion as she fired out her words. "How dare you speak to my father before me!"

Ottie turned her back on him. Surprised by her outburst, Alberto staggered up from the floor and brushed the grit from his palms. He noticed her heaving shoulders and his hand rose to touch her back. But stayed in mid-air, unable to break through the resentment that he felt radiating from her.

"Look at me, Octavia. Tell me it meant nothing. Is that something you do often?" His voice was bitter, hurt seeping through.

"How dare you think that of me! I thought you could be killed.

That I might never see you again! It was the first, the last, the only time ever! What gives you the right to make decisions about my life." Tears of frustration erupted with her words.

Alberto held his hands up in surprise. This wasn't his intention. He was confused, and he regretted what he had said. The evening wasn't panning out as he hoped. He knew how foolish he would look when he took her back home, where everyone was ready to celebrate their engagement.

Ottie realised how she had been manoeuvred into this situation. Salvo, leaving them alone, should have raised her suspicions. Given time, this choice might be tolerable; marrying Alberto could work. He was good enough. She just needed more time. She needed the war to end. How could she decide amidst such dire circumstances? Ottie did everything she could to push her fears down and out of her mind. Facing Alberto, she saw the resignation on his face. The last thing she wanted was to hurt him. It would be hard to go against her father's wishes. She was hesitant to let her life change, at least for now. She liked her new independence, her job, and being at home with her sisters. Maybe she just wasn't ready yet. A pang of regret hit her—Alberto looked so hurt and lost.

"I just need more time."

Alberto studied her upturned face, noting the cleft in her chin he loved so much. A strand of hair had fallen across her eye, and he gently tucked it behind her ear.

"Sorry, did I hear you right? You need more time? Does this mean we have a chance?" He couldn't hide the desperation in his voice.

"I can't marry you—not yet, not while we're at war, not like this. But I accept your proposal if you're willing to wait until it's all over."

Alberto lifted Ottie and spun her around, kissing her full on the mouth.

"My beautiful, darling, muddle-headed fiancée! I'm the luckiest man in Carva!" He shouted up to the sky.

Ottie couldn't help but laugh; Alberto's happiness was infectious. He kissed her again.

"I've been saving up for a ring. We can choose one together," he said, full of excitement.

She reached out to him. "No, I don't want one. Please, Alberto, isn't being engaged enough?"

Alberto pulled a mock sad face and spoke with his bottom lip protruding: "If you insist, my lady."

Ottie made out to punch him and Alberto feigned discomfort as he rubbed the spot she had aimed at. He held out his arm for Ottie, and she placed hers in the crook of his elbow.

"Come on, my girl, let's go find Salvo at the bar. I want a celebratory drink. I am the luckiest of men."

7

The Good Samaritan

S o far, so good. Fi had booked a single ticket online from Ashford Central to Paris Gare du Nord. She had hastily packed her favourite bag, the wheeled floral travel bag. Ashford had just two departures daily, and she preferred the early one. The train was relatively empty, which gave her the opportunity to change seats three times before she felt comfortable–a habit no amount of cognitive behavioural therapy could change. Her allocated seat was next to a craggy-faced pensioner who had spread her belongings across both seats. The woman glared as Fi hesitated by her reserved spot. Fi quickly found a more suitable place within the carriage, away from the narky pensioner.

The Kentish terrain looked a gloomy grey in the overcast light. The train flashed through the county, revealing a momentary glimpse of the English Channel awash with sunlight, casting a sun path on the silver sea before the train burrowed below the water level. Fi tightened her fists into a *mano fico* gesture in a bid to reinforce the sun's good omen. It had seemed like such a good idea this morning — a simple train journey. But now, the impulsive decision was sinking in, and a wave of panic swept over her. What the hell was she thinking? What an idiot! Apart from reaching Paris, she had made no other plans.

Seeking relief for her empty stomach, she ventured towards the catering carriage. Fi returned to her seat with a rippled, beige, cardboard takeaway coffee cup topped with an ill-fitting plastic lid and a Meal Deal sandwich, that tasted as plastic as its wrapper. She pushed herself back into her seat, trying to make herself small and inconspicuous. She had turned off her phone to avoid any distractions. She would call Quin in the morning, when Macau's local time was in the afternoon. It would be a more sociable hour; she didn't want to worry him.

***

Fi had been a shy, pensive child. Her Aunt Nella had given her the epithet "China Doll." It was an apt description. As a child, Fi had delicate porcelain features, soulful grey eyes, and a head full of loose yellow curls. Nella loved taking her out to show her off, until Fi's juvenescence faded, and she became a gawky, awkward, moody adolescent. That was around the time Nella left. She emigrated to Australia with her latest suitor, a man she had met just a few weeks earlier. Impulsive, svelte Nella, with hair so black it tinged blue in the sunlight. Fi had watched her go on that fateful day in the early morning light.

Fi reminisced; her thoughts encouraged by the gentle rocking of the train. That day, she had watched Nella clumsily navigate her large, overstuffed suitcase, scattering the rose and fuchsia bloom petals that overhung the garden path. Taking one final look, Nella bid farewell to her lifelong home. She gazed upwards and caught the forlorn sight of Fi in the corner of her bedroom window, hazed by the mist of her breath shadowed on the glass from the early morning chill. Nella smiled up at Fi and twisted her finger into her cheek—a nod to her Neapolitan heritage, expressing her love to her niece. And then she was gone.

Nella married her lover, and it wasn't long before they had children. The whirlwind of excitement and novelty between the couple soon gave way to the everyday mundanity of suburban life. Seeking a better outcome, Nella left her husband for his younger, wealthier colleague. Hal and Ottie were heartbroken when their only remaining child moved so far away. Their strained relationship became as distant as the miles between them.

It must have been hard for Nella when her sister, Tilda, died days after giving birth to Fi. Fi was the surviving twin, the first to be born, taking her mother's remaining life force with her. Her twin sister fared worse, and their mother followed within days. They were buried together, their grave tended weekly by Ottie, who kept it swamped with irises, freesias, and roses—Tilda's favourites. But Nella never forgave Ottie for how she had handled Tilda's unplanned pregnancy. Despite their differences, the sisters had been close. They always stood up for each other, bound by shared experiences and kinship. Nella's fiery, impulsive spirit had been tempered by Tilda's calm, intuitive nature. Nella's dark features were a stark contrast to her sister's fair complexion.

As Fi grew up, Nella found some comfort in the similarities between her niece and her late sister. But as Fi matured, inheriting her mother's Titian hair and striking features, it became too painful for Nella—a constant reminder of her loss. She gradually distanced herself from her niece.

"When I am gone, the only problem you'll face is Nella," Ottie had warned as she gazed out from the open conservatory door into her beloved garden, taking in its heady scents and the soft hum of a train in the distance.

Fi tucked the blanket tightly into the chair around Ottie.

"Nonna, don't say such things, you're gonna live forever. We all need you." Fi kissed her forehead as she rose.

"I can't live forever. No one can."

Ottie smiled at her granddaughter. Fi saw a glimmer of Ottie's twinkle that was always saved for her. Ottie's prophecy had been correct. Nella had arrived just a few days later, causing problems with her demands and tantrums. In the week before Ottie's death, Nella spent most of her time in the garden, chain-smoking and steadying her nerves with Ottie's cooking sherry. She had become as rotund as she was bitter, counting down the days until it would be over, and she could return to Australia. The family had arranged the funeral around her departure flights, and Nella had strutted through the house on the eve of Ottie's wake, choosing the pick of her mother's possessions, which Fi shipped to Australia at her own expense. Nella never spoke to Fi again, enraged that the family home had been left to her.

***

The outskirts of Paris came into view as the train fast approached its hub. During the last twenty minutes of the journey, Fi had talked herself into getting on the next train home. She alighted the train and became caught up in the crowd's ferocity, carried along by its sheer force. She needed a moment to breathe, to think. Fi recognised the logo and sign for *Eurostar billetterie*. The kiosk had a hand-written cardboard "*Ferme* "sign propped against the inside of its window. Fi sought help from a passing station attendant, and he casually indicated toward an endless queue of fellow travellers at the ticket office in the distance.

This wasn't how it was meant to be, she thought, and hurried out of the busy station. Outside, she took a left turn away from the crowd, her luggage trailing behind her, its wheels rumbling across the uneven cobbled streets. Not sure where she was going, Fi walked through the streets of Paris deep in thought, oblivious to her surroundings. *She had talked herself into pressing on—what was she hoping to find here? Closure? A distraction? The answer remained as elusive as ever.*

It took her a good forty minutes of walking before she found herself in the Latin Quarter, strolling along Boulevard St Michel. She took a detour from the main busy street, away from the hustle and larger branded shops and cafes, and stepped into one of the many smaller, quieter side streets. Following the narrow pavement, she turned a corner and was met by Hotel Galou.

It was a tall, narrow, Georgian-style building, its name in white writing printed on the billowing blue and white awning. Window boxes with dusky pink geraniums decorated its lower windows. The hotel had a pleasant ambience about it. She felt it would be alright here. She felt a sense of calm; the walk had relaxed her.

Her room was snug, though somewhat gloomy, as it faced out onto the neighbouring building's brick wall. Nonetheless, it was clean and had been decorated in tasteful yellow shades. The friendly receptionist, with *Lianne* written in bold on her gold badge, had offered her the double room overlooking the street. But Lianne's attempt at upselling failed. Fi had declined and took the cheaper single room. The room was based one floor above, where the lift stopped. Fi had assured Lianne she was more than capable of carrying her luggage up a flight of stairs.

Fi wasn't sure how she had ended up here—in a modest two-star hotel near central Paris—but here she was. She felt a flicker of pride. Despite her doubts and second-guessing, she had convinced herself to press on. *She paused, eyes fixed on the ceiling. The tension in her muscles slowly unwound, replaced by a dull ache of hunger.* All her nervous energy felt used up, and she fell backwards onto the bed. Its frame creaked.

Exhausted and famished, she decided to go out and try solo dining in a nearby café: Why not? Eager to test her newfound confidence, she wanted to dine alongside fellow travellers and cosmopolitans. Fi had collected some euros from an ATM on her way to the hotel. She hid her purse above the wardrobe, deciding it would be safest to take cash and her phone. With the help of Google Maps, she could sit and plan the next leg of her train journey, making dining alone less daunting. She switched on her phone to check she had enough battery. No one had tried to contact her, which was a relief. She didn't want to have any distractions from her mission. She made a mental note to call Quin on her return to the hotel.

Fi walked past a few cafes, looking for one that she felt would be suitable for a single female traveller. The sun was beginning to dip, and she felt a cold bite in the air. She vowed to go into the next café, not wanting to stray too far from the Hotel. Le Karib Creole looked good enough. It was situated on a corner of two streets and had brightly painted benches adorned by cushions with elephant motifs and matching blankets for the colder evenings. Background reggae music added to the casual mood of the place. The rich aroma of spices—ginger, garlic, and grilled meat—wafted through the air, mingling with the sweet scent of plantains frying in hot oil.

Fi sat outside and found a corner spot sheltered under a silver propane patio heater. She was handed a plastic wipeable menu written in French; it had the standard pictures of the food to make it easier for tourists to understand. Rita, the server, returned with the beer that Fi had ordered. With the tray held above her head, Rita's ample hips gently sashayed between the tightly packed tables, causing them to wobble. Fi pointed to what looked like a picture of goat curry and rice. The photograph displayed the meal with plantains neatly encircling the dish. Rita sucked in the air through her red lipsticked mouth and nodded in approval.

"*C'est très bien,*" Rita commented as she placed the beer and complementary peanuts on the table.

Fi studied the other diners. The assorted group consisted mostly of Afro-Caribbean customers. Fi hoped that this showed the food would be authentic and decent. She noticed some students and a few scattered tourists. A British family with young children were the noisiest group. In the corner opposite her, another diner sat alone. It was clear he was well known to the restaurant staff, Fi watched as Rita bent forward and hugged him into her ample bosom. Her infectious laugh from a shared joke trailed off as she sauntered away with his order. Fi and the stranger exchanged glances, and his face opened up into an affable smile. She returned it awkwardly, before casting her eyes down and using her mobile phone as a distraction.

The goat curry lacked the same precision in its presentation as the pictured version. She ordered another beer—well, why not? Her dish was hearty and tasted good. She confirmed this to Rita with hand signals and rubbing of her stomach. This clearly amused Rita: her ebullient laugh carried with her as she moved over to the man in the opposite corner. He smiled over to Fi and mimicked the stomach rub she had given Rita. Fi felt herself relax in the comfortable environment. She requested the bill with the universal pen-to-hand gesture. She needed to get back to the hotel and work out tomorrow's leg of the journey. Unless, maybe, it was easier just to slip back home. She felt the uncertainty swell up inside her.

Fi reached for the cash in her bag to pay the bill. She had enjoyed

Le Karib Creole and wanted to leave a generous tip. But where was the cash? She had zipped it in her bag's side pocket. Or maybe not. Why do bags have so many pockets? She emptied all its contents—lipsticks, receipts, and hairbands amongst the paraphernalia—but still no cash, to her dismay. She attempted to explain to Rita, but it was a challenge: Rita's demeanour was not so friendly now. Rita folded her arms and scowled down at Fi. No amount of slow speech, body language or pointing to an empty bag was going to make her understand. Fi had been robbed of the sum of one hundred and fifty euros; all her cash had gone, and she could not pay her debt. If Rita would just let her return to the hotel, she could get her bank card and return to pay. But Rita's barricade-style posture would not enable this to happen.

The man in the opposite corner noted the shift away from the harmonious vibe between Rita and the demure white woman who had eaten alone. He had noticed her earlier when he glanced up from rolling his joint and saw her slipping into her seat in a sideways, self-conscious way. She had stood out to him, as she wasn't the usual visitor to this part of Paris. Pale and elegant, her large eyes casting nervous, gazelle-like sideways glances. Still, she seemed to relax with Rita's warm hospitality and had reciprocated his smile, albeit fleetingly. The words that carried across to him now were in English. He tuned in to a few of the keywords that came through over the cafe's general babble: "robbed", "pay later", and "no money".

"Can mi help? Is there a problem?"

Fi noticed that the man held onto his vowels when he spoke; his voice had a natural silky quality.

"*Avez-vous un problème?*" he asked Rita in an authentic French accent.

Both ladies directed their stories at him in unison, speaking in two different languages. He quickly picked out the main threads and spoke rapidly with Rita, none of which Fi could understand. Rita left with a disapproving shake of her head, sucking her teeth.

"Thanks for helping," Fi said. "I'm not sure what you told her. I can't believe it—I had money. I only went to the supermarket before

I came here. It was busy, and I got knocked into–I think that's when someone took my money."

"A pickpocket, it would have 'appened in seconds. It's okay, it's sorted with Rita. Don't worry." He placed a reassuring hand on her shoulder. "Relax: no matter."

"Well, I can get some cash and bring the money straight back. I want to pay," Fi insisted.

"Cha, calm yourself, it's cool. Rita's bill is sorted," assured the man. Fi twigged what the man meant.

"You paid! My goodness, thank you. Please wait here while I get some cash. I am Fiamma, by the way." She spoke rapidly as she extended her hand out towards him.

Her bag and coat tangled around her arm as she rose from her seat. His handshake was as cool as his skin felt.

"I'm Doc. And it don't matter none,"

"No, no, please. I insist. Wait here. I will pay, and I would like to buy you a drink."

Fi had gone, her voice trailing behind her before Doc could reply. *As she hurried back to the hotel, her mind raced—had she been foolish to continue this trip? What was she even searching for? Maybe it wasn't just about returning the locket; maybe it was about finding a connection to her own past, something she hadn't admitted even to herself.*

Fi returned within twenty minutes, flushed and out of breath. Doc refused the money but accepted a beer. Rita's friendly disposition had returned, realising that Fi's circumstances were genuine. She had seen all the tricks in her time as a server in Paris. Fi offered her a drink, too, but Rita declined and gave Fi an affectionate rub on the head; her faith restored a little in humankind.

"Dat sishta don't trust no one," Doc reflected as they watched Rita walk away.

He adjusted his tam, scratching his scalp. A trickle of grey ran through his dreadlocks. Fi studied his face. Deep smile lines framed his eyes, emerald flecked with yellow, which gave them depth. The effect compelling, contrasting with his dark skin.

"And you?" Doc held her gaze. "Wah gwan?"

"Mi deh yah," replied Fi.

Doc chuckled at her use of his dialect.

"Ha, you speak my tongue, girl."

They high-fived each other.

"A little. My fiancé shares your heritage."

"Well, I guess it's yours too now. But that's not where you're from ?"

"No, I'm English, but part Italian, too. I'm kinda on my way to Italy. Well, that was the plan when I left home this morning..." Fi's words tapered away.

Doc placed his hand on his chin and leaned in towards her as he spoke. "Girl, yuh seem a bit vex. Mi no mean to be bright with ya."

"It's okay, it's not rude. I don't mind you asking. It's just, well, this morning, it felt like the right thing to do, and now I am not so sure. My grandmother did the reverse just after the war - she came to England from Italy by train. I thought I would be brave like her, but I am not. I guess it's different nowadays."

Fi felt the light hand of Doc pat her shoulder. Doc leaned in closer, and as she turned to meet his eyes, she felt the heat of his breath skimming her face. His warm eyes compelled Fi to stare into them—they seemed to hold so much history. *She felt a strange, almost spiritual connection, as if an old soul beyond its mortal years was reaching into her past, unearthing her deepest thoughts.* Doc dropped back into his chair without lifting the deepness from his gaze.

"Me tinks yuh come dis far to be right here girl." Doc gave a knowing nod.

"Who, me?" Fi held her hands towards her chest to emphasise the point. "Erm, I dunno. I mean... I'm not impulsive, you see, but I want to impress Quin, my fiancé. He travels all over the place. And I found this locket, which I need to give back to my great aunt. There is a photo of a man in it. I don't recognise him and want to know who he is."

"Does it matta? Sometimes, past best left where it tis. Here and now is di only ting that's real."

"Hmm." Fi considered Doc's words before she continued. "I wish I could be like you. I can't seem to let go of my past. I daren't think of my future. It doesn't look too great." She gave a short laugh. "Huh, I, well, I am about to lose my job. And it's not *my* past—the locket is my aunt's, and I just think it will be nice to return it to her."

"Fi, we ancestors' keepers, dat's for sure, but we don't need to know all the mysteries of our family. Yuh cum yah fi drink milk. No cum ya fi count cow." Doc paused, letting Fi take in the essence of his wisdom. "Don't waste time, do what yuh need. Wi run tings, tings no run wi."

Doc was a man who worked within his means. Despite a meagre pension, he had been fortunate enough to choose an early retirement. Throughout most of his adult life, he had lived nomadically, travelling and working in Europe and the Third World, primarily for Médecins Sans Frontières. Instead of focusing on his pocket, he had always aimed to nourish his soul. Faced with hardship, Doc provided counsel and support to others. His experiences equipped him with great acumen; he was street-savvy and compassionate. Hence, the name "Doc" was bestowed on him. Knowing life's fragility, Doc stopped taking it seriously long ago.

"Goat deh sweat, but long hair cover it," Doc continued. "My madda used to say dat. People don't share their real feelings, everything is nice, all is well. Underneath most of us, wi got our problems. It's gud whatever yuh do, don't sweat it none."

"I tend to overthink a little. This never used to be who I was." Fi felt clumsy as she tried to justify herself.

"Wen coco ripe, it muss buss." Doc wanted to reinforce his encouragement, but Fi looked puzzled. He offered an explanation. "Its bud will burst. What yuh do speaks louder than what yuh could ever say." Doc paused and smiled. "Maybe it's di kaya talking—this old man talk some shit. It's time guh sleep. I heading your way. Let mi walk yuh back."

Doc offered the crock of his arm to Fi as he rose from the chair. Fi looped her arm into his, and the new companions headed towards Hotel Galou.

Fi lay on her bed in the semi-darkness. She took a draw on the joint

Doc had given her. It took her back to her teenage years. It felt good. Doc had handed her it as they had exchanged their goodbyes at the front of the hotel.

"Have dis relax some. If yuh need mi tomorrow, mi be sat with Rita having coffee in dah mawning. If mi don't see yuh, mi know yuh be gawn."

She followed the smoke rings she attempted to make and giggled. She considered calling Quin as she drifted off to sleep.

8

Elena

"Come on, Lofty, let's have one for the road." Taffy raised his beer towards Hal as he spoke, spilling its contents in the process. Hal felt drunk but had enough nous to realise he wasn't as far gone as Taffy. Stan, barely conscious, had been slumped over the bar for the last five minutes. He was celebrating what was likely a brief reprieve from Cassino. The engineers were required to clear the river paths for his unit, while the infantry served as cannon fodder. From what he heard, the Texans were making a brave attempt to cross the fast-flowing Rapido under German mortar attacks. All attempts aimed to get him closer to Monte Cassino, a hellish place on top of a mountain.

"Taff, we gotta get on that truck. It's the last one outta here. Give me a hand with Stan, will ya?"

Taffy lurched himself down off his stall. He burped loudly.

"I need a piss," he said, slurring his words.

He placed his empty glass on the bar and staggered through the crowd toward the toilets.

"Right Stan, me ole fella, let's get on that truck," Hal spoke over his shoulder in Stan's direction.

Hal turned to aid his friend, only to discover that Stan had disappeared. The bartender caught Hal's eye and waved outside. Hal nodded a thank you towards him and left in search of his absent friend. He caught sight of a recumbent figure leaning over the fountain's wall. Hal quickened his step and came into earshot of the sound of Stan vomiting into the water. He noticed a young woman sat on the fountain wall to the left of Stan, nervously trying to edge herself further away from the scene. Hal pulled Stan by the shoulders out of the water and retrieved his soaking wet cap before it floated away. He smiled apologetically over to the young woman.

"Oi-oi!" Taffy shouted across the piazza.

"Taff, come on, help me here," Hal shouted back.

Hal and Taffy carried Stan in between them, his feet dragging behind him. Taffy sang at the top of his voice, accompanied by a laughing Hal.

"*Tongues of fire on Idris flaring, news of foe-men near declaring, to heroic deeds of daring, call you Harlech men!*" Taffy sang vehemently, his choir boy tones rusty, a touch off-key. Stan, lucid for a moment, chipped in at the end. "*You Harlech men!*"

They reached the truck and lifted Stan up onto the back of it, where he disappeared amongst his comrades. During the tussle, someone knocked Taffy's cap onto the floor.

"Mind my bleedin' head," Taffy commented as he replaced his cap and hitched his leg up, ready to swing into the truck.

The action jogged Hal's memory.

"I left Stan's cap by the fountain. He will need it tomorrow. I won't be a minute, wait for me," Hal shouted up to the driver.

The driver waved and nodded.

"Hey up, make way for the little Welsh git," quipped one of the lads from the depths of the beer-infused truck.

Hal figured he'd dragged Taffy and Stan out of enough scrapes by now—this was just another night, another story for the boys back home. He returned to the fountain. He noticed the young woman was still sitting in the same place on the wall. The area of ground near where he had fished Stan from the fountain remained sodden, the soil darkened. He was sure he had placed Stan's hat on the side. He caught the anxious young girl looking at him. She was holding a dripping cap out towards him.

"If you are looking for this, it fell back in the water," the girl explained in Italian.

"Ah, *grazie*," Hal replied, taking the hat from her. He made to leave but paused for a moment before he inquired, "Are you alright? It's just that it's unusual seeing a local girl out here alone."

She gave Hal a level, demure gaze before answering, "I am waiting for my brother. He is a little late."

"Oh, I see. Can I help at all?"Hal asked, seeing the girl shake her head, he continued, "Well, don't stay out here too long. It gets a bit rowdy when the bar closes. No place for a young lady like yourself."

"Thanks. Hopefully, he will be along soon."

Hal dipped his head in a polite farewell, flashing her an open, friendly smile.

"Thank you for finding my friend's hat. Sorry about the mess he caused."

The girl returned the smile; she found his kind, handsome face reassuring –making his towering stature feel less intimidating. The truck's horn interrupted them with a loud honk in the distance. Hal jumped at the noise, holding up the hat as he waved to leave.

"I must go," he called out, then sprinted towards the truck, catching it just as it started to pull away.

With the help of outstretched hands, he clambered aboard, settling in amongst the lads. Hal safely on board, the group erupted into a singsong as they made their way back to base.

***

Elena felt the emptiness left behind by the affable, tall soldier's departure. The soft undertones of laughter and music drifted from the bar. A warm glow from its windows spilled onto the piazza, reflecting in the rippling water of the fountain. She shivered, against the sudden night chill that hadn't previously existed, she pulled her cardigan tightly around her. Elena wished Marco would hurry up. She was annoyed with him.

Brothers, who needs them? He was supposed to be her guardian. He was more preoccupied with the contents of his pants, canoodling with Carmela behind the church while she waited, cold and alone. Carmela and Elena worked together as waitresses at Coco's. Elena liked Carmela: she was fun to be around. She was also beautiful, with all the curves in the right places, hence Marco's willingness to be Elena's regular chaperone. When picking Elena up and dropping her off at work, he would flirt with Carmela. Well, tonight, his persistence had paid off. At last, the opportunity arose for him to discover the alluring curves of Carmela. He'd pleaded with Elena to wait by the fountain, promising he wouldn't be long.

Elena looked over to the church positioned behind her on the piazza opposite to the bar. Still no sign of Marco. It struck her how these two places—a church and a bar—seemed to silently confront each other across the fountain.In the corner next to the church, its salmon-pink walls turned a dull white by the moonlight; she saw the dark gaping hole which led to the park. The overhanging branches of the park's trees jutted out onto the piazza, creating foreboding shadows.

She turned towards the bar to focus on an altercation that had broken out. She recognised the Pardi brothers, Enzo and Gianni, being physically escorted out of the bar. They shouted abuse at the bar staff as they walked away. Elena dipped her head, hoping to go unnoticed as she moved further into the shadows behind the dolphin statue. She knew the brothers lived nearby and would likely cut through the park—the quickest way home. The Pardi brothers were not her favourite people, particularly the older one. Enzo, he gave her the creeps. His intentions were always far from innocent. Tonight, luck eluded her. Enzo swaggered straight towards her, peeling off his shirt.

"I need to cool down," he said to no one. "That was a good fight."

Gianni laughed. "You're crazy."

Enzo noticed the sodden area in front of him speckled with traces of Stan's vomit and moved to the left of the fountain. He caught sight of Elena.

"Well, well, what a nice surprise: the lovely Elena," he jeered, puffing out his bare chest. "Do you like what you see?"

With a curious, concerned smile, Gianni appeared beside Enzo and asked, "Hey, what are you doing here?"

Elena directed her answer at Enzo, fighting to keep the strength in her voice. "I am waiting for Marco."

She shouted Marco's name in the vain hope that it would encourage her brother to hurry. But Enzo lunged at her, clamping a firm hand over her mouth

"Shh, now. We don't want to disturb the neighbourhood, do we?"

Elena attempted to push his hand away, but it only seemed to enflame Enzo's alcohol-endorsed ardour. He tightened his grip on her, pulling her closer.

"Hush now, calm down. Just a little kiss. Be a good girl now."

Enzo pulled her tightly towards him as he spoke. He smelled of stale beer and tobacco.

"Let her go. Come on, let's go home." Gianni spoke calmly as he gently tried to pull Enzo towards the direction of the park's entrance.

Enzo stared menacingly into Elena's chocolate eyes, near black, her pupils large with fright. He was enjoying the fear he could see in her. He pushed her up against the fountain wall and lifted her skirt. She clamped her thighs together. He attempted to pull them apart, freeing his hand from her mouth to do so. She was able to let out a scream. Gianni stepped in, clasping his hand over her mouth.

"Be quiet now, Elena," he pleaded." Don't be a fool Enzo, you will get seen. Let's go home through the park."

"The park! Good idea, bro."

Gianni, relieved, removed his hands from Elena. But Enzo grabbed his shirt and thrust it into Elena's face, covering her mouth and tightening his grip. She felt panic at being unable to breathe, his fingers digging into her cheeks.

"Now, be a good girl. When I take this off, I don't want to hear a sound. Do that, and you won't get hurt." His voice was low and threatening.

Enzo looked into Elena's eyes, and she managed to nod. Enzo mirrored her nod as he took his hand away.

"Now, I want you to come with me to the park," he continued. Enzo held a tight grip around her shoulders as he spoke. Elena had no doubt about Enzo's intentions.

She appealed to Gianni. "No, please, please. I don't want to." Elena started to cry. "Let me go, I won't say a word. I promise."

Unaffected by her tears, Enzo gripped her face in his hand, his words menacing. "You won't say anything. If you do, I will pick on little Rosa next. No one will want you. I will make sure of it. You'll be used goods. You are best to keep it to yourself."

Elena tried to scream, but her voice shrunk, and she emitted a pitiful mumble. She felt Enzo's fist strike her jaw and then everything went dark. Gianni felt a surge of panic as he witnessed his brother's aggression.

"What have you done? She's out cold." he hissed, his eyes wide with fear.

"Come on, help me get her into the park," Enzo commanded.

Gianni stared at him in disgust, unable to move himself. He knew he should stop Enzo—everything inside him screamed to intervene—but the fear of what might happen next rooted him to the spot.

"Come on, we can't leave her here! You've got to help me—you're a part of this!" snapped Enzo.

Right now, Gianni hated his brother. He liked to watch Enzo fight, using his boxing skills and sheer wickedness to win, and he enjoyed the kudos from being his kin. But this was different. This was on another level. It made him sick to his stomach. However, he was afraid of his brother and the potential consequences if he went against him. He liked Elena more than he let on to anyone. He felt the dilemma rise within him.

"Come on, Gian, grab her on the other side," Enzo appealed to his faltering brother. "We will just lay her on the park's edge, and she will come round. I gave her a knockout punch. She won't remember a thing."

Unable to fully comprehend the situation, Gianni stood dumbly in front of him.

"Do it!" Enzo ordered, now becoming agitated by his brother's lack of support.

Enzo's malevolent behaviour made Gianni even more on edge. He supported Elena on the other side of Enzo, her warm body slumped against him. She was very light, and they got to the park's edge within seconds. Enzo pushed Gianni onward further into the darkness of the park. He steered off the pathway and instructed Gianni to help lay her down behind some shrubs.

"Now go and wait by the path and whistle if anyone is coming," ordered Enzo.

"Why? What you going to do? Let's go home now." Gianni clutched his brother's arm to reinforce his request.

"Just do it! Get fucking gone! Now!" Enzo threw a punch at Gianni with each word.

Gianni obeyed and turned to wait at the path. He retraced his steps through the park. His hands were shaking, his knuckles white from clenching his fists. He felt enraged, sick to his stomach, and wished he had stayed home. Stupid girl, out on her own like that–what was she thinking?

"Elena!"

Gianni heard Marco's call. He twisted round to warn Enzo. His brother must have heard, too. Gianni made out Enzo's form in the semi-darkness, making his way back across the park and adjusting his belt as he walked. Silently, they headed home together. Gianni's jaw clenched, his eyes fixed on the ground. He couldn't bring himself to look at his brother.

***

"Elena!" She heard Marco call her name. It took all her physical strength to raise herself from the ground and head towards the light coming from the direction of the piazza. Her body ached all over, and she was in a daze, but she staggered on. The voices around her merged into a distant hum, words slipping through her consciousness like water through fingers. She realised she was crying; her face felt wet with mute tears. She could not elicit the reason behind her trauma. She made it to the entrance of the park, and relief washed over as she saw the familiar shape of her brother running towards her. Her legs buckled, and she fell to the ground.

"My god, Elena, what's happened to you?"

Marco cradled his sister in his arms. He noticed the blood seeping from her skirt and down her legs. His hands trembled, fury building behind his eyes. His rage heightened as he deduced what someone had subjected his sister to. Not far behind Marco, Carmela arrived at the scene. Her eyes widened with the realisation of what had happened.

"Go and get some help! Go to the bar. She's been raped." Marco fired out his instructions.

He kissed Elena's hair and rocked her gently. Carmela returned with a small group of staff and customers, and they encircled the huddled siblings.

"We called the police," Carmela said.

Elena started to cough and come round.

"Here, give her some water," urged an onlooker.

A glass was passed through the crowd. Marco put it to Elena's lips. She took just enough to moisten her mouth.

"Who did this to you, Elena?" Marco asked, gently coaxing her.

Elena remained befuddled. The crowd around her ebbed and flowed and moulded together. She tried to focus on her brother's face. It kept changing shape, so she homed in on his smile. It was kind. The tall soldier, he was kind, too.

"Soldier...tall...fountain." Elena slowly produced each word, then felt herself slip back into unconsciousness.

Marco shook her by the shoulders, his voice cracking with panic. 'Elena! Wake up!' he shouted, his fear growing as her head lolled, unresponsive.

He shouted into her face, slapping her cheek. But his efforts did not rouse her.

The bartender returned, having gone to check around the fountain. "I saw a soldier here earlier with his drunken mate," he said. "You couldn't miss him. Tall as a giant, an English guy. The ground's all wet near the fountain. Big footprints in the mud, too, bigger than most men's feet. Makes sense, what the girl says."

The police arrived. They checked the scene and dispersed the crowd. The news had already trickled through Carva. Elena had regained consciousness but wasn't making a great deal of sense. The police advised Marco to take her home, let her rest, and let them know if she remembered anything else. They would be in touch over the next few days.

9

Twins

The cups clattered in the background at Le Karib Creole café. Morning commuters lined up for their takeaway caffeine fix. Grabbing an on-the-hoof breakfast as part of the hamster wheel life they found themselves in. The Paris sky was heavy with rain. Doc sipped his coffee, leaned back in his seat and inhaled the aroma. A smile traced his lips, and he nodded as he finished his third cup of the day.

"Beat dem bad, Fiamma," he whispered.

Doc dropped his money for Rita on the table and ambled up the street, against the flowing tide of city workers.

***

The Basel station was bright, its intricate ironwork stretching across the high ceiling. Light streamed in through the skylights, casting golden patches on the ground. The station's structure rebounded the echoes of human activity, producing a soft hum of sounds. Fi stepped onto her connecting train for the last leg of her journey to Zurich. Doc's image flashed across her thoughts. She linked her little fingers, sending a silent gesture of friendship into the breeze. She had pre-booked a hotel for the night in the Langstrasse a neighbourhood just a ten-minute walk from the station. Fi felt more confident now that she had made it this far. The train gathered speed as it pulled out of the terminal, and town buildings ebbed away, revealing an abundant green countryside. Fi wondered if Quin had ever been to Switzerland during his European travels. Surely, he must have, she thought, and the question tugged at her heart. She wanted to ask him. He had loved telling her about his adventures and the different modes of transport he'd used to journey around the world: from the luxury of first-class cabins to hitching rides on farm carts. His last epic train journey had been just a few months before he had met Fi. He'd travelled from Moscow to London by train—a two-day journey, born more out of necessity than choice. With him, he'd carried a plastic carrier bag stuffed with notes—over a hundred thousand pounds in hard-earned cash from working three long winters at Moscow's largest casino. Fi thought of the small studio flat he'd purchased with the funds. It was empty now, but she still cherished the two original artworks he'd gifted her—paintings that once hung on the flats deep red walls. Quin had bought them on a whim as he'd passed by an art gallery.

"They are for our home, my butterfly. When we get married, wherever we go in the world. We can hang them up and enjoy them together." She sniffed, smiling softly as she recalled his terms of endearment. Fi's mind curled round and settled on Ottie; her image was hard wired into Fi's psyche. Ottie had often spoken about her train journey through the Alps. Switzerland had been the first foreign country Ottie entered after leaving Italy just after the war. Fi considered how epic Ottie's first journey to England must have been, a young mother, heavily pregnant, with a toddler in tow. The thought filled her with courage to continue her own journey. Not one for crowds, she was thankful the carriage was empty. Trains always relaxed her—they allowed her to sift through her ruminating thoughts. The past remained her comfort, and she held onto it with a tight grip. She needed to work things out, to free herself, and to start living again. Doc's advice had hit home.

She thought of her present life, her daughters, and the young women they had become. She was thankful that the girls were well and that the family curse seemed to have lifted with her. Her great-grandmother, Nella Matanti, Ottie, and Fi's mother had all endured the loss of twins. Ottie had rarely spoken of her own experience—it was a subject too painful to broach. However, it became more pertinent when Fi herself was carrying twins.

Fi had borne her pregnancy well and safely delivered two healthy daughters. Agatha was the firstborn. Fi thought of little thoughtful Aggi, recalling how, as a newborn, she had been laid across her chest by the midwife. She had watched Aggi yawn, her big almond-shaped eyes looking around with calm, wide-eyed curiosity at the world she had entered. Edith came soon after, kicking and screaming, the smaller of the two. The nurses handed the wriggling, baby to her father. A cloth screen in hospital green separated the new parents from the gruesome sight of the surgery on Fi's abdomen.

The girl's father barely ever entered her mind these days. Their marriage had no chance from the beginning. It was too volatile between them; they were both young, inexperienced, and under pressure. He wasn't exactly the most loyal guy. They parted ways when the girls were just three weeks old.

Fi was drawn back to the present by the presence of another person in the train carriage and the stagnant smell of coffee in her nostrils.

"*Etwas zu essen oder zu trinken?* "Asked the youth, nodding toward the trolley laden high with provisions.

He hesitated, studying the blankness in Fi's wide-eyed expression for a moment longer before he coughed uneasily. Fi came to her senses.

"Oh, sorry, I was miles away. Erm, I don't speak... I mean, no thanks. *Nein, danke.*"

She gave him an apologetic smile.

"*Du bist Englisch?* Yes?" Seeing the affirmation in Fi's body language, he continued, "You sure you don't want something from the wagon? Coffee, maybe?"

"Oh, go on then, yes, okay, why not?"

Fi reached into her bag and fumbled in her purse for cash.

"Give me one of those croissant things, too."

"Mmm, yes, they are very good; I like those. Are you on holiday or business, maybe?"The youth asked, efficiently managing the sway of the train as he exchanged goods and produced change from his apron.

"Thank you," Fi answered, steadying the hot coffee handed down to her.

She noticed the youth raise his eyebrows, expectantly waiting for her answer.

"No, I'm not."

"Oh, I see, a woman of mystery."

He dropped her croissant down on the table, lowering his head to meet the level of her face. She observed the fuzz of pre-stubble across his upper lip. She felt a pull at her maternal strings despite his attempts at flirting.

"No, not quite. A woman who feels a long way from home, more like."

"I would love to leave home. I share with my brothers. No private space, you know?" His eyebrows arched with an inkling of indecency. "Well, enjoy," he finished politely.

Fi watched him as he headed towards the next carriage. She grinned, amused by the tomfoolery of young manhood. The train lulled her back into her reveries. Her thoughts turned to her family home, now sold. Fi cursed herself for grieving a house. A house without the people who shaped and formed it was just that—a house. But it felt as though she had lost the last link to her past, leaving her adrift.

Before leaving England, Fi had stood at her grandparents' grave in the cemetery. It had been a crazy notion, saying goodbye before her travels, and she had felt foolish standing there alone in the early morning mist. Running her fingers over the new headstone, she admired the ceramic oval picture of them together—a common feature of Italian memorials. She leaned over and kissed the image, the stone's chill lingering on her lips. The picture was a formal, almost totalitarian depiction of her youthful grandparents, perched together on a corrugated silver metal dustbin. She heard Hal's voice in her memory: "Just put some grass down, luv, and mow over me when I'm dead and gone," he'd chuckle, a roll-up dangling from his lips.

Ottie, of course, had done nothing of the sort. Instead, she covered his grave in flowers that bloomed throughout all the seasons, visiting every week without fail. A constant battle ensued between Ottie and the graveyard's resident squirrels, who enjoyed digging up and eating the various bulbs that she had planted. Fi laughed out loud at the memory of Ottie taking her shoe off to throw at the squirrels, shouting Italian expletives at them as her shoe soared into the branches of the trees. How Hal would have laughed too.

Walking back together from the cemetery one balmy summer Sunday, having just festooned Hal and Tilda's graves with flowers, Fi casually asked the question,

"Why is it just written *and a baby* on Mum's grave?"

Ottie glanced sideways at Fi as they walked arm in arm. Aggi and Edie skipped ahead in unison, their little bobbing blonde heads haloed by the lowering sun's rays.

"They never baptised the baby." It had no Christian name, so, in the eyes of our church, it didn't exist."

Ottie stopped in the shadow of the cemetery's ancient yew trees. She watched Fi curiously as she spoke. "Besides, I couldn't. Tilda never gave me any names. It was hard enough choosing a name for you."

"How did you pick my name?"

"Nella and I chose it. Grandad helped without realising. He called you 'little fiery one'. Your hair was very red when you were a baby, and you'd never settle. Fiamma means 'flame', so Nella and I thought it suited you."

"Well, it's unusual. Then again, so is your name."

Fi poked Ottie in the ribs and strung out the consonants in her name: "Oc-ta-vi-a." Fi said it a second time and skipped backwards in front of her grandmother.

"Yes, that was my Papa's choice." Ottie laughed out the words, amused by her granddaughter's antics. "He chose 'Octavia' as it signifies eight.

I was the eighth child to be born, you see."

"I knew none of this! We have meaningful names Nonna."

"I guess we do. Thankfully, Mamma overruled Papa's other choice, which was Italia."

"That would have been very grand! Being named after your country." Fi paused, and when she spoke again, her tone became more serious as she probed her grandmother further: "Did you name your own twins, Nonna?"

"I did. I named them, but I never got to bury them."

Fi waited patiently, hoping Ottie would continue, but afraid she might have pushed too far. In the end, Ottie broke the silence just as it began to get uncomfortable.

"It was the middle of winter when my boys were born at home. Hal went to get the midwife in the snow. No phones, you see, in those days. They had come early, like twins usually do. I had Hal's mum with me. Do you remember her? She lived next door. You called her Little Nanny. Her back had gone with age, and she was near doubled over. I guess it made her look little stooped over like that.

Anyway, Hal came back with the midwife. She was a mean-looking ole thing: arms like tree trunks and a face that never smiled. She said Mediterranean women were noisy and that I would be screaming the house down soon. I told her straight that it didn't happen with my Tilda, and it wouldn't happen this time. She felt my stomach and said the babies were facing the wrong way up. She turned them with her bare hands, pushing and pulling away at me. I thought my innards were gonna fall out. The pain made me near faint. The old bat was surprised by how well I coped. She said she had to get the doctor, who was at home having lunch. She went to fetch him from his house. Told me to keep panting and hold it together, told me she wouldn't be long.

Well, it blew a blizzard outside, snowing thick and fast. It was freezing, and we lit the fire in the bedroom. I did all I could to hold on to those babies until the midwife returned with the doctor. It was nigh on over an hour when she got back. My waters had broken, and I had started to push. I couldn't stop myself–the first boy's feet were sticking outta me. Neither of 'em would touch the baby, said it would shock it. Stood at the end of the bed watching me, they were. I could see the worry on their faces. I called the first boy Davy. Dr Pitt took him quickly out of the room to where Hal was waiting. I wanted to see him. I never saw him; they didn't let me.

Then it happened in seconds. Before I had time to think, the next baby was on his way. He came headfirst. He was the one that should have been born first. But Davy moved in the way. I pushed and pushed, but he wouldn't budge. The cord, you see, it was wrapped around his neck three times. It just got tighter the more I pushed. The midwife had to cut the cord before he could be born. He came out quick then. Limp and blue, not crying. We called him Stanley.

Hal said that Dr Pitt wrapped the boys up together in newspaper and put them on top of the piano in the front room. When it was time to leave, he put them in his bag. Away they went. I never held them. Never said goodbye. Hal told me they had thick, black, curly hair. I think of my brother Angelo–it's the only face I have. No grave, nothing. Tell you what, though, that midwife had her work cut out. She had changed her tune by the end of that night. When your Aunt Nella was born, she came on her day off. It was a hot summer day, that time."

Brave Ottie, a product of her time. Fi was thankful for having her in her life for as long as she had. She wished it could have been the same with her own mother.

Fi swallowed the last dregs of her coffee, and the grains hit the back of her throat, leaving a bitter aftertaste. She felt uncomfortable in her seat. Fi pulled out her compact mirror and studied her features: large, pale grey eyes, auburn hair framed with high arching eyebrows, a small flat nose, and a pale complexion. Her mother's likeness reflected back at her. Tilda's black-and-white picture, with its muted bronze frame, had always held pride of place on the front room's mantelpiece. The years had passed, and her mother looked down from the mantelpiece, ageless and forever young.

The best room in the house, reserved for visitors, was the front room. It was a room that only glimpsed the sun early in the morning, remaining shadowed and cool throughout the rest of the day. Ottie had decorated the walls with a fan-patterned, cream sheen wallpaper. An Artex ceiling in a similar pattern to match, reminiscent of the *Great Gatsby* era, and Hal's framed canvases and sketches covered all four of the compact room's walls. The giant, ornate oak mantelpiece, painted over in a heavy white gloss, dominated the room with a ceremonious presence. Intricate scrolls and whirls adorned the wood, with a large, bevelled-edge mirror positioned at its centre. Tilda's picture was positioned on the top shelf, gradually joined by more pictures of deceased loved ones until the shelf below had to be cleared to make room for even more. Ottie had outlived all bar one from her generation: Zia Nari, the great aunt with the infectious laugh. What sad news Fi was bringing to her.

She reached deeper into her bag and found the locket, which she placed around her neck. She studied the face of her young aunt within it. The almond-shaped dark eyes, the full Cupid's bow mouth and black hair adorning a delicate face - she was undoubtedly beautiful. Zia Nari had come to England to help when Tilda was due to give birth to her twins. By then she was a rounded, middle-aged woman with eyes always holding onto mischief. She was happy to visit England for the first time, blissfully unaware of the tragedies ahead for her niece. Ottie and Hal never recovered from the loss of Tilda. They carried their guilt as individuals. It wrapped around their hearts with a tight grip and eroded a part of them forever.

She could see it now—the way Ottie kept herself busy, her hands constantly occupied with work, as though she feared what idleness might bring. And Hal, with his long, quiet silences by the fire, the roll-up dangling from his lips as he stared into the flames. They had never spoken of their loss, not openly, but Fi had always felt it, like a shadow stretching across the family.

Fi wished for more. A memory she could hold on to, her mother's voice, her laugh, or her touch. But all she had were fragments pieced together from Ottie's stories and Hal's silences. The rest was lost to time, like so many others in the family.

Fi studied her reflection again. Looking back into her compact mirror, the locket rested neatly against her collarbone, a quiet reminder of everything her family had endured and everything they had lost.

10

Pea Thief

Factory work suited Ottie. She soon became adept at her job and enjoyed the daily routine. Despite Alberto's protests, she was determined to continue; besides, the money was useful. Most of her wages went towards the upkeep of her family, she kept a little aside to treat herself. Geno, obviously for a price, had procured a pretty pink rouge cream for her.

She enjoyed working with Annamaria, too. Their conversations on the rides to and from work made the journey pass quickly. Ottie still liked to take lunch on her own, enjoying the downtime and observing the activities in the camp. During her break, she often watched the comings and goings at the food store. It had become apparent that during lunchtime; the stores were generally unlocked, as the kitchen staff required access. Most staff, however, were either busy serving or eating food at this time. Deliveries, she had noted, always arrived at the start of the week.

"Today would be a good day," she muttered to herself.

She touched the soft cotton apron scrunched up in her lap. The edges were decorated with a scalloped crochet border added by Fina. The previous night, Ottie had folded the apron in half and crudely sewed the sides up to make a large pocket. She needed to tie the apron around her waist underneath her baggy overalls. She sniffed the pale pink material, which smelled of washing soap and ingrained cooking smells, reminding her of home and Mamma.

It was an overcast, chilly day, discouraging anyone from sitting outside. Nobody else had come to sit on the bank for their lunch - not that many ever did. It would only take a moment to go into the stores. No one would see her. Anyway, who would miss an apron full of smuggled food? Food was so scarce at home, even Salvo was struggling to catch any rabbits these days. Ottie egged herself on; now was the time.

Before standing up, she stuffed the apron into her pocket, undoing her overall to the waist. She needed to be discreet; drawing any attention to herself was the last thing she wanted. With confident, purposeful strides, she walked as though heading for the latrines around the corner of the factory building.

At the edge of the building, she switched direction, scurrying across the dusty patch of land between the two buildings. For a few seconds, out in the open, she felt utterly exposed. She eased herself through the large metal double doors, which had been left ajar just enough for her to slip in without moving them and making any noise.

The store had a well-designed layout with a raised vaulted ceiling that kept the temperature much cooler than it was outside. Produce was stacked high in crates, and sacks were propped against the walls. She scanned around quickly, looking for a word she could recognise on the hessian sacks. One sack had been neatly folded open for easy access: it contained dried peas, with a metal scoop sunk into the middle of the spherical, pale sage peas.

She checked once more over her shoulder before kneeling down. She wanted to ensure that no one would detect her visit to the stores. Carefully, she began to fill the apron pocket, steadying the fabric with one hand and scooping with the other. She worked methodically, avoiding spills that might give her away. Before leaving, she planned to check for footprints on the dusty grey floor to ensure no trace of her visit.

Uninterrupted, she persisted, her focus sharp, until a shadow fell across her. She froze, the air around her suddenly colder. Slowly, she turned and found herself face-to-face with a tall soldier standing behind her. His hands were in his pockets, his head cocked slightly to one side, watching her with a calm but unreadable expression.

Ottie's heart hammered in her chest. He could only have been there for a few seconds. Ottie froze under his gaze. She gently dropped the scoop back into the sack and raised herself up off her knees to face him. He beckoned for her to hand over the sagging apron, now heavy with contraband. Ottie handed it over to him and dropped her head with shame. He motioned towards the door.

"Go on, get back to work. We will deal with this later." He said in a steady, measured tone.

Ottie didn't wait for further instruction she ran past him, her face hot with humiliation.

Throughout her shift, she kept an anxious lookout for the tall soldier. He marched up and down the factory, sometimes stopping at a work-bench to speak with a worker. Thankfully, he didn't come near her. She caught his eye a couple of times and quickly turned away.

When the siren sounded three times, signalling the end of her shift, the workers prepared to leave. Ottie joined a group of female companions gathered in the square, waiting for their truck driver. Nearly home, she thought. So far, so good.

Then she saw him. The towering image of the tall soldier coming across the busy square soon made her think differently. She noticed a flick of pink cotton in his hand, swinging as he walked. He had spotted her and was making a beeline towards her. Her legs didn't know whether to cave in or run away. Instead, she jutted her chin into the air, faking confidence. He halted in front of her, his shadow stretching across her and the group of women. The chatter around her quietened, curiosity filling the silence. He held the pink apron up to his shoulder height.

"It is Octavia Matanti, isn't it?"

"Yes, I am her," Ottie replied, raising her face up toward him, her heart racing.

"I believe you misplaced this."

He held the apron out toward her. Ottie reached for it, but just as her fingers grazed the fabric, he raised his arm higher, keeping it out of her grasp. Then, with a flick of his wrist, he lowered it, allowing her to snatch it from him. Ottie stuffed the apron into her pocket as quickly as she could, her face blazing with heat. She despised being the centre of attention and longed for the conversation to end.

"Thank you, I must have... I am so sorry. I..." Her words lost themselves under her tongue; redness started spreading up into her cheeks.

Before she even had time to gasp, she felt herself being lifted off the ground. The tall soldier had clasped her arms tightly against her sides and hoisted her into the air as though she weighed nothing. Ottie froze, her body rigid with fear. He carried her a short distance before depositing her inside a large ring of stacked truck tires that came up to her shoulders. She stared up at him, her humiliation complete as a small crowd gathered, their laughter echoing in the square.

His dark pewter eyes locked onto hers before he looked away. He glanced casually at her headscarf and flicked at the stiff cotton bow with his finger. Then, to her utter disbelief, he leaned down and pressed a warm kiss onto her forehead.

"Let that be a lesson to you, Signorina Matanti." Mirth bubbled beneath his words.

The small crowd erupted into hysterical laughter. Ottie watched as he walked away, restricted by the tyres. Annamaria, assisted by a couple of women, rushed to her aid, helping her climb out of the tyres.

"What did you do to deserve that kind of attention?" asked Annamaria.

Ottie felt flummoxed by the events and relieved it was all over. She left Annamaria's question unanswered, still trying to fathom it out for herself.

11

The Cobbler's War

I t had been an arduous day. Despite it being evening, Annamaria
felt like another hard day lay ahead of her within the routine of her
home life. She reflected on the day's events, her thoughts returning to
poor Octavia. Why had the tall soldier placed her in that stack of tyres?
    When it had happened, Annamaria had felt uncomfortable, as though
she had witnessed something she shouldn't have. The humiliation he
inflicted felt like an abuse of authority. She didn't trust the British. She
didn't trust any man in a soldier's uniform. Annamaria firmly believed that
the best way to survive the war was to keep her head down and blend in.
Something that her friend Octavia didn't seem capable of by any means.
    She stepped from the street into her home, entering through the
large wooden door worn down by overuse and exposure to the sun.
Annamaria paused, giving herself a moment to adjust to the darkened
room. The damp air and the familiar coolness layered onto her skin.
    It was too quiet; her family was nowhere to be seen. Just as she was
about to question their whereabouts, the door opposite suddenly burst
open, casting its light before her. Figures appeared, silhouetted in the
door's frame. Her children scurried in towards her, shouting for their
mother. Little Lucia trailed behind, clutching a chestnut-brown chicken
against her chest. Her arms disappeared into its feathers as it fought to
free itself, its feet almost dragging on the floor.

Guilio ran toward her, forcefully pushing her back as he threw his arms around her waist. "Mamma! We have a chicken! Nonno says we will have eggs for breakfast," he exclaimed, his face bright with excitement. Annamaria ruffled his hair and looked across at her other son, Filipo. He held back, at the grand age of thirteen, he felt it wasn't done to display such affection to his mother.

"Filipo brought it," Guilio continued excitedly. "Nonno said we can keep it in the yard, and we will have a feast!"

The chicken had managed to escape Lucia's grasp, landing on the table with a thud. A monochrome poo escaped from its behind onto the tablecloth just as Master Lucien appeared at the door. Hindered by his arthritic knee, he leaned onto his walking stick for support.

"Filipo, where did you get it from?" Annamaria demanded, her voice sharp.

Correcting his adolescent slouch, Filipo glanced at his grandfather, he moved to stand by the door, giving himself time before he mentally confirmed his dialogue, and then replied to her: "Uh, I just came across it."

He caught his mother's frown, the one where the fold above her nose deepened—the way it always did when she was cross.

"When I finished work." Filipo dropped his head and swung his foot as he spoke. "It was the farm. It followed me as I walked home."

"Take it back," demanded Annamaria. "It belongs to the farm!"

"But, Mamma, you can't take Tata back. I like her." Lucia protested. "Nonno said he can build a little house, and I am going to help him. I drew a picture. We will paint it yellow."

Lucia's big eyes looked up, tears teetering on their edges as she pulled down on her mamma's skirts. Exasperated, Annamaria threw her hands up towards her father.

"Papa, why are you encouraging this?"

She bounced her hands off the side of her head in frustration.

"Argh, I do not have time for this."

She reached for her apron and tied it around her waist in sharp, angry movements.

"I best start dinner. Get that thing out of here. Shoo Shoo! ," Annamaria shouted, waving her arms at the bird.

The chicken nonchalantly dropped to the floor.

"Filipo," Master Lucien said gently to his eldest grandson, "please take Tata into the yard."

Filipo was unable to pick up the bird but managed to chase it outside. The chicken zigzagged across the room, flapping its wings and making feathers fly into the air, much to Lucia's delight, she squealed with laughter at the chicken's antics.

"Where's Valentina?" said Annamaria, ignoring the chaos around her. "I told her to prepare the sauce."

"She managed to get some work today," replied Master Lucien.

"Huh. What work will a seamstress have in these times?"

Master Lucien's response surprised her. "About the same amount as a cobbler."

Master Lucien watched for the wince he knew would follow. Work in his trade was also scarce. In the years of the war, he turned to cobbling, mending the shoes of the less fortunate, and sometimes soldiers' boots.

"She's managed to get some work at Signore Pardi's place," Master Lucien continued, when Annamaria did not bite at the bait.

He watched his daughter scurry about the kitchen; her stormy mood reflected in the way she stirred the sauce and prepared the vegetables. She wiped her brow with the back of her hand, an action that made clear her weariness.

"Annamaria," he mumbled as she buzzed to and from the stove.

"Annamaria!" He raised his voice a notch.

She turned but continued stirring the sauce. Her dishevelled hair, flecked with grey, framed her face. Dark circles prominent beneath her hazel eyes.

"Come, sit," Master Lucien requested.

"But, Papa..." She waved at the bubbling sauce on the stove.

"It will keep a moment. Sit with me, please." He requested again, pulling out a chair beside him.

Reluctantly, she wiped her hands on her apron and sat down. He momentarily removed his black felt beret, scratching his thick hair, a scatter of white against the brown.

"You work too hard. Let Valentina come and work at the army base too. Then you won't have to do so many shifts."

He had suggested this before and was hoping she would relent this time.

"No, she needs to be here to help you and look after the children. She shouldn't have gone today and left you."

"She wants to help. I can manage them."

Annamaria lowered her head and anxiously picked at her nails. Her thoughts drifted to her former life in Naples with her husband, Aldo. She reflected on the immense upheavals that had taken place when she lost both her home and Aldo within a matter of days.

Just after hearing about Aldo's heroic death in battle, Annamaria's entire neighbourhood had been destroyed, reduced to ruins by relentless bombings. On the day her home was lost, she had been visiting her dying mother and made it back to the family house just in time to say goodbye. Lucia had been kicking deep inside her belly then, a bittersweet reminder of life amid so much loss.

She had ended up back in the house where her life had started, with nothing left. Though grateful for a roof over her head, she couldn't ignore the burden her return placed on her father. A strong sense of duty compelled her to stay, even as she acknowledged the extra stress she brought into his later years.

"The soldiers treat you well there, don't they?" Master Lucien asked, his black eyes sharp and studying her face. "You have no cause for concern. Valentina… she wants to help."

"As well as any, I guess," Annamaria replied, not meeting his gaze. "One went a bit too far today, though."

Master Lucien raised an eyebrow, intrigued. He leaned forward as she recounted the day's events—the humiliating scene where Octavia was lifted into the tyres in front of a crowd. Annamaria noticed her father's lips curl in amusement at the image, which irritated her.

Just then, Valentina burst through the open door, carrying a string of onions in her arms. Their brown skins flaked off as she moved.

"Ha, what are you two colluding about?" Valentina joked; her pale skin flushed rosy from the exertion of striding home.

She held up the onions proudly, displaying her prize.

"I got these as a gift from Signora Pardi. What do you think of that?" Valentina dumped them onto the table.

"I think you can make me a nice onion soup like my *grandmere* used to make when I was a boy in Nantes." Master Lucien quipped, his grin broad as Valentina kissed his cheeks.

Annamaria stood up to continue making the meal. Her sister promptly came to her side, and as was their usual habit of cooking together, they swiftly prepared dinner. The family soon gathered around the table, tucking into their filled bowls. Annamaria reminded the children about their table manners, though the excitement about the chicken dominated the conversation. When the meal wound down, Annamaria recounted Octavia's story to Valentina, who, to Annamaria's dismay, found it just as amusing as their father had.

"I see Octavia's brother, Salvo, in the bar sometimes," Valentina, remarked casually. " He's not at all like his father or brother; he's really quiet."

Master Lucien leaned back, stroking his stubble thoughtfully.

"I can't believe how quickly time has passed since I made little Octavia her first shoes. She was such a tiny little dot with a head full of curls. Renzo, her father, came with her. Without fail, he would bring each of his children to me for shoes, and he always paid upfront. There's no doubt he was a tyrant, but I always saw the pride in his eyes when he left with a new pair for his child."

Master Lucien gained his reputation as a skilled shoemaker, earning him the name Master. He reflected on his years as a cobbler. Before the war, he had been known for crafting custom Italian shoes from the finest leather. He had come to Italy from his native France to work for the king, with dreams of travelling the world fuelled by his incredible talent and ambition.

Instead, he had stayed, settling down after meeting Giulia, who worked as a maid in the palace. Sitting in his black widower's attire, he reflected on the love they had shared and the family they had built. Master Lucien leaned back, watching his family as they chatted together. Amidst, the general mayhem of the daily routine of tidying up and preparing the children for bedtime. Lucia interrupted his thoughts, her small arms wrapping around his neck as she bid him goodnight.

She whispered into his neck. "Look after Tata. Don't let Mamma throw her away."

Master Lucien comfortingly patted her back, as Annamaria gently lifted Lucia into her arms and carried her to bed. The moment she walked back in, Annamaria felt her father's gaze upon her, a silent question hanging in the air.

She met his look and answered before he could ask. "I will think about keeping the chicken, but I don't want Valentina to work at the base."

"Well, that's a start, I guess," he replied.

Master Lucien collected his cobbler's tools while Annamaria stood with her arms folded, watching him. He knew his daughter well, pressuring her further would only increase her resistance.

"You know, I have not always been a widowed shoemaker. I haven't always been an old man in this failing body. I, too, have been a soldier. Yes, Annamaria, your own father, for thirty-eight long months, fought in the French army's fiercest battles in the last war.

I fought in places that were obliterated, filled with destruction and death. I survived the worst of the worst, cheated death many times. I felt death in every part of my life. If it wasn't death, it was boredom. Boredom almost killed me at times, boredom and fear. The endless marches, the sleepless nights, the game of waiting. Tired, with mud up to my ankles. I watched suffering on both sides.

Sometimes, the boredom was so great that we broke the rules. We left our trenches to meet with the Germans, exchanging cigarettes and chatting like comrades. They were just like us. The true enemy wasn't them—it was our own officers, and the leaders above them.

I will never forget my fallen comrades. Never will I forget the sound of their cries against the initiators of that bloody war."

Annamaria stood in silence, absorbing his words. She had never heard this story before. Master Lucien took his little wooden working bench and the tools of his trade outside into the street. As the evening sun cast a warm glow, he began repairing the old shoes he had acquired, planning to sell them to passersby. He hoped he might manage a sale this evening.

12

Ice Cream With Strangers

The central station in Zurich, Hauptbahnhof, gave a grand reception to the city. Its entrance featured a large archway supported by two pairs of mock Roman pillars. Positioned atop its arch was a clock with a circular face made of enamel. Elegant female alabaster statues adorned the roof of the building. The figures held onto the Swiss flag, that proudly flapped in the light breeze. The red flag stood out against the clear blue sky.

Fi had already mapped out her route on the train and turned right towards Langstrasse. Her steps felt bolder than they had in Paris. The area around the train station was bustling with people, mainly families. Fi remembered it was a Saturday, which accounted for the significant presence of children in the crowd.

She headed towards the yellow-painted zebra crossing, taking note that the road across the street tallied with her directions. As she approached the pavement's edge, she glanced up at the street name, trying to work out its pronunciation. Out of the corner of her eye, she saw a car speeding toward her. In an instant, she realised the driver wasn't paying attention. A yellow flash of hair crossed her eyes as the person in front of her also flicked their head towards the car. Fi's instincts kicked in, she grabbed the person in front and pulled them towards her. The car's brakes screeched to a halt as Fi and the other woman tumbled to the ground together.

A small crowd immediately formed around Fi and the stranger. Their handbags and various body parts had become tangled and intertwined. Fi's luggage case had split open and spewed out her possessions onto the road, one of its wheels still spun slowly around. The woman on top of Fi, was heavy and reeked of cheap perfume. The woman's tone was unfriendly as she rolled off Fi, muttering words Fi didn't understand. Holding their mobile phones, some in the crowd started recording. Her face turning crimson with rage, the woman screamed at the crowd. The crowd of onlookers quickly scattered.

The door of the car—a silver BMW—opened. From the open door came the sound of blaring music and the screech of young children. The driver, a sophisticated woman in her mid-thirties, emerged and walked over to the human bundle sprawled on the road. Fi had just managed to separate herself from the other woman, who was now seated on the pavement's edge. The stranger clutched her ankle, which was starting to swell, the flesh spilling over the ties of her rope-design wedge sandals.

The exchange between the two women was curt. The sophisticated woman handed her business card over to the road victim. The yellow-haired woman took one look at it and threw it back at her. She spat on the ground to confirm her disdain. The elegant woman peered down at her in disgust she shook her head vehemently. She strode back to her car and drove off with a loud screech, the yellow-haired woman giving her a rude salute as she passed

An elderly gentleman with a distinguished silver moustache assisted Fi in picking up her things. He cast his eyes down at the woman on the floor, who was now attempting to raise herself from the pavement, he gave her a disdainful look. She had outstretched her hand towards him for support to raise herself, but he did not seem willing to help and ignored her by looking up at Fi. Fi thanked him for his help, and he soon departed.

"*Scheisse!*" cursed the yellow-haired woman after him.

Fi guessed its meaning and extended her hand to help the woman up. "You English, *ja?*"

She scaled Fi's body and lifted herself to meet her gaze. Fi noticed that her pale blue eyes were smudged with black kohl. She wore a foundation two shades paler than her natural skin, which had settled in the creases under her eyes.

"Yes, I am. Your ankle looks painful. Do you need to go to the hospital?" They both looked down at her left ankle, bulging around the crisscross rope ties of her sandal.

"No, I just need ice on it and rest. You help me home? I live just around the corner." The woman's voice had a smoker's throaty tone.

Fi noticed that her red lipstick had bled into the smoker's lines around her mouth. The unlikely pair headed awkwardly across the zebra crossing in the direction the woman pointed to. Fi, while supporting the woman on one side, was also attempting to wheel her case with her free hand.

"My house is just round this corner, third door along. I am Yara. What's your name, English girl?"

Fi introduced herself as they clumsily made it across the road, they paused for a breather, leaning against the wall. With every step, Yara's full weight pressed onto Fi, tugging at her shoulder. With her heeled shoes on, Yara was about a foot taller than Fi. Despite her ankle swelling, she refused to take her heels off.

Making two additional stops, they reached the third door on the partially tree-lined Schienengasse. Fi cast her eyes up at Yara's apartment block. The building had seen better days. The concrete cladding hung onto the grime of the street, resulting in muted ochre shades. Heavy metal shutters blanked out the lower windows. Yara leaned against a car that had parked illegally on the pavement and rummaged through her bag for the front door keys. The metal-and-glass front door had a chipboard panel at its base, where someone had obviously attempted to kick it open.

Fi scrutinised Yara as she perched up against the car. She was muttering under her breath with frustration, rummaging through her bag, unsuccessful in locating her keys within its jumbled contents. Her belly hung over the top of her white, near see-through, skintight jeans as she bent forward to peer into her bag. Her low-cut, black shirt revealed a red bra, her bosoms, speckled with the marks of sun damage, spilling out over the top. Her head was bent down, her yellow hair over her face. Fi could see the tidemark of black roots close to her scalp.

"Ah, here they are!" Yara exclaimed, dangling a bunch of keys from her scarlet-painted nails.

They stepped into the building's darkness, leaving the noise behind. Colourful pamphlets littered the worn coconut coir matting on the floor. The corridor echoed the building's gloomy exterior: a line of grease ran along the wall, parallel with the rising stairs.

"It's the first door upstairs." Yara directed.

Yara managed the stairs herself, hopping up each step and supporting herself against the bannisters. Fi kept close behind her in case she toppled. Once inside, Yara hobbled, supporting herself by holding onto furniture. She fell heavily onto a worn, burgundy velvet sofa and lifted her ankle up onto the coffee table, knocking magazines to the floor as she did so.

"Please, get me peas in freezer," Yara asked, pointing towards the kitchen area. "Oh, and get the ice cream. Two spoons in a draw. *Guete.* Excuse, I need to make call."

Fi moved to the kitchen, which was part of the open-plan sitting room. The sink was overflowing with dirty dishes. At the far end of the counter loomed an enormous fridge-freezer.

Yara proceeded with her phone call while Fi searched the freezer. Yara's voice seemed to blend into the background, rising and falling as she spoke in her native tongue on the phone. Fi found a tea towel and used it to cover the peas, then placed them on Yara's ankle. She went back to grab the spoons and ice cream.

The door to the other room caught her attention. She caught sight of Yara's bedroom. The king-size bed stood at its centre, covered with a tiger-print throw. On the red-painted wall above it hung two gilt cherubs playing musical instruments. Between them, a leather strap dangled, with handcuffs clipped to its end. A bottle of baby oil sat on the bedside table. She became aware that Yara was no longer talking and felt her eyes penetrate her back. Fi let out an uncomfortable cough and turned round to face Yara.

"Erm, so I have the ice cream." Her voice felt small.

She waved the spoons in the air, attempting to distract Yara, who folded her arms over her escaping bosoms. Her eyes narrowing.

"You look in my bedroom; you see where I work. I am sex worker." Yara's manner and tone was confrontational.

Fi's cheeks flushed. "Oh, that's really... interesting." Fi was aware of the awkwardness in her voice; she had never met a sex worker before.

She held up the tub of salted caramel ice cream.

"Shall we?"

Hesitation hung in the air between the two women until the fridge interrupted the silence, emitting a mooing sound. Yara's red lips curved upward, and they both couldn't help but laugh. Yara patted the sofa's vacant seat next to her.

"Come, Fiamma, funny English girl, sit with me. We eat ice cream like girls in American movies."

Fi obliged, and they tucked into the softening ice cream straight from the tub.

"I just lost client today, with this sore foot...Is it 'arnkle', you say?" Fi nodded. "Ankle."

"Ankle, *ja*. He comes here this time every week. I handcuff him, I spank him, he likes, he goes. I look after myself and earn my own money. Here in Zurich, sex worker can do this, but now they come and traffic girls, young girls. I do this work thirty years, but now it's not so good."

She lifted the frozen peas off her ankle to have a look.

"Ay, it's sore." She continued, "I have no regulars for next two days. I can't go out and work with this! Oh well, it should go down if I rest it for these days."

"Well, we had a lucky escape," Fi offered.

"Huh, you think! That stupid bitch in her nice car. I lose money now until I can work!"

Fi, a little irritated by Yara's negativity, added. "It can always be worse. You know, you have a sore ankle. It will fix itself."

Yara frowned and shook her head. Her response carried an undertone of anger.

"Easy for you to say. Life always hard for me. And people? Pah! They disappoint. People are weak, and if they are not weak, they are cruel."

Removing her right trainer, Fi lifted her leg and placed her prosthetic foot on the coffee table beside Yara's injured ankle.

"I lost my foot in a car accident last year. I didn't work for six months. Luckily, I got some sick pay, but that doesn't replace my foot."

Yara leaned in, her curiosity piqued. She inspected Fi's foot closely, touching the lifelike silicone toes with a featherlight graze.

"That is very clever foot... Were you crossing road? You're not very good at it...are you?"

"No, I was driving a car with my fiancé, and we went into the back of someone at speed on the motorway. I got my foot crushed by the car's engine. Both of us ended up in the hospital. It was a pile-up."

Fi felt a lump rise in her throat. The two women concentrated on their ice cream for a moment before Yara broke the uncomfortable silence.

"Ah, life, I need smoke." Yara said, delving into her bag and pulling out her cigarettes.

She offered one to Fi, who declined, before lighting up and taking a big draw.

"So, where is your man now? You're here in Zurich alone, aren't you?"

Yara let out a puff of smoke, which swirled in front of her. She waved the air to disperse it and directed her gaze into Fi's eyes.

"He is away in China on business."

"Huh, men. You trust him when he is away? I entertain men who are away on business all the time. Why you here alone?" Yara waved her own question away dismissively. "Actually, I don't care why. But you are a fool if you put your trust in a man."

"I trust him completely." Fi said firmly.

Yara continued relentless. "*Ja*, really? When you last speak to him?"

Fi clenched her jaw, trying to contain her annoyance.

"A while ago. He is a long way from me. I can't just call. It's not that easy."

"No call? No text? You crazy. Give me phone, I call. Then you know, you'll know, by his voice!"

Fi hesitated but handed her phone to Yara, already finding Quin in the contacts for her.

"It's late in China now. He will be working. He works in casinos; you won't get to talk to him."

"Casinos! Casinos are all about sex and drugs."

Yara studied Quin's photo on the screen.

"I see he is handsome. Pah, you have no chance lady."

She pressed call and listened for a moment.

"Hmm, voicemail is full," she said, handing the phone back to Fi.

Fi placed her head in her hands.

"I know," she mumbled.

"Listen, I really need to get checked into my hotel. Can I get you anything before I go?"

"No, you go," Yara answered with a flick of her wrist. "It does not pay to help people. You have done enough."

Fi sensed a trace of sadness in Yara's words.

"There are moments in life when we all need help."

"Kindness is weakness," Yara persisted. "You need to be strong, Fiamma. Otherwise, you will be used up." Yara's comment sounded more like a criticism than advice.

"Maybe. Take care of yourself. And thank you for the ice cream."

Yara stretched out her hand to say goodbye. She grasped Fi's hand firmly with both of hers. Fi sensed the warmth and compassion hidden beneath Yara's tough exterior.

13

Passage To Napoli

Ottie was grateful to have a break from work after the events of the previous day. Her father had granted the day off solely because her sister Mina had come to visit from Naples. Salvo had borrowed a beaten-up old car and offered Mina a ride. Salvo was determined to make the most of the trip, and stock up on black-market goods from Naples. Contraband had significantly increased since the Anglo-Americans had arrived in the city. The scarcity of flour in the countryside had forced the Matanti bakery to resort to making marzipan sweets to replace the bread they could no longer bake. Salvo brought back Mina and as many supplies as the compact car could carry - flour, coffee, chocolate, and tobacco. Later that evening, he planned to take Mina back to Naples and bring back even more flour.

Mina was thankful for the chance to see her brother and visit her family but wished her boys could have come along. The cramped space of the tiny car and the dangerous Naples roads made it impossible, so her boys were left at home with their father and grandmother. As she left, she had watched them waving goodbye from the apartment balcony. Aged two and four, they pressed their cheeks against the railings watching, their eyes following their mamma as she disappeared from view. Despite her reluctance, Mina knew she needed to visit her family—it had been far too long.

The uprising in Naples, known as the "Four Days of Naples," led to significant events in the city. It remained fresh in her mind. Corpses had littered the streets in the aftermath of the riots and even weeks later, the authorities still hadn't finished removing the bodies. Nearby churches stored stacks of them, waiting to be laid to rest.

Salvo was taken aback by the destruction he encountered upon entering Naples. Blocked roads forced him to take detours. The stench of sewage seeped up through cracked flagstones, making it impossible to ignore the city's suffering. Salvo saw the toll the city had taken mirrored in Mina herself. Her face was almost skeletal, her eyes weak. Her lankiness was intensified by her lack of body fat. The vibrant energy that defined Mina was gone; her signature carefree laughter, such a crucial aspect of her personality, was missing.

During their journey to Carva, the two siblings exchanged news. Riots involving Partisans, Fascists, and the criminal Camorra were still common in the recovering city of Naples. Though things were finally calming down, Salvo hoped this meant Mina would be safer in the city.

Being back with her family briefly, Mina's previous radiance re-emerged. The camaraderie and gossip between the sisters transported her to a more innocent time. Nari, always enamoured with Mina's gorgeous auburn locks, insisted on styling her hair. She pinned Mina's hair into elegant rolls, finishing the look with care, while Ottie added a touch of her new rouge to Mina's cheeks. Mina wore her sole decent dress for the event, which now hung loosely on her diminished figure.

With only a few ingredients available, such as wild mountain herbs, chicken heads, and feet, the sisters cooked together and used their inventiveness to create a meal. Even with limited ingredients, the sisters cooked a decent meal, and the Matanti family sat down to enjoy it together. Papa brought out the red wine he had saved for a special occasion.

The time passed too quickly, and Mina soon found herself saying a tearful goodbye to her clan. She climbed into the front of the compact car, ready to return home. Ottie and Geno were also hitching a ride with Salvo to Carlotta's house. Once again, Geno sought to regain

Carlotta's affection by asking her to the dance at Coco's. Ottie was going to join them and meet with Alberto. There was nothing Ottie loved more than dancing.

Salvo sounded the horn outside Carlotta's house as Ottie stood at the door, peering up towards Carlotta's apartment. Carlotta's mamma appeared on the balcony, waving down to Ottie to signal that Carlotta was on her way. Ottie waved back, but her smile faltered when she noticed Carlotta's mamma tighten her shawl and cast a disapproving glare over her shoulder. Turning, Ottie saw the cause—Geno had stepped out of the car to open the door for Carlotta.

After leaving the building, Carlotta got into the car and sat between Geno and Ottie in the backseat. She wore a full-skirted primrose yellow dress, a white cardigan and a matching flower pinned to the side of her head.

"You smell and look beautiful, my Carlotta," Geno said, leaning in to kiss her hand.

His siblings groaned silently, but Carlotta, sweet Carlotta, was immediately won over.

"Thank you, Geno. I am so looking forward to tonight. Are you coming as well?" Carlotta directed her question at Mina, and Salvo sitting in the front.

Mina shifted her position to look at Carlotta, who was cramped in the backseat with her knees raised because of the tight space.

"Sadly, no. I can't remember the last time I went to a dance. Salvo is taking me back home to Naples."

"Oh!" Carlotta sounded surprised. "Haven't you heard there is a roadblock outside Carva? Anyone heading towards Naples is being sent back."

"Do you know why?" asked Salvo, bending his head towards her, unable to turn as he was driving.

"I am not sure. I think there has been another riot."

Panic surged through Mina's veins. She was determined to get back to her sons, no matter what. Salvo, perceptive to his sister's distress, calmly placed a comforting hand on her shoulder. It was the first time she had been away from her children for longer than a few hours.

"Don't worry, Mina. I am sure they will let you through when we tell them why you must get home." Salvo's words lacked sincerity, merely a ploy to pacify Mina.

Mina sank into her chair, sceptical yet willing to embrace hope. They reached their destination, Coco's. Ottie had decided to come to the roadblock; she had no intention of dancing when her sister needed support. With puffs of black smoke, the car trundled away toward the roadblock as Geno and Carlotta waved goodbye. A miffed Alberto sat in the back seat next to Ottie, preferring to be with her than wait alone at Coco's. He readjusted his slacks and sports jacket to get comfortable in the cramped car. Alberto had carefully selected his outfit for his date with Ottie in a bid to impress. The evening wasn't unfolding as he had imagined. Ottie's actions were not out of the ordinary though. Despite seeing no benefit in her joining her sister, he was aware that it was useless to try and discourage her.

The main road out of Carva was closed by a roadblock, and the sight of the vehicles ahead being denied passage didn't inspire confidence in the car's passengers. As they rolled up towards the barricade, a carabinieri placed his arm across the top of the car and peered into the window. He informed Salvo in a manner that indicated he had been repeating the same information for most of the evening that access to Naples was not possible. Villages leading up to Naples would be accessible, but not Naples itself. Salvo stressed the importance of allowing Mina to return to her children.

Mina, on the verge of tears, continuously pleaded and repeated the same words. "Please let me get back to my sons."

She raised her face towards the carabinieri. While listening, he sympathetically stroked his moustache. Being a father of young children himself, he empathised with the mother's situation, but he couldn't permit them to pass. His duty was to protect the public, he had heard news that the riots were particularly aggressive. Although he was concerned for her children in that situation without their mother, he couldn't jeopardise her. The drivers behind them honked impatiently, causing the carabinieri's colleague to step forward and attend to the other cars. Taking advantage of the officers' distraction, Mina leaped from the vehicle and sprinted towards the barricade. The carabinieri held onto Salvo's door and instructed him not to move. Ottie, who had been sitting behind Mina, frantically tried to lift the seat so that she could chase after her. Alberto shouted at her not to be so stupid, but Ottie continued unsuccessfully to try and raise the seat. With great effort, she manoeuvred her slender figure through the narrow space, resulting in her dress ripping and her limbs getting scratched. Once she was out of the car, she dashed towards her sister, who had already covered a considerable distance.

Ottie observed the army trucks beside the barricade as soldiers poured out and surrounded Mina in a pincer movement. Ottie kicked off her heels so she could run faster despite the rough road tearing into her feet. With his arms locked around her waist, a soldier pulled Mina towards him, pressing her against his abdomen. Her arms and legs were flailing wildly, and her russet hair, no longer styled in Nari's curls, was whipping near the soldier's face. He curved his back to keep the hair out of his eyes. Ottie recognised his stature immediately. He was at least a head taller than the other soldiers. Out of breath, she slowed down and walked towards the scene, mortified that she was to find herself in another awkward situation with Lance Corporal Hal Bennett.

Hal released Mina, and she stood next to him with her chest visibly heaving. In sharp contrast to her typically well-groomed look, she appeared wild and dishevelled.

"Tavi, tell them, please," Mina pleaded. "My babies. I have to get home."

Ottie took her sister in her arms. Mina wept on her shoulder, her tears staining the light blue satin of her dress. Her gaze defiantly met Hal's as she looked up at him.

"If you do not let my sister through, she will either swim to Naples or climb over the mountains. Such is the need for her to be with her children. She is a mother. You can't do this! Can't you see? She is broken!" Ottie's voice trembled with the resentment she fought to conceal. The soldiers had now encircled them. Hal observed the dishevelled duo, who appeared very distinct from each other. With angular facial bones and vibrant hair colour, Ottie's sister had a striking look, her current wartime body alluding to her former Amazonian figure. In contrast, Ottie was petite, with dark hair, and possessed delicate facial features. The only thing they had in common was their big, expressive, mascara-streaked chestnut eyes that looked up at him like baby owls in a nest.

Hal caught a glimpse of Ottie's blood-stained bare feet, with torn stockings curling at her ankles. Noticing the direction of his gaze, she glanced down at her only pair of stockings and saw that they were now in tatters.

"Octavia, Naples is unsafe. We can't just let people through," Hal explained.

Mina wailed, and Ottie, still determined, continued, "This is different. This is her family!"

The arrival of the moustached carabinieri, with Salvo and Alberto, led to the dispersal of the group that were surrounding the girls.

"You know them?" The carabinieri asked Hal.

"I know her." Hal waved his hand towards Ottie. "They are credible."

"Gentlemen, allow me to return my sister to Naples," Salvo implored. "I am willing to take a risk. Just let us through."

Hal admired the dignified demeanour Salvo maintained amidst the surrounding chaos, acting as a protective brother to his sisters. Though he wasn't so sure of the irritable-looking man standing behind Salvo, who sidled up to Octavia and handed over her shoes. The man pulled her close and tenderly touched her arm, his eyes fixed on Hal the entire time. The carabinieri signalled for Hal to come aside for a private conversation. Salvo watched as they talked, heads bent towards each other. The carabinieri patted Hal on the back and strode back towards them.

Hal expressed defeat by raising his hands and giving a subtle nod to Salvo. The carabinieri returned to the group and gave his verdict.

"You can take her as far as the barricade at Naples, and then the carabinieri will escort her home." He gave a slight smile and then said to Mina. "I wish you a safe journey back to your children, *Signora*. We will radio through to Naples, so they are expecting you."

Mina threw her arms around the carabinieri. He patted her back and felt her protruding ribs against his hand. Mina and Salvo made their way back to the car as the police lifted the barricade for them. Ottie caught sight of Hal in the distance as she waved and blew goodbye kisses at Mina. As she turned away from him, she felt Alberto's hand in hers.

The couple began the long walk back to Ottie's house. Her outfit was no longer appropriate for the dance, and it was too late to change. Walking silently, Alberto's evenings disappointment contrasted with Ottie's worry for her sister's well-being. Eventually, their feet throbbing, they reached the Matanti front door.

"Thank you, Alberto. I am sorry the evening didn't quite turn out as planned. It would have been nice to have had a dance."

Alberto leant forward to kiss Ottie, but she turned her head to place the key in the door. The moment passed, he stepped backwards, his hands still in his pockets.

"Well, maybe next time," he muttered, his head lowered.

Ottie gave a noncommittal nod as she slipped behind the front door. Closing it behind her, she rested her back against its wooden surface, lifted her head to the heavens, and let out a sigh. The sigh had barely escaped her lips when Geno presented himself, a towel in his hand, his upper body sodden, his white shirt with large lapels stained a murky brown.

"Mamma Mia, what happened to you?" Ottie exclaimed.

Geno gave his hair another rub with the towel and checked it in the hall mirror, flicking it into place and admiring himself.

"I have learnt a very good lesson this evening. That is, to always look up. Always look up when you are under your future mother-in-law's balcony, kissing her daughter goodnight." Geno laughed. "Clean water would have been more polite, don't you think? Besides, you are a fine one to talk. Look at the state of you. What happened? Is everything okay?"

Ottie explained the evening's events to Geno as they sat at the kitchen table drinking hot milky cocoa, courtesy of Salvo's recent food supplies from Naples. Deep in conversation, they caught the car headlights brushing past the kitchen window and heard the recognisable popping of Salvo's car exhaust. Ottie poured another cup of cocoa in preparation for Salvo.

***

Salvo was not allowed to pass through the last barricade near Naples. The two carabinieri officers assured him they would safely escort Mina back to her sons. His original reason for the trip–to gain further contraband–now seemed insignificant compared to his sister's safety. He watched Mina climb into the back of the police car alongside the armed officers. Just before leaving, she turned her face towards him one more time, offering a small smile as a way of acknowledging him. He disliked entrusting her to strangers, aware of the vulnerability it placed her in, but he had no choice.

Mina was all too familiar with the scars that Naples had etched into its structures. Broken and crumbling, the austere grey and terracotta buildings stood amidst a landscape pockmarked by bomb craters. Yet, the spirit of the Neapolitan people endured. Since the time of the ancient Greeks, Naples had been one of the oldest continuously populated cities in the world. Their pride in their heritage drove their determination to fight until the last Neapolitan remained standing.

Living on the outskirts of Naples, Mina was informed by the carabinieri that the disturbances were mainly occurring in the city centre and were expected to subside by morning. Previously, Mina had sheltered in the catacombs with her family amongst the ossuaries, the antique skulls of the dead banked up against the walls. She prayed her children were peacefully asleep in bed, blissfully unaware of the nearby violence.

While driving through Naples, the carabinieri had to navigate obstacles such as debris from damaged buildings and the bodies of both the dead and injured. Despite these sights, Mina clung to hope, her thoughts fixed on her sons. When they arrived at her apartment, it was intact, with the shutters securely fastened. She rang the bell. The buzz for her to enter was instantaneous. She thanked the carabinieri and prayed for their safe return, entrusting their journey to Santo Cristo's protection. Mina hurried up the stairs, taking them two at a time, eager to be with her family. Her husband Paolo was waiting for her at the door, holding it open and visibly relieved to see her.

Paolo, anticipating her worries, whispered softly. "Mina, our sons are fast asleep. It's late, you have had a long day, let's go to bed."

Mina refused to rest until she saw her sons. She crept into their room and watched them sleeping, curled up together, two dark manes of hair peeking over the covers. Her heart swelled with both relief and a mother's love as she gently pulled the blanket higher to keep them warm.

14

The Corporal And The Pea Thief

I t wasn't until lunchtime that Hal finally spoke to Ottie. She was sitting in her usual spot on the grassy bank, her lunch laid out on a gingham napkin on her lap. She detected Hal's shadow as he approached, and she forcibly swallowed a large mouthful of bread. The sun cast a halo around Hal as he stood over her.

"I thought you'd want to know—your sister has been returned home safely. I'm guessing you haven't heard, communications being what they are at the moment."

Ottie craned her neck up towards Hal, shielding her eyes from the sun's glare before she spoke. "Oh, thanks. Papa was going to try and get news from the carabinieri today, which isn't always easy."

Ottie picked up her panini, indicating that she wished to continue her lunch break.

"That looks nicer bread than we get in here,"

Ottie inspected the panini as if she were seeing it for the first time. "It's from my family's bakery. We can't make as much bread as we used to, but what we do make is the best." She bit into it as soon as she finished her sentence, tearing a piece off with her teeth.

"I guess your brother made it back alright last night?" Hal continued, finding a reason not to leave just yet.

"Yes, he did. My family is grateful for your help in getting Mina back to her boys." Ottie spoke through a mouthful of panini, her words slightly muffled.

Hal watched her bulging cheeks and smiled at the sight.

"You've got the carabinieri to thank for that. Looked like it spoiled your date, though?" Hal said, his voice light, though his eyes lingered on hers a moment too long.

"Oh, you mean my fiancé. I guess he'll get over it."

"Do you smoke?"

Hal took out a packet of Lucky Strikes, placing one in his mouth as he offered the pack to Ottie.

"No, not at the moment, thanks."

"It's kinda nice chatting with you over lunch. Could we do it again sometime, or will that cause a problem with your fiancé?" Hal grinned as he held onto his last word he tried to pull off a comical expression, raising his eyebrows to make his ears wiggle just like Stan Laurel.

The siren called the workers back, and Ottie raised herself, finishing with a slight bounce to shake the breadcrumbs from her lap.

"I guess not," she finally said, brushing past Hal.

Hal took a slow draw on his cigarette, gently exhaling as he watched her walk away.

***

Over the next few weeks, Fina noticed Ottie's appetite increasing, her sister constantly requesting a double portion of lunch to take to work. Ottie seemed distracted, humming happily to herself. Fina knew the signs all too well and kept her observations to herself.

For Ottie, learning about Hal and England was always fun—life there seemed so different from Italy. Ottie looked forward to her breaks with him more with each passing day. They would sit together on the bank, sharing her lunch while Hal told stories about his mother, his dog Bonnie, and the work he did on the farm. One day, Hal mentioned his father's suicide at the beginning of the war.

His voice lowered as he spoke. "Found him in the barn. I was only thirteen," he said, pausing to pull on his cigarette. "He'd been... off, you know, for years. Said people were out to get him, that someone wanted him gone. The things he witnessed during the last war made it even more difficult to cope."

Ottie watched him silently, her panini forgotten in her lap.

Hal's voice grew quieter as he added, "Doctor said it was some kind of... I don't know... a sickness of the mind." He stopped, his gaze fixed on the horizon. "I guess some things run in families."

The last sentence hung in the air, and Ottie leaned forward.

"You're not your father," she said softly, her voice filled with certainty. "You're strong, Hal."

Hal snorted lightly, flicking ash from his cigarette.

"We'll see about that," he murmured.

Ottie then shared her own grief, describing how the loss of Mamma had pulled her down. She told him about the days she couldn't bear to rise, the empty ache that nothing seemed to fill. As she spoke, Hal watched her intently, nodding when she paused.

Their shared sadness seemed to draw them closer. Each day on the bank became a little longer, a little harder to leave behind.

15

Partisan Alle Vongole

The Inn Hotel, a stylish 19th-century structure, was painted sleek slate grey and complemented by clean white window frames. Symmetrical black curved balconies made of wrought iron adorned its sides. Fi stepped inside the hotel. The interior had an appealing, light, and airy atmosphere, featuring a modern décor with clean lines and a colour scheme of white and various shades of blue.

She was informed about breakfast serving times by the helpful young trainee staff duo. Fi wondered if they had been hired for their appearance, as both wore severe, ash-blonde bob haircuts and dark plum lipstick. The attentive team asked whether she would like a table or room service for the evening, mentioning that solo diners typically opted for the latter. Fi declined, inquiring about nearby dining options. The concierge, who joined the group in a supervisory capacity, suggested Fi head towards Piazza Cella for various dining choices. The Italian connection piqued her interest and gave her confidence to venture out.

Fi had booked a single en-suite room. Located on the third floor with a window overlooking a busy street, it turned out to be surprisingly roomy. Unsurprisingly, it was bright and very white. Fi found a way to stick her head out of the window, despite its safety locks. She wanted to see the sun setting over Zurich and hear the soft bustle of the street below. Her neck grew uncomfortable from the awkward position, so she twisted back into the room.

Before facing another evening dining alone, Fi showered and changed. On a whim, she picked up her phone and messaged Quin:

Sorry, I tried to call you earlier. I guess you're working. I know your voicemail is full, and I can't leave you any more messages. I just really miss you. It doesn't get any easier being apart for this long.

She paused, added three kisses, and hit send. She scrolled through Quin's previous messages. His texts always ended with an absurd number of emojis, insisting there weren't enough emojis in existence to convey his immense love for his butterfly.

"Fin time" was a phrase Quin used often, a reminder of the warmth and connection they shared, moments that made life feel complete. Quin's quirky expressions were always amusing, making her smile every time. Fi considered messaging her daughters but decided against it. She didn't want to answer the inevitable questions or worry them unnecessarily. This was unpredictable behaviour for her, and her girls would naturally be concerned. She preferred them to be blissfully unaware and occupied with their busy lives.

She indulged in the luxurious walk-in marble shower. The hot jets soothed her, calming her thoughts. As she relaxed under the hot water, her thoughts wandered. She hoped Yara was ok. She believed she was a woman who always got by.

Piazza Cella was within walking distance from the hotel, passing by bars with bright lights advertising exotic girl shows. When Fi arrived, she found the piazza underwhelming—nothing like a typical Italian square. The piazza was named in memory of the Italian immigrants who had faded into obscurity. Except for one immigrant, a restaurateur named Erminia Cella who was honoured with a small blue plaque. The Italians had relied on her restaurant as a central hub in the piazza for decades. The death of Cella's descendants and the integration of each generation within Swiss culture meant that the Cellas and their kind existed in memory only.

Fi noticed a side street veering off from the main road. Her eye caught the green, white, and red of the Italian flag, under which flashed a green sign: "Nonno's Kitchen." She altered her course, drawn by the familiar sight. The taverna-style restaurant had empty tables adorned with red gingham plastic tablecloths. Condensation trickled down the yellow-lit windows. Inside, Fi heard murmurs of conversation, the restaurant looked busy. Her shyness threatened to take over as she hesitated, her legs leading her away. To calm herself, her eyes fixated on the menu showcased in the window, featuring the familiar types of traditional Italian dishes she knew so well.

Just then, the tavern door flew open, and a waiter appeared. Sporting an impressive, waxed moustache and a glistening bald head. Despite his small size, he carried himself with a proud, upright posture. He spoke to Fi directly; at first, Fi could not understand him.

"Sorry, I do not understand. I'm English," Fi stammered.

"Oh, hello!" He bowed slightly. "Welcome! I see you looking." He pointed at the menu. "Our food is delicious. We have a nice corner table outta the way. If you wanna come in."

He held the door open with his foot and gestured into the restaurant. He had a friendly face with a smile that settled in his dark eyes. Cooking smells wafted out the door and into Fi's nostrils. She shivered, it was getting colder outside, and her stomach was rumbling.

Fi hesitated, then smiled.

"Erm, okay, yes, yes. I will. I'd like that."

The waiter clapped his hands together.

"Come, Signora! May I take your coat?"

It was clear that the waiter was pleased to serve another customer. He bustled between the busy tables. He led her to a corner table at the back of the taverna. Fi, a creature of habit, went for the corner seat. The restaurant had a simple Swiss charm, its yellow walls and candlelit tables glowing warmly, intensified by the honey pine cladding. Ladder back rattan chairs set around gingham-covered tables laid in a triangle style. Chianti bottles held candles with days' worth of dribbled wax clinging to the sides of the bottles, adding character to the place.

The waiter returned with bread, olives, and house red. He theatrically stretched his arm, pouring globs of olive oil and balsamic vinegar from a great height into the glazed terracotta bowl.

"What would you like to order, Signora?" he asked, twirling his moustache.

"Vorrei spaghetti alle vongole bianche, per favore."

The thespian flair continued, the waiter threw his hands in the air, gesturing a kiss with a delighted expression on his face. He ceremoniously produced a pen and notepad, ready to record her easy-to-remember order.

"Parli Italiano! I should have known, you have those beautiful Italian eyes!" he added.

He dramatically scribbled down her order.

"Dove in Italia—where are your family from?"

"Vicino Amalfi," Fi answered, smiling. "A place called Carva."

"I know it! My great uncle was there during the war," he exclaimed proudly. "That is the last time my grandfather, his brother, heard from him. My grandfather, Bruno, came to Zurich at the start of the last war. We had family here–they had come over generations before to build the tunnels through the Alps, where the Bernina train goes. You know it? It's magnificent! The scenery and all that." He highlighted his words with a wide-armed gesture. "My grandfather opened this restaurant. It was called Fratello Rapino back then. He always hoped his brother would come and join, but eh,"–the waiter shrugged his shoulders and lifted his palms skywards–"he never came."

"Wow, my Zia Fina used to sometimes talk about a partisan they sheltered. They sheltered a few, but one had family in Switzerland. I am sure she said that."

"Come, come, I show you pictures of them."

He led her to a wall lined with family photos, by the corridor near the toilets. Black-and-white photos of the Rapino family were scattered all over the wall. A few faded colour photos were at the display's borders, and Fi recognised the waiter as a young man in a tight, red, polo neck jumper with a smaller moustache and a full head of hair, his arms draped around a rotund, older man's neck. Among the sepia tones, he pointed to two brothers: his grandfather, Bruno and his Great uncle Matteo, the partisan.

"Next to him here, yes, here he is, that's his brother, the partisan. My grandpa put these pictures up next to each other when he took over the restaurant, and they've been there ever since."

He put his finger on a faded photo. An earnest young man with dark hair and soft features stared out at them. Fi studied the photo, her heart inexplicably drawn to the young man with dark, brooding eyes and thick-rimmed spectacles. Why did she feel he had somehow been a part of her? She dismissed the thought as impossible and pushed it aside.

"Yes, that's him, my Zio Matteo. I never met him, but I still have his war time letters—the ones he wrote to my grandfather. He wrote whenever he could. In his last letter, he spoke of a girl he wanted to marry from Carva," the waiter added softly.

Fi shared with the waiter the sad motive behind her journey. She was travelling to Carva by train as a tribute to her grandmother. His warm smile dimmed slightly as he listened, and they exchanged a shared moment of unspoken understanding. With sadness for their respective losses, she returned to her table.

A plate of spaghetti with clams awaited her arrival, the steam carrying a delicate briny aroma that made her mouth water. It tasted as fabulous as it looked. She rolled the pasta up on her fork, and the oil ran down her chin as she ate voraciously. She finished by tearing a piece of bread, using it to sweep the plate clean, as if leaving any part uneaten would have been disrespectful.

The waiter returned with a complimentary shot of limoncello, his eyes twinkling with a conspiratorial delight as he placed the glass before her, ignoring her polite protests.

"Signora, I feel that with our history, we are almost family. I insist. On the house," he said, his voice warm and resolute.

Fi hesitated only briefly before raising the glass, knowing it would be discourteous to refuse such a heartfelt gesture.

"Grazie. Saluti," she said, smiling as she raised her glass toward him. "To our grandparents," she added with a soft but firm voice. "To their pasts that paved the way for our futures."

The air held her words, a hushed acknowledgment of time's relentless march. The waiter nodded deeply, seeming to feel the weight of her sentiment.

With a full belly and a happy heart, Fi expressed her gratitude to the waiter with a warm embrace and a kiss on both cheeks before leaving Nonno's Kitchen. The scents of garlic and lemons still clung to her senses as she stepped out into the cool night air, her cheeks warm from the limoncello and the connection she had felt within those walls. Feeling a little tipsy after being convinced to have two more limoncellos, she made her way back to the hotel.

Pondering her past and her family's story, she realised how their twists and turns had led her to her present situation: in Zurich, embarking on a solo adventure to her grandmother's country. Her thoughts returned to the waiter's story, his words laced with pride and sorrow, a reminder of how the past lingers, shaping each life in ways both visible and unseen. It struck her how deeply the roots of history entwined, connecting them all, even across generations and borders. Destiny, she thought, had to be embraced—not merely accepted but shaped by choice where possible, even as circumstances wove their own patterns.

Tonight, Fi Bennett felt fully in charge. Tomorrow, she would embark on the picturesque Bernina railway route through the mountains, its path carved in part by her ancestors' toil. Her journey would carry her across the border into Italy, drawing her closer to Ottie's spirit.

She would do it for herself, for her family. She would do it because she had the privilege of freedom in her lifetime, and she could do it just for fun, and why not? She tilted her face to the sky, a small, defiant smile playing on her lips, a gesture of gratitude and hope.

16

Sketches

Hal arrived early at the grassy bank. The sky was clear and cloudless, the sun shining brightly, with a cool breeze drifting down from the mountains. Hal breathed deeply, the crisp air filling his lungs, and let himself relax into the moment. He opened his sketchbook, softened his pencil at his lips, and lost himself in his drawing. He began with the walnut tree before him, studying its form carefully, the leaves licked by sunshine, the dappled shade dripping down from its gnarled boughs.

From her concealed spot, Ottie observed him silently. Hal's attention was wholly absorbed by his sketching, oblivious to his surroundings. She was captivated by the outline of his broad shoulders, the way his black hair fell forward as he leaned over his sketchbook, brushing it back from his forehead before looking up again at the landscape. Her gaze lingered on him, enjoying the unusual luxury of observing him without interruption. It felt indulgent, almost decadent, to admire him so freely.

Her stomach growled, reminding her it was lunchtime, she stepped away from the building's edge. Hal caught sight of her from the corner of his eye and lit up with a beaming smile. She felt herself grow taller with each step as she approached him.

What are you drawing?" she asked, her arms crossing tightly over her chest.

"Oh, just the trees. I wanted to catch them in blossom."

The sharp snap of his sketchbook closing cut through the air as he turned his attention to Ottie.

"Let's see," Ottie said, dropping into the spot next to him.

Hal glanced briefly at his sketchbook and then shook his head with a knowing half-smile.

"No," he replied.

Ottie pulled her chin back in mock disbelief.

"Why not?"

Hal didn't answer, letting the moment simmer as she began laying out their lunch between them.

"Want some?" she asked, holding out a jagged bread crust and waving it playfully under his chin. Her head tilted as her gaze met his.

Hal stretched his interminable limbs before finally snatching at the offering. Ottie threw back her head and laughed, the sound bright as sunshine.

Hal felt something stir inside him, a warmth rising at the infectious sound, his need to make her happy inescapable. His eyes traced the curve of her neck as she laughed, taking in the soft shades of burnt sienna and ochre created at the notch between her collarbones. Oh, how he missed his palette. Pulling himself back to the moment, he took a bite of bread.

Without warning, Ottie abruptly fled from her spot, coming to a stop a few feet away, taunting him with his red sketchbook held high in the air. Hal jumped to his feet and reached her side with one stride.

"Give it back," he implored.

Ottie dashed toward the trees for protection, flipping through the pages as she ran. Hal followed at a steady stride, resigned to the fact that it was too late to stop her. With dread, he watched her flipping through the pages, glancing between him and the book. Ottie slowed her pace, looking through the pages more deliberately now. Hal trailed behind, his hands clenching and unclenching as he braced for her reaction.

"Oh, my... Why, these are really good!" she exclaimed, glancing between him and the book. "Wow, that's Bonnie, your dog... The flowers look so lifelike."

She flicked further through more pages, then stopped, her gaze fixed on a particular page.

"What's this?" she asked, stepping out from under the tree canopy. Confusion creased her brow as she slapped the back of her free hand against the open pages.

"What's this?" she said again. "What prompted you to do this?"

Hal approached slowly, his voice soft. "I like drawing. You're good to draw."

"But you never asked," she replied, her tone a mixture of accusation and intrigue.

"I'm sorry... You're just... Well, you...you inspire me to draw. I have you in my thoughts, and, well, it just kind of flows." Hal stopped talking, silenced by Ottie's glare.

Ottie stepped out from the tree's umbrella, disturbing blossom that flurried in her wake as she moved. She held out the book towards him. She looked at him, her emotions shifting like the light filtering through the leaves.

"Why didn't you tell me?" she asked, her voice quieter now, almost vulnerable.

Hal stood rooted, unsure how to reply. She held out the sketchbook, her expression unreadable.

"Thank you," Hal muttered, taking the book and using the moment to gently brush his fingers against her hand.

Ottie stepped forward into his space and raised her chin to him. She felt the warmth of his breath between them as he leaned closer to her.

"Hey, Lofty!" The sharp call was followed by a shrill whistle.

Hal turned to see his fellow soldier, Ken, tapping impatiently at his bare wrist, miming a watch. Hal sighed, gave a thumbs-up, and took a step back from Ottie.

"I have to go," he said with a small, regretful smile.

Ottie shrugged, trying to appear indifferent.

"Sure, okay."

As he walked away, a thought flickered through her mind. She cupped her hands around her mouth and called out.

"Hey, Hal, have you seen Vesuvius yet?"

Hal stopped at the edge of the building, turning back.

"No, not yet."

"I can't begin to tell you. It's like the entire sky is one enormous firework."

Hal nodded, his gaze thoughtful. He'd heard about the eruption and had seen the illuminated night sky in the distance. The idea intrigued him.

"You should come and see it from the top of Carva," Ottie called out again. "Quite a crowd gathers at the top of my road at night. It's amazing."

Hal paused, her words lingering in his mind. He thought of the quiet intensity of the sky and the way her voice carried a note of excitement. Carva was definitely closer to Vesuvius, and she would have an amazing view.

"Maybe I will," he said with a faint grin pulling at his lips as he turned the corner.

17

The Little Red Train

"Will you two stop jumping on the sofa!" Lil shouted in frustration at her children.

She glanced over towards Garth's back. He was sitting on the back step, leaning forward, his forearms resting on his thighs. Lil vigorously stirred the boiling pan on the hob, turning it to a simmer.

"She ain't coming. You know what she's like," Lil continued, raising her voice over the children's playful shrieks. "Girls!! If I have to tell you again... there will be trouble!"

Lil gestured, exasperated at her daughters, who were running around the sofa. The smallest sibling, wielding a clandestinely acquired dirty wooden spoon, chased her sister.

"She ain't been right since the accident and then losing her nan. I told you when you invited her for lunch this Sunday. She wouldn't show up...Right, that's really enough, Caitlin! Look what you've done to your sister."

Garth leaned back to glance at the commotion. As usual, Lil had everything in hand. He stayed where he was, rolling his cigarette between his fingers. He wasn't surprised by Fi's no-show. She'd had a rough time lately, and he figured she just needed space.

Still, he pulled his mobile from his jeans' back pocket. He'd texted Fi last night to remind her about lunch, but she hadn't replied. That was unlike her, and it nagged at him a little. With a quick tap of his thumb, he typed another message: *Wats up. Even pigs grunt when u poke em.* He pressed send. When the reply flashed back almost instantaneously, he smiled.

Oh, no :-(I can't come today. V Sorry. You won't believe me if I tell you! I am not going to be at work Monday either!

A small sigh, followed by a smile, hovered at his lips.

Good to know ur alive and kicking kidda. Don't stay away too long! :-)

***

Fi smiled at her phone before slipping it back into her bag. Her gaze swept across the station platform. Having just debarked from the Zurich train, she was now waiting at Chur station. A scattering of individuals populated the quiet platform. Mountains dominated the skyline, and the Swiss air felt light in her lungs.

The little red Bernina Express soon arrived, its panoramic windows curving over the roof. Fi found a corner seat and settled in as the narrow-gauge train twisted and curled through the Alps. Chocolate-box villages embedded in green pastures passed by, gradually giving way to patches of snow as the train climbed higher. Babbling rivers and lakes, their colours turned black and white by the land's minerals, glittered as they came into view.

The train track curved and headed up into the glorious mountains. The sky a vivid blue in stark contrast to the jagged peaks. Tourists were crossing sides and jostling across each other, vying for the best view. Mobile phones and cameras at their faces, watching the view through a lens. Fi, sat back and took in the breathtaking sights firsthand. She couldn't remember the last time she'd allowed herself to simply *be*—to exist without the weight of expectations, responsibilities, or grief.

She felt exhilarated, thrilled to be returning to Italy. It had been too long. Watching Switzerland pass by, she imagined Ottie seeing the same views decades earlier. Had her grandmother felt this same awe?

The train slipped across the border.

Fi felt the tinge of a migraine at her temple. She reached into her bag for some tablets to ease the pain. Years ago, when her migraines first surfaced, Ottie had insisted on placing a bowl of water under her chin and dropping olive oil into it. As the oil separated, Ottie would define the shapes, searching for the *malocchio* symbol. She'd make the sign of the cross on her chest to remove the curse that had caused Fi's headache. A small smile tugged at Fi's lips as she remembered her grandmother; she missed her care and protection.

The little red train terminated at Tirano. Fi stepped onto Italian soil and walked a short distance to another train station that would take her further into Italy. She had decided to head to Verona, planning to spend a few nights there before meeting Zia Nari. Verona, was a city she had always dreamed of visiting; and her growing sense of adventure spurred on by her newfound confidence whispered, "Why not?"

Fi grabbed an espresso outside the station before boarding the train to Milan. At Milan, she had to switch trains, rushing across platforms with only a few minutes to spare. In what felt like no time, she was walking out of Verona Porta Nuova station. The building was covered in scaffolding—part of a regeneration project for the station, which hadn't been touched since its post-war resurrection in 1946.

Verona's bustling energy greeted her as she ventured into the heart of the city. Fi was determined to see Juliet's balcony before she found a place to stay. She wasn't worried about not booking a room in advance this time. Her Italian was a little rusty, maybe Neapolitan being the bulk of the language she understood, but hey, she had been okay so far she told herself. Italy resonated deeply within her; it felt familiar and comforting.

As she walked the streets of Verona, the sun's warmth pressed against her back. She dragged her case over the old, bumpy roads, casting her eyes up to admire the stunning architecture that took her through the city's different ages from Romans to Renaissance, with modern-day buildings mixed up in between.

Juliet's balcony sat in a small courtyard with a bronze statue of Juliet at the centre of the courtyard's patterned pebble stone floor. She was demurely posed, one hand clutching her skirt, the other resting delicately on her chest. The metal at her breasts gleamed brighter than the rest of the fair Capulet's body—the mark left by superstitious tourists touching at her bosoms for luck in love. Fi looked up at Juliet's balcony, small and solid, with little arches carved into its sides. Occasionally, a tourist's head jutted out from the top, glancing down at the small crowd below, searching perhaps for their Romeo.

Fi had no interest in paying for the tour of Juliet's fictional house. She glanced around the walls of the small courtyard, covered in chewing gum, used to attach notes. She read a few; love was etched on the notes in its many guises: the lost, the gained and the unrequited.

"Wanna buy some paper so you can add your bit o' love to the wall, eh." The accent was south London.

Fi turned towards the request at her shoulder. The man was young and Mediterranean in appearance, handsome in a high-maintenance way. He had his sunglasses perched on his forehead.

"Or some gum, maybe?"

"You've come a long way from home to sell gum," Fi declared.

The young man snorted, leaned back on his heels, and gave a cursory look over his shoulder. He ran a hand through his hair, checking out his well-defined bicep, that flexed under his tight t-shirt as his arm raised to his eyeline.

"I'm visiting my family 'ere. Thought would earn a bit o' cash, too. You could call it a workin' holiday."

He smiled from his eyes, his mischievous charm unmistakable.

"I was thinking you don't look typically English."

"Might as bloody well be, hun. My parents moved from 'ere to England when I was a kid." He finished with a flash of his white teeth and turned away for a moment to sell some paper to a group of Chinese tourists. "You catching the sights of Verona then?" He continued.

"Sort of passing through. I am on the way to visit my Zia," Fi answered.

"Ha, well, you certainly don't look typically Italian." He answered her in Italian, as he gave her titian hair a flick with his finger to highlight his reasoning.

Fi replied in the same tongue. "Very true, I guess not. I am looking for somewhere to stay for a couple of nights. Where would you recommend going? Fairly central, not too pricey."

"You come to the right guy, darlin'. You're gonna love this. My Nonna rents out a few rooms. I'm sure she can set you up for a few nights in her gaff. Tell her, that her favourite grandson Rocco sent you. It's literally a ten-minute walk from 'ere. She'll give you a good price. You want anything else, a tour or museum tickets?" He continued, despite Fi's shaking head. "Or opera. What about the opera? You look like an opera kinda girl. Aida is on at the Arena. I get tickets at the best price."

"Opera would be nice. I've been told that they stage amazing open-air shows in that beautiful amphitheatre."

"Atta girl. Have some fun while you're 'ere. I'll drop a ticket over later. Now let's write Nonna's address down for you on one o' me notes. No charge," he winked. "I'll give her a tinkle. Let 'er know you're on yer way."

He handed the address over to Fi and gave her verbal directions, his gestures punctuated by animated hand movements as he spoke.

Twelve Via Segh proved easy to find. It was situated across the river, down an uneven, cobbled street. The lofty buildings provided welcome shade through the narrow passageways. The buildings were so tightly stacked together that neighbours could shake hands from their balconies across the street. Washing lines full of clothes crisscrossed above Fi's head between the apartments. The vivid laundry fluttered amidst the deep shadows, and uneven patches of broken rendering on the walls revealed powdery terracotta wounds.

Nonna Salerno was a welcoming host. She opened the weathered front door, barely hanging onto the last of its black paint, to reveal a neat little courtyard behind it. She placed her broom down and gestured for Fi to follow her. A small archway led to stone steps, their middles worn smooth from years of use, which wound up to Fi's apartment on the second floor. It was dark inside, with a vague musty smell. Nonna Salerno pushed open the green wooden shutters and light spilled across the tiled floor illuminating a charming, albeit somewhat old-fashioned room with its solid dark wood furniture.

Nonna Salerno beckoned her to the balcony, where two chairs and a small round table were arranged. At the centre of the table sat a red geranium plant, its vibrant petals adding a cheerful touch. The main room was spacious, featuring an old king-size metal bed against the back wall, with a picture of the Madonna and child hanging above it. A quaint, cotton-covered sofa faced the balcony, planted in the middle of the room. Fi wandered into the bathroom and noticed an old-fashioned porcelain toilet, its brass pull chain swaying gently. The galley kitchen had open-shelved units lining one wall, with the lower shelves hidden behind handmade curtains. The kitchen walls were adorned with vibrant seventies tiles.

Nonna Salerno gave a thorough explanation of the apartment's quirks, from the oven to the toilet. To flush, Fi needed to pull the chain twice quickly, then once more for a longer duration. After ensuring everything was clear, Nonna finally left Fi in peace.

The bed creaked under her as the lumpy mattress pressed against her back. The fresh scent of clean white linen wafted up as she kicked off her shoes, letting the cold tiles cool her bare foot. Her hand flopped over the bed's edge, and she closed her eyes, feeling the weight of travel fatigue. A warm wetness touched her hand. Turning her head, she found herself looking at a dog's face, perched on the bed.

"Well, hello, little dog; where did you come from?"

The dog wagged its tail enthusiastically and rolled onto its back, revealing a pink belly. Its grey fur was soft to the touch. Fi noticed a bone-shaped dog tag around its neck. On one side, it read *Ruffie,* and on the other, a phone number. She realised her apartment door was ajar and slipped her shoes back on. Padding over to the door, she tried encouraging the dog to leave, but it sat back and whined. After a few unsuccessful attempts, she decided to find Nonna Salerno, with Ruffie trailing close behind.

Nonna Salerno was in her ground-floor apartment, mopping vigorously. Her gold hoop earrings jingled with her movements. She stopped and grinned at Fi.

"Ah, Ruffie, he came to see you."

"Yes, he did. He won't leave my side. Are you his owner?" Fi asked, glancing down at the dog, which remained close, looking up at her with sad eyes.

"He likes you. Me, his owner? Oh, no."

"Who is? Shall I take him to them?"

"His owner is dead," Nonna Salerno replied, resting against her mop. "She was an old lady. She lived in your rooms. She was in her bed four months ago. I give him food sometimes. So do other residents, but no one wants him. He enjoys being in the rooms where you are. Where she died."

Fi felt slightly uneasy at the thought. Putting her mop down, Nonna Salerno searched the pocket of her floral apron.

"My handsome Rocco," she chuckled, pulling out a ticket. "He has brought the ticket you wanted for the opera. It's for tomorrow's performance. You can pay me the euros."

"Yes, of course. What shall I do with the dog?" Fi asked as she took the ticket and handed over the money.

"The dog is free," Nonna Salerno chirped.

She made the common Italian gesture of pinching her fingers together, both hands raised in Fi's direction, to say, *what more do you expect from me?* Then, picking up her mop, she resumed her chore. Her sturdy little frame moved purposefully as she swished the mop across the floor, standing with her shapeless legs firmly positioned a hip-width apart.

Fi shrugged at Nonna's indifference, turned her back, and left with Ruffie padding close at her heel.

18

Ash Cloud

Vesuvius erupted with billowing smoke, fire, and intense heat. Thick lava dribbled down the volcano's sides, rolling silently, slowly engulfing the villages that stood in its path. Ash rained heavily from the sky, its weight collapsing roofs and bending trees over onto their backs. A sooty powder coated the Campania region, bringing havoc to its inhabitants. Initially, the land was levelled by the relentless lava, then the ash storm worsened the destruction, wiping out towns and villages, leaving them devoid of any trace of life. Side by side, civilians and soldiers used shovels and excavators to clear pathways and attempt to restore normality.

On the second day of the ash storm, Hal went to view the volcano from the top of Ottie's road. The crowd that evening was modest compared to previous days, the novelty having worn off, fire and brimstone was more of a crowd-puller than the display that now stretched up towards the heavens. The ash billowed from the top of Vesuvius, forming cauliflower-shaped blooms towering over the entire region. From the vantage point at the top of Ottie's road, a sprawling plain stretched for miles, the striking silhouette of Vesuvius' cone-shaped crater dominating the horizon. The momentous ash cloud loomed above, bent over by the elements, forming an ominous, solid mass.

It was easy to spot Hal in the crowd. Tall and broad-shouldered, he stood out among the New Zealand regiment soldiers nearby, his uniform distinctly different. He chatted with the soldiers, finding them to be a friendly bunch. They had recently returned from Cassino, and their gruesome accounts of battle made Hal uneasy. The vivid descriptions of death and destruction lingered in his mind, and he silently hoped his friends were still alive.

Ottie stood huddled amongst the knot of locals gathered closer to the mountain's edge, distancing herself from the intimidating Pardi brothers. Enzo was noticeably on edge, his obsequious brother close at his heels. Ottie caught sight of Elena and wanted to speak to her, but Elena disappeared as quickly as she had arrived. The moment Ottie spotted Hal, she wasted no time and made a beeline for him, Nari trailing closely behind.

"Why are we headed in this direction?" Nari questioned.

"I want to say hello. You don't have to come. Why don't you go home?"

"You're no fun lately Tavi!"

Nari, with a look of annoyance, stopped following Ottie and walked away in the opposite direction. She crossed her arms over her chest, a common Neapolitan gesture of disapproval. Ottie had already turned away and did not benefit from her sister's rebuff.

Hal, at least a head above most in the crowd, noticed Ottie weaving towards him. Her raven hair was elegantly styled, and she clutched her black patent bag tightly to her chest as she manoeuvred through the throng until she reached him. Hal held his palm up to the sky, letting the ash settle onto it.

"I don't reckon much to this dirty snow," he commented.

The ash flakes drifted and settled, Ottie brushed some off her hair.

"I think your friends left you behind," continued Hal.

"Oh, that's not my friend. She's just my sister."

"Whoa, how many of you are there? There's only one of me. Don't tell me you're related to half the people here!"

Ottie laughed. "Just a few of them."

"Good, I didn't fancy getting lynched." Hal grinned, exposing his impeccable teeth accentuated by the tiny gap in his upper set.

Ottie lightly prodded him in the ribs.

"I'm glad you made it to see Vesuvius… eventually. But I have to head home before it gets too dark. Otherwise, my family will come looking for me, especially since I'm supposed to be with my sister."

"Hey, well, we don't want that to happen. There'll be a swarm of Matanti folk scouring the mountain for you."

Ottie giggled at the thought, clutching her bag into her chest as she did so. She glanced towards the fading light, a hint of worry crept in. Her brothers wouldn't take kindly to her being late, but the thought of leaving Hal's side was just as troubling.

Together, they moved away from the crowd, walking downhill towards Ottie's house. The tree branches were dusted with ash, their monochrome appearance resembling a black-and-white photograph. Time slipped away as they stopped near Ottie's, engrossed in conversation. As the temperature dropped and darkness settled around them, Ottie instinctively drew her jacket tighter around her. Hal, noticing, checked his watch. Laying a finger on its dial, he pointed out they had been talking for over an hour. Ottie joked about rushing home before someone organised a search party. Hal insisted on escorting her all the way to her doorstep, determined to ensure her safety. It dawned on Hal that he was also running late. If he didn't hurry up, he would miss the final truck returning to base.

"It's been a lovely evening Hal," Ottie said, her brown eyes filled with warmth as she looked up at him.

"Yes, it's been really great."

Hal watched a flake of ash settle on her cheek. Ottie brushed it away with the back of her hand, leaving a smudge of soot across her face. Without thinking, Hal placed his hand on her cheek to remove the mark. He locked onto her eyes, his large hand covering half her pixie face. Ottie laughed softly, she put her hand over his and pressed it into her face. Hal leaned in and kissed her softly, testing her reaction. As their kisses deepened, the intensity of their desire left them both stunned.

Taken aback, they both moved away from each other in equal surprise.

You're an incredible woman, Octavia—Ottie, my Ottie. Will you be my Ottie?"

Murmuring softly, Hal pulled her close, his hand gently threading through her hair. His silver-grey eyes glinted in the fading evening light.

"Ottie," she whispered, repeating his words. "Ottie… that sounds good."

"It won't be long before I'm called to Cassino. Knowing you want me to return safely would mean the world to me." Hal hesitated, his voice faltering.

He wasn't used to showing sentiment, it made him feel exposed and vulnerable, the thought of Ottie waiting for him gave him a rare sense of hope.

"I'm not going anywhere Hal, unless it's with you," Ottie replied, her voice filled with affection as her eyes locked with his.

Hal planted a firm kiss on the top of her head.

"You'd better get indoors. I'll see you in the morning, my wonderful Ottie."

He grabbed her shoulders, turned her around, and pointed her toward the front door just a few yards across the street. He watched as she slipped inside, waving goodbye before gently shutting the door. Hal responded with a wave before quickly turning and sprinting away. He had limited time to catch the final truck back home. The last bit of daylight clung to the fading sky.

***

Hal knew he would not make it if he took the main road. To save time, he had to cut through the orange grove. The low fence felt rough under his hands as he vaulted over it, the familiar scent of citrus enveloping him immediately. Hal waded through the undisturbed ash surrounding the trees, his footsteps muted, making the grove eerily silent.

Hal paused to catch his breath, leaning forward with his hands on his thighs. Out of the corner of his eye, he saw something move. A shadow flickered in the dim light, shifting between the trees. Before Hal could straighten up, a sharp punch landed in his right kidney. He staggered sideways, his breath knocked out of him. A prickling sensation up his spine alerted him to the presence of others closing in, their intentions clearly hostile.

A voice from the trees spoke. "You dirty English soldier! Rape our Elena, and now you think you can take another!"

"Stay away from our women," another voice snarled.

Hal tried to respond; his words caught in his throat. He threw a punch, connecting with one of his attackers and sending the man sprawling onto the ash-covered ground. He spun around, his heart pounding in his ears, his gaze flitting anxiously across the surroundings in search of the others. The trees concealed his assailants, and he couldn't pinpoint the source of the potential attack. He was aware that the man who had fallen over behind him had quickly got back on his feet and limped off, possibly to bring back reinforcements.

Hal's voice boomed in the darkness. "I've never harmed women!"

Out of nowhere, another man launched himself towards Hal. Hal, twice his size, picked him up and forcefully slammed him against the trunk of a tree. With his head slumped onto his chest, the man stayed in the same position where he had fallen.

Hal's senses heightened as the grove grew deathly quiet again. His pulse hammered in his ears, and his breath came in sharp bursts. Hal readied himself for the next assault, lifting a large log jutting out of the ash-covered earth. He held onto it like a cosh, ready to take on whatever came towards him. When the next man charged, Hal swung the log, deflecting the blow and sending the attacker reeling.

But before Hal could catch his breath, another assailant launched himself onto Hal's back. Hal quickly got rid of his weapon, threw his hands behind him and grabbed the assailant straddled on his back, he forcefully threw him on the ground in front of him. Hal didn't hesitate. He brought his hobnail boot down on the man's forearm, feeling the bones crunch beneath the force. The attacker's scream pierced the air, but it was cut short as another sharp blow struck Hal's shoulder from behind. Hal dropped to one knee, the sudden pain making his vision blurred. Before he could react, a final strike came down on the back of his skull. His body crumpled into the ash, his head hitting the ground with a dull thud. Hal remained face down in the ash, a dark stain of blood spreading beneath his head, stark against the grey soot.

The perpetrator threw the log back into the ashes next to Hal. He kicked the prostrate body. Hal remained motionless.

"Is he dead?" The individual with the injured arm asked.

"Who knows? We best get out of here quick. Come on, let's go."

***

Ottie lay in bed, her thoughts swirling as she stared up at the darkened ceiling. Beside her, her sisters stirred in their sleep, their soft murmurs breaking the stillness of the room. Fina wriggled closer, muttering a name—Matteo, whoever that was. Ottie gently pushed her sister back into her own space.

Her brow throbbed as she touched it, she winced, recalling the strike she had endured earlier. She hoped the dark, angry bruises could be completely concealed by her makeup in the morning. She didn't want Hal to notice. The thought of him warmed her heart, but the memory of her brothers' harsh words soon eclipsed the feeling.

Unable to sleep, Ottie laid back with her hands behind her head, her thoughts drifting between Hal and the turmoil brewing within her family. Salvo and Geno had been waiting for her when she returned home. Their disapproval of her tardiness and her time with Hal was palpable. Ottie shuddered to think what would happen when Papa returned, and her brothers reported her actions to him. She knew she had to tread carefully, but deep down, a defiant part of her didn't want to give up what she felt with Hal—not for her brothers, not even for Papa.

Her brothers' anger hadn't been a surprise. It was their actions that haunted her—their lack of hesitation when they lashed out at her. She touched her temple again, her fingers brushing the spot tenderly. The sight of her fraternising with the English soldier ignited rage and disgust in them. Their questions had come like rapid-fire bullets, not waiting for her answers.

Despite the ache in her head, Ottie couldn't help but replay the evening's events with Hal. His smile, his kindness, and the way he had kissed her as though she were the only woman in the world. The memory softened her worries, if only for a moment.

19

Aida

Arena di Verona was meticulously decorated and prepared for its Aida performance, featuring a captivating replica of a pyramid at its core. The vast amphitheatre had just opened its doors, and the arena was gently filling up. Fi had come early. She made her way past the line of punters, who had been waiting patiently for hours, clutching their cushions, eager to get a cheap seat on the stone steps at the back of the theatre. Fi felt a twinge of smugness as she passed them. The bar code on her ticket bleeped her through into the arena. She climbed the steps towards the back of the amphitheatre, pausing briefly.

Fi admired the ancient beauty of the extensive Roman relic, which had been preserved and used for performances for countless generations. She was glad to be among the first to see the amphitheatre that evening, its glory unhindered by human activity. Being ahead of time meant she didn't draw attention to herself having arrived alone. Fi occupied a seat near the rear central archway and glanced around at the scene, feeling slightly nervous and self-conscious. As she looked out at the empty stage, she concluded that Rocco had found good seats. Her seat was positioned next to the 'poltronissime' - the gold standard of luxury seating. She felt her pelvic bones already pressing through her backside on the plastic chair and cast an envious eye over to the burgundy plush cushioned seats with gilt gold frames. Only a few steps away, yet an entirely different world. She noticed the divide had been further emphasised. The first two rows of seats were sectioned off with sweeps of corded red rope.

A figure in the centre of the roped area sat motionless. She could see his profile side on and caught the edge of his refined features. She was close enough to make out the hairs on his well-groomed chin covered by grey stubble. His granite-toned hair swept casually back from his face, falling onto the collar of his indigo jacket. He wore a scarf in a similar shade tied in an a la mode style. He turned his head a degree and caught her watching him. His piercing pale hazel eyes cracked at the corners as he nodded lightly towards her, a smile playing on his lips. Fi reciprocated and then averted her gaze respectfully.

She pulled Nonna Salerno's pashmina shawl around her shoulders, feeling underdressed. Fi had created a makeshift outfit by cobbling together different garments. She packed a stretchy black Lycra skirt that she pulled up to her armpits to create a strapless mini-dress, but she'd had to forgo wearing a bra. Nonna Salerno lent her the wine-coloured shawl, disapproving of the amount of flesh Fi had on display. Fi had found a scarlet lipstick in her bag, which she slicked across her lips. Her hair was haphazardly pulled back into a loose chignon. Her efforts to look presentable now felt glaringly inadequate compared to the polished crowd filling the arena.

Fi shifted back into her seat and tried to relax. Over the arena, she observed the setting sun sinking behind the stage. Her thoughts turned to her grandparents; they would have loved this venue. Memories of listening to opera on scratchy vinyl records flooded back, played on Hal's record player in the best room at the front of the house. Hal would share the stories behind the songs with her. Typically, these were usually love stories with tragic endings.

He had once recounted taking Ottie to the opera during the war. For a rare night out, they had visited the partially bombed Teatro San Carlo in Naples, its performances continuing despite the structural damage. Allied troops made up the main audience. Ottie had been excited to go, dressing up for the occasion. Hal had told Fi that it had been an opening night—a grand affair with Gigli himself performing. The memory of that evening still amused him.

As the lights dimmed, Hal read the introduction for the first act. The programme described a svelte figure skipping through the forest. When a hefty, heavy-footed soprano lumbered gracelessly to the front of the stage, Hal couldn't contain his chuckles behind the pamphlet. Ottie had nudged him to stop, casting baleful glares. As the soprano launched into her high-pitched aria, Hal's stifled laughter only worsened. Consequently, the couple were asked to leave before the great Gigli even appeared. Ottie took years to see the funny side.

Fi came back from her daydreams. The floodgates seemed to have opened, and the crowds poured in, filling the arena.

"It's up here, honey. I got it." The American tourist shouted unnecessarily, his family right by his side.

Laden down with cushions and provisions for their family expedition, they arrived at the row Fi was sitting in. A young couple stood up at the end of the row to allow the family to pass. They were pushed uncomfortably against the back of their seats as the family squeezed themselves and their equipment through.

"Here we are, seats twelve to fifteen—that's us," confirmed the American.

He positioned himself next to Fi. She glanced up, noticing his salmon-coloured trousers, the black belt half-hidden beneath his abdomen. Her stomach dropped as she realised the tickets in his hand included her seat. Fi groaned internally. She was sitting in seat thirteen and was now fully aware that the tickets in the man's hand also contained a ticket for the same seat. Looking down at her from above, he peered over the bundle in his arms. A small droplet of sweat hung from the end of his nose. He locked his eyes on her, patiently waiting for her to move. Rocco came into her thoughts, along with a few select curse words.

"It appears we have a ticket for the same seat," Fi said, holding up her ticket for him to see.

His wife pushed forward and rudely snatched the ticket from Fi's hand.

"Why, Earl, it sure is—look," she declared, pointing a podgy finger at the two replica tickets.

"Well, we bought these from this very box office... four days ago. So, you got yourself a dud missy," the man added, his Southern drawl dripping with smug certainty.

An usher appeared at the opposite end of the row, having noticed the commotion. The Americans shouted over to him, loudly informing him—and the entire block—that Fi had a counterfeit ticket. Blushing, Fi stood and manoeuvred her way past the seated crowd. She purposefully refrained from glancing at the American family, who had already settled into her seat and expanded into the surrounding space with their belongings. Fi handed her ticket to the usher.

"It got me through the barrier. I thought it was okay—I bought it from a street seller."

The usher inspected the ticket, holding it at arm's length.

"It's a good copy," he said thoughtfully. "Some of these do get through—it's often the last-minute seats. A bit of a gamble. People sometimes get away with it if they find a vacant spot instead of the one they booked. But unfortunately," his tone softened, "I'm afraid this is an unofficial ticket."

The usher's demeanour was charitable. Which only contributed to Fi feeling more humiliated.

"I'm afraid I have to ask you to leave," he repeated, gesturing for her to follow him.

Fi felt her stomach churn. Her family's story of being thrown out of the opera felt like it was repeating itself. She stepped forward but abruptly stopped, colliding with what felt like a brick wall of a man. He blocked the entire gangway, towering over her. Fi was taken aback she regarded it as superfluous to bring a bouncer to escort her off the premises.

The man addressed them both in a deep, authoritative voice. "Madam, Visconte Falcone requests the pleasure of your company this evening.

He asks if you would be so kind as to join him in watching this evening's performance."

His Italian accent rolled over his words, the delivery well-rehearsed. Fi looked across the seated heads towards the poltronissime area. The roped-off chairs were still unoccupied. The handsome man in his suit stood up to acknowledge himself to her. With an enigmatic smile, he swept his hand toward the seat beside him, inviting her to join him.

The usher beamed. "Well, in that case, there's no problem at all. Please, madam, you must take your seat. The performance is about to start."

The bouncer led Fi toward the poltronissime, holding the rope aside as she entered. He seated himself in the row behind her and the Viscount, a discrete distance from them, surveying the crowd with hawk-like vigilance.

Fi turned to Visconte Falcone, her voice tinged with disbelief. "Thank you—thank you so much. I don't even know what to say."

He brushed off her gratitude with a graceful nod, his expression one of dignified detachment. The performance began, and Fi found herself swept away by the hauntingly pitch-perfect voices that filled the arena. The sound resonated perfectly throughout the arena, captivating the audience. Fi marvelled at the sight, as the sun continued to tuck itself away and disappear underneath the amphitheatre. The stars replaced the sun's rays, covering the night sky with a sparkling canopy, adding further magic to the performance. The interlude arrived all too soon, and Fi clapped enthusiastically. A waiter arrived carrying a silver tray with two champagne flutes.

"Please, be my guest," the Viscount said, his English almost perfect but for a faint trace of his Italian heritage, hanging at the end of his sentence.

Fi accepted the glass with a small smile, sipping the crisp champagne. She noticed his well-manicured hands as he lifted his flute.

"How remiss of me," he said after a moment. "I haven't properly introduced myself. My name is Sergio."

"Sergio, pleased to meet you," Fi replied, clumsily shifting her flute between hands as she extended one for a handshake.

Sergio took her hand briefly, lowered his head, and kissed the top of it. Fi was taken aback by his chivalry—such gestures were rare among men her age.

She fumbled over her words. "My name is, erm… Fiamma. I—I'm visiting from England."

"Ah, an English rose with an Italian name meaning 'Fiery One,'" he said, raising an audacious eyebrow.

"Yes, that's right. My grandmother was Italian. She named me. She would have loved to be here—it's… wonderful."

"It is," he agreed. "I live in Verona, and every year, I must see at least one performance here. Food for the soul. Speaking of food," he added, holding her gaze, "I would be honoured if you joined me for dinner this evening."

"Oh, you've already been too kind. I really can't impose on you further."

"No, it is my pleasure. What harm could it do? Besides, Fiamma, you are an enigma to me. I would like to hear your story. Are you not intrigued by mine?" He cocked his head to one side as he spoke, gauging her response, handling her rebuff with beguiling aplomb accustomed to getting his own way.

Fi studied his rugged features. He was right—he had captured her interest. She had never met anyone quite like him.

"Then, in that case, how can I refuse?" she said finally.

The interlude ended, and the final act began. It was as sensational as the rest of the performance. The encore lasted for what felt like an eternity, the audience showering the performers with cheers and applause. Before the final ovation, Sergio's bodyguard discreetly led them out of the arena.

To Fi's astonishment, they entered a secret tunnel, reserved exclusively for the elite. At the end of the passageway, a sleek German luxury car waited with its engine already running. The chauffeur opened the door, and Fi slid into the white leather seats, still hearing echoes of the crowd's enthusiastic applause as they pulled away.

20

The Truth

E lena was glad to have escaped the group of onlookers admiring Vesuvius. A reluctant Rosa dragged at her heels, purposely lagging behind. Elena had felt uneasy the moment she arrived. The sideways glances, the whispering behind hands, the pitying looks—it was unbearable. She preferred those who did all they could to avoid her entirely. At least their absence gave her peace. She wanted to get back to Mamma, domestic chores with her were a welcome distraction. They were the one constant in her life since the assault. Even Zio Giacomo and her brother Marco behaved differently toward her. The last few times she had sought comfort in Zio Giacomo's arms, she had been met with a change. His body stiffened in her embrace, and as he pushed her away, he commented that she was too old for such affection. As for Marco, the guilt he carried over her attack was etched into him, his spirit dimmed. Marco was drinking too much these days, and his nights out often ended in fights at the local bars.

Elena settled herself on a fallen tree, sheltered beneath the thicket's canopy, waiting patiently for Rosa to catch up. She idly probed at the burnt orange lichen attached to its bark, the barren tree giving its surface up for another species' existence. Rosa stopped close by, silently watching her sister, lost in thought as she picked at the log. Elena physically looked the same to Rosa, but she wasn't the same anymore. Her smile had disappeared, replaced by a shadowed sadness that Rosa didn't understand. Elena was melancholy, no longer the happy, fun girl Rosa had once known. No one would explain what had happened. Rosa was aware of the rumours; she had overheard whispers that an English soldier had harmed her sister. Was it idle gossip? Rosa felt left out. There had been hushed conversations behind closed doors, fleeting glances exchanged over her head as though she were invisible. Why was she the last to know anything? She was fourteen—a young woman—yet they still treated her like a child.

***

Among the crowd today was the tall soldier. He hadn't seen Elena, but she had noticed him. How could anyone not? He ranged above his own kind and was at least a foot taller than most Italian men. Elena's mind remained fogged, her memories of the attack clouded and incomplete. Her physical wounds had healed, but her emotions remained in tatters. She had tried to remember, but the harder she was pressured, the more difficult it became. From a distance, she glanced across at Hal. She regarded him without fear, only mild curiosity. She recalled how he had warned her to be careful—that was her last memory of him from that night. Fragments of that evening flashed before her; a hand gripping her arm, the sound of shoes on gravel, the taste of blood in her mouth. But then it all dissolved again. Elena caught Ottie's eye as she looked back at Hal. A nod of recognition passed between the two women. Ottie was busy talking to her sister-in-law, Anna, poor Anna widowed too soon after Marcello. Elena knew Ottie would come to her next, full of curiosity and superfluous concern. The weight of Ottie's pity was too much. She left before Ottie could approach, unwilling to endure her questions.

Elena continued poking at the lichen, aware that she was being watched. She looked up and saw Rosa close by, staring at her. Elena noticed the dirt streaked on Rosa's legs from the knees down, evidence of her careless swooshing through the fallen ash.

"Your best shoes are filthy. What will mamma say?" Elena chastised. Rosa looked down at her feet and then defiantly at Elena.

"Who cares? They're only shoes," she challenged.

Inhaling deeply, Elena carefully contemplated her response.

"I agree with Rosa."

Another voice echoed from the depths of the thicket. Its source stepped into the clearing. Enzo—and the never far behind, Gianni—stumbled out from the foliage. Enzo strutted forward, asserting his presence in the space between the two girls. Gianni lingered at the periphery, his body language uneasy, as though he wished to melt into the shadows.

Enzo studied Rosa for a moment, then placed the tip of his finger under her chin, tilting her face toward him, closely inspecting her face. Elena moved to get off the log, but Enzo challenged her with a sharp glare. She froze, fright paralysing her. Enzo resumed his original task, his attention returned to Rosa, his gaze predatory.

"Such a beautiful woman, Rosa. It's not your shoes that men notice." Enzo cast his eyes over Rosa's body before continuing. "There's much more to a woman than that."

He used the same hand under her chin to rub his thumb provocatively across her lips. Rosa trembled under his touch, intensifying his pleasure at the control he wielded.

Elena found her voice. "Leave her alone."

Enzo turned his attention toward Elena. He gave Rosa a sinister look and instructed her not to move. Placing his braced arms on the log beside Elena, he caged her in. Leaning toward her, nose to nose, he sneered.

"Why, Elena, are you jealous? Not getting enough attention?" He leaned closer, his breath hot against her cheek, and whispered in her ear. "Do you want more of what you had before?"

Elena's eyes widened in realisation. The smell of him brought back a flash of memory—rough hands pinning her down, his cruel laughter. It came flooding back all at once. She pushed him away, her hands trembling. Enzo feigned hurt, pressing a hand to his heart as he smirked.

"Oh, be careful. Remember, you're used goods now. I wonder if your sister will be more fun?"

His smile grew menacing as the idea took hold.

"I hear someone coming," Gianni warned.

Gianni had been pacing anxiously on the edge of his brother's show-ground and heard the snap of a twig, followed by distant voices. Rosa snapped out of her fear and ran to Elena, clutching her tightly. The sisters, gripped by a chilling fear, watched the two brothers leave.

"Let's get out of here." Elena breathed out her words, each syllable a sigh of relief.

She grabbed Rosa's hand, and half dragged her out of the thicket. They ran together, towards home, only stopping to catch their breath when the roof of their house came into view.

"Enzo hurt you badly, didn't he Elena? That night, you came home late with Marco and the police... it was him, wasn't it?" Rosa's voice trembled, her words bursting with urgency.

Elena did not answer, her lips trembling as her eyes welled with tears. Rosa pressed on, her breaths quick from running.

"Elena, answer me! What did he do to you? Why haven't you said anything? You can't keep this to yourself anymore."

"I... I couldn't remember. But now, seeing the tall soldier and then Enzo, it came back to me. I must..." Her voice cracked, and she broke down, the tears streaming from her face, her nose running. She wiped her face against her sleeve, her sobs shaking her entire body.

"You must what Elena?" Rosa crouched down to meet her sister's eyes, her voice softening but still firm. "Come, Elena. We are going to sort this out. Mamma needs to hear this."

Rosa took her sister's hand firmly, pulling her toward home with an unshakable resolve.

***

Mamma, her hands sticky with gnocchi dough, looked up sharply as her daughters entered the kitchen through the open back door. She noticed their dishevelled appearance and the way their eyes darted nervously, both focused intently on her. Sensing trouble, she set aside her preparations, rubbing the flour from her hands onto her apron as she braced herself. She pressed her daughters to account for their apparent woes.

"What's happened now?" she asked.

Rosa did most of the talking, her words tumbling out in a rush. She described the incident in the thicket and the revelation Elena had shared. Mamma's face tightened as she listened.

She turned to Elena, her voice steady but commanding. "Is it true? Did Enzo...?"

Elena's face crumpled as she nodded, covering her face in shame. "Yes, Mamma," she whispered, her voice barely audible. "It's true."

Mamma said nothing for a moment, her expression unreadable. She finally sent the girls to bed with the last of her cocoa ration.

"Drink this and sleep," she instructed. "I need to think. Tomorrow, we will deal with this."

Left alone in the kitchen, Mamma pressed her elbows onto the table, and let her forehead drop onto them, deep in thought. What a calamity, an utter mess. The Pardi boys. Enzo so arrogant, Gianni so spineless. Neither were like their father—a man she had held in the highest regard. Signore Giacomo Pardi, her late husband's cousin, had been a pillar of support since her widowhood, even creating a job for Marco in his vineyard. His generosity had kept them from poverty, and she owed him much, but this... this was beyond forgiveness.

She waited, the minutes dragging, until Marco returned. They needed to sort out this mess. Thankfully, Marco was neither too late nor too drunk on this occasion.

***

Marco's brain was banging against his skull when he eventually regained consciousness. His body ached from the fight, his spine stiff as if every vertebra had been bruised. He felt dazed, nausea kept hitting him in waves. At his feet, the tall soldier lay motionless, a thin layer of ash settling over his back like a shroud. Failing to scramble to his feet, Marco gripped a tree trunk for support and hauled himself up. He wiped his mouth with the back of his hand and forced himself to move. The trek home felt endless, each stumbling step a battle against his own guilt and exhaustion.

When he finally reached the back door, he felt a fleeting rush of relief to see Mamma still awake. She rose quickly, her sharp eyes scanning his dishevelled frame.

"Marco!" she exclaimed, rushing to him. "What happened? Have you been fighting again?"

Marco groaned, leaning heavily against the doorframe.

"I fell on the way home from the bar," he mumbled, avoiding her gaze. "Took a knock to the head."

Her lips pressed into a thin line, but she said no more, accepting his explanation for now. She placed a steaming cup of lemon tea in front of him.

"Drink this."

As he sipped, she told him about Elena's confession. The words hit him like a blow, his grip tightening on the mug until his knuckles turned white. Marco knew Elena wasn't lying. He knew what kind of man Enzo was. Yet he had let himself be swept into Enzo's scheme, fuelled by his own blind anger. Together with Cesare and Gianni, they had ambushed the tall soldier, convinced he was the man who had hurt Elena. But it had been a lie. He wanted to kill Enzo, the cunning bastard. Marco had brought Cesare, his best friend, along for support; the four of them followed the soldier into the orange grove and then battered him. Now, Marco's stomach churned with the weight of what they had done. They had beaten an innocent man, perhaps killed him. And he had allowed it to happen.

***

At first light, Marco and Mamma marched to Zio Giacomo's house. His mousy wife, Marta, let them in before she timidly scurried away. Giacomo Pardi sat at the kitchen table with his latte, idly dipping stale bread into the milky foam. A second mug had been set on the table for Marco, ready for the two men to have their usual shared breakfast. Morning conversation over coffee formed a part of their working day at the vineyard. He looked up, startled, at the sight of Pina and Marco entering unannounced. He raised himself from the table and gestured for them both to take a seat, shouting for Marta to fetch another latte.

"Pina," he greeted her, standing. "This isn't the usual time for a visit. What's the matter? Please, sit."

"No, Giacomo. We won't be staying long." Pina's voice was cold and resolute.

Giacomo had a strong affection for Pina Fragopane that stretched back to their youth. In those days, she had been a striking beauty, her looks matched by a natural warmth that drew people to her effortlessly. Though the years had taken their toll, every time Giacomo laid eyes on her, she still made his heart skip a beat.

Today, however, she looked exhausted. The grey streaks framing her temples, the dark circles under her eyes, and the firm set of her jaw told him that this was no ordinary visit. He studied her quietly, a pang of regret surfacing. He had often chastised himself for not seizing his chance with her before his charming cousin had swept her off her feet.

He loved her daughters as if they were his own, in contrast to his feelings toward his own sons, who had become a source of deep disappointment. Their mother had coddled them, and he had afforded them a privileged life—too much ease, too little discipline. They had grown into men he barely recognised or respected.

As his gaze shifted to Marco, he sensed the younger man's irritation. Giacomo's sharp eyes noticed the purple bruise on Marco's temple, the telltale mark of another fight. It was becoming all too common since the trouble with Elena. Still, for all his faults, Marco never shirked his responsibilities at the vineyard. Whatever else he was, Marco was no coward and no layabout. Marco stepped forward.

"Zio," he said, his voice thick with emotion. "I come with bad news. News that will tear our families apart."

Giacomo leaned his elbows on the table, his hands pressed together in a prayer-like gesture. The tips of his fingers resting under his chin brushed his grey beard as he straightened his back, exhaling slowly, steadying himself before speaking.

"Those are strong words you use, Marco. Tell me—what news is it that you both bring to me?"

Across the table, Pina's unwavering stare pierced into the back of his eyes.

"Your sons," she said, with a moment's pause as she considered the weight of her words. "I think Enzo is the main one. But both are responsible for Elena's assault."

Giacomo fell back into his chair, his fists clenching tightly as he exhaled loudly and looked to the heavens. His shoulders sagged, the enormity of the allegation sinking into his chest.

"That's a strong accusation," he said, his voice low and measured. "Are you certain?" His gaze returned to Pina, though he already knew her answer.

"I would lay my life on it," she replied, her tone unwavering, every syllable heavy with conviction.

"Marta!" Giacomo bellowed, his voice echoing through the house.

She appeared at the doorway, her hands clasped tightly in front of her.

"Get those lazy boys out of their beds and bring them to me!" He commanded.

She hesitated, her lips parting as if to ask a question. Giacomo raised a finger and silenced her.

"Then I want you out of this house," Giacomo added sharply. "Run chores, do whatever it is you do all day—just get out!"

She let out a slight whimper at his anger but hurried away to carry out his orders. Moments later, Enzo and Gianni appeared bleary-eyed in matching cotton pyjama bottoms and white string vests. Enzo roused to his senses the quickest of the two brothers, immediately miscalculating the circumstances.

He verbally lunged at Marco. "You traitor!" You told them about last night." Without waiting for a reply, he added defiantly, "I'm not sorry, Papa. If that soldier is dead, he deserved it!"

"What are you talking about?" Giacomo barked. "This has nothing to do with last night. Marco, tell me what happened."

Marco's voice wavered as he addressed his mother. "Oh, Jesus, this is terrible. Mamma, I'm so sorry. I wanted to tell you. Believe me. Last night, with Cesare and these two, I attacked an English soldier. They made me believe he'd raped Elena. But now I know better."

"You idiot, Marco! You scum of the earth!" Enzo interjected, his voice dripping with venom. "Papa, I'm not responsible for the soldier. It wasn't me…No, he did that!" He pointed at Gianni as he spoke.

Gianni turned pale. "I never meant to kill him," he stammered. "He knocked out Marco and broke Cesare's arm. I had to… I hit him on the back of the head with a log. He would have killed us!"

Marco's voice erupted in fury. "No, Enzo, you're party to this! You ran off like a coward and left us! Not as easy a target as raping my sister, was it? And now you threaten Rosa? You bastard!"

Marco rose, his fists clenched, and lunged toward Enzo, but Pina quickly stepped between them, her arm raised to block him.

"Sit down, all of you!" She commanded, her voice sharp and unrelenting. "You all disgust me!"

"I didn't touch your sister," Gianni whimpered, tears spilling down his cheeks. "I would never do that. I love her."

"You're pathetic," Marco snarled, his voice heavy with contempt. "You let it happen, and then you covered up for Enzo. Be a man, Gian. Tell us what happened."

"I told him not to!" Gianni replied pathetically.

"Shut up, Gian," Enzo hissed, his words sharp and biting.

Gianni made a feeble attempt to defend himself. "He made me take her to the park and stand watch while he—"

"Enough!" Giacomo roared, slamming both fists onto the table as he rose to his feet.

"You boys dishonour our family. You bring shame upon us!" His eyes homed in on Enzo, his eldest son. "Enzo, you are the lowest of them all. You are no longer a son to me. I am sending you to Crispiano to work the olive groves with your uncle. If, by some grace of God, this war ever ends, you will board the first ship to New York and never return to Italy."

Enzo's face twisted in shock. He knew his uncle's reputation, a harsh man living in poverty with his brutish sons. They lived like animals in the middle of nowhere; he was an oaf. The work was hard, monotonous, and gruelling. The thought of a life spent in hard labour, mocked and ridiculed by his cousins, left him speechless.

"I need to fetch my things," Enzo muttered, as he made to leave.

"You won't move from that seat!" Giacomo thundered. "You will take nothing but the clothes on your back. Marco will accompany me. We leave as soon as I've finished speaking."

"You make one false move. Or I ever see your face again. I swear I will kill you Enzo." Marco snapped.

Giacomo's eyes flicked to Marco.

"You," he said, his tone icy. "You've been a fool, blinded by anger. If it weren't for your mother's situation, you'd never work for me again. Step out of line once more, and you're gone. Starting today, you'll never to set foot in a bar again."

Marco bowed his head in shame, unable to meet his uncle's glare.

Finally, Giacomo turned to Gianni.

"And you," he said, his voice filled with disgust. "You have murder on your hands."

Gianni's lips trembled as he spoke. "Oh, father... I'll go to the police. I'll tell them everything. I deserve whatever punishment they give me."

"No," Giacomo said sharply. "None of this is to ever be spoken outside of this room. I want you, Gian, to go back to the grove and see if the soldier is still alive. So, we know what we are dealing with. Then you have a choice. Leave today and never return or stay here and work as hard as Marco. You'll be paid a wage, but part of it will cover your food and lodging. You are no longer my son. Both of you are disinherited. When I die, this vineyard will pass to Elena. It will be her decision whether you've proven yourself worthy to stay."

Gianni's face fell as Giacomo delivered his final blow.

"Pray the soldier is alive. I doubt it. But if you have an ounce of decency left, you'll own up to your crime, and you'll bear the blame alone. But I know you are weak, Gian, just as your brother is cruel. Try for once in your life, to do the right thing and be the one dutiful son for your mother, as her eldest son will now be dead to her forever. If you stay here, you live as one of the workers; that is how I will always treat you. I give you all more than you deserve."

21

Close Call

I t took Hal a moment to reconnect his brain and comprehend what had happened. He was alive—of that, he was sure. He tried to move, but everything hurt. Raising his head, he carefully sat back onto his haunches. The ash fell away from him; thick clumps remained stuck to his bloody skull. He surveyed his surroundings. There were no other bodies, a new layer of ash had covered any tracks that might have been left. He was lucky to be alive. The volcanic ash had cocooned around him while he was unconscious, keeping him warm through the night's chill. Hal cautiously touched the back of his head, feeling a lumpy mat of hair. He examined the dark, congealed blood on his palm. He noted his bent little finger—a lifelong reminder of his days working as a garden boy in the Manor house. He had fallen hands-first into a glass cold frame full of cucumbers after hopping over the kitchen garden wall as a shortcut, nearly losing his little finger.

His mind was fogged, and he kept losing focus, the trees melting together. This time, he had to handle more than just a partially severed little finger. He had to use every ounce of strength to get himself up and out of the orange grove. Each step jarred his aching body, but it wasn't just pain that gnawed at him—it was the memory of the ambush. The cries, the punches, the way the ash swallowed the world whole. He shook his head, trying to banish the images. Judging by the slight chill and low sun, it was early morning. He looked at his watch to verify. The dial was cracked, the hour hand loose behind the glass. Swaying, he got to his feet and staggered toward the main road—a journey he had intended to make last night. He needed to get back to base. He needed to get cleaned up. But right now, he had to get away from the orange grove. If those bastards returned, he knew he wouldn't stand a chance this time.

He made it to the road and blindly stepped into the open space, still concussed, dazed by the brightness that was unforgiving, away from the shadows of the trees. The glare of the sun made his head throb, and the sound of gravel crunching under the truck's tires barely registered over the ringing in his ears. With a shriek of brakes and the honk of a horn, a large delivery truck stopped within inches of Hal. The driver's sign language through the windscreen was easily understood. Hal shook his head, too worn out to react. He stepped into the passenger seat, delegating the driver with the responsibility of taking him back to base. The driver was taken aback by Hal's beat-up appearance. As luck would have it, he was passing by the base anyway and willingly obliged. The truck driver dropped him off a short distance from the camp. With a thank you, Hal raised his hand as the truck continued its journey, leaving a dust trail in its wake.

Hal stumbled up the hills incline to the spot where he knew the fence had been tampered with—a small hole concealed behind a scraggy juniper bush, useful for soldiers, in the know. While attempting to squeeze his large frame through the hole in the fence, Hal cursed the bush's prickles that leaned forward and spiked into him. On the other side, he managed the last leg toward his Nissan hut, taking big strides, pleased to see hut twenty-seven in his sights. Hal fell against the door, desperate for his bed. His fellow soldier, Ken, stood covered in shaving foam, a brush in one hand.

Surprised to see Hal burst through the door, he exclaimed: "Hal? … Is that you? …Bloody hell man."

Ken moved toward him as he spoke, unsure of the filthy figure in front of him despite the British uniform. Ken recognised Hal's tall, slightly stooped silhouette, which was evident, as he entered the room. Hal was covered from head to foot in dirt, making it hard to make out his features. The whites of his eyes were prominent against his skin, stained dark by the ash. Hal sank onto his bed, exhausted. The commotion roused the other soldiers in the barrack. Hal was struggling to keep hold of his senses. He thought he heard Taffy's Welsh brogue. He believed he must be hallucinating or dreaming—or both.

Hal slipped into darkness. He came round with Taffy's freckled face at the end of his nose.

"He's awake," Taffy called over his shoulder before turning back to Hal. "Jes man. You look like you've been down the pits with my tad."

Stan's voice came from the background. "What the hell happened to you? It's us cannon fodder that's been in battle, not you."

Stan appeared from the back of the room, looming above a kneeling Taffy.

"Oh, fellas. It's good to see you," Hal said, gulping his words between sips of water offered by Taffy.

He told them about the ambush in the orange grove. Stan and Taffy listened, encouraging him to get up as they did. They informed Hal that the Captain had been in while he'd lain out cold on his bunk. Hal needed to get himself over to him sharpish. The Captain had ordered that Hal was to be cleaned up and seen by the medics. Hal did as he was commanded, albeit begrudgingly, requiring another push from his mates.

The Captain's eyes narrowed as Hal stumbled into his office, his uniform still streaked with ash.

'What in God's name have you been up to soldier?' he barked, slamming his fist on the desk.

Hal straightened as much as his ribs allowed, muttering a clipped explanation about the ambush.

The Captain glared, his tone softer but no less sharp. 'We will investigate your allegations. But don't think you're above discipline. Report to the cookhouse at 0600 hours. Now get yourself to the medics before you keel over."

Within the hour, he found himself in a less dazed state, walking across the square, having left his dressing down from the Captain. The doctor had nonchalantly advised Hal that he may have a broken rib or a hairline skull fracture, which would heal without intervention. This was wartime. He was alive; he had all four limbs, and he could shoot his Enfield as well as the next Tommy. It wasn't the first time he had been patched up and sent back to the line. At least this time, he wasn't stooped down in a trench trying to sleep standing up.

He had been given extra cookhouse duties for his tardiness and told his allegations would be investigated. Rising early to peel potatoes all day wasn't a chore he relished. As his mates reminded him, it could have been worse, a fact he was well aware of. If ever he caught one of those bastards again, he wanted to give them a good hiding.

Seeing Stan and Taffy was a bonus. They had very few stories about Cassino, mostly painful memories, all of them grim. The battle was harsh. The losses were many, and the progress was nil. They wanted to forget, but were glad to have returned alive. Hal felt grateful for the rest of the day off.

Tomorrow began with an early start in the kitchen. He sank into his bunk, bone tired. Ottie was due at work tomorrow, and he needed to get a message to her. He had written her a note and added a little sketch around the edge of the pages. This gave him the enthusiasm to continue drawing. He sketched her face on a separate page. Stopping in between, to ease his sore knuckles, bruised from the fight. His pencil brushed on the paper. Her features unfolded in front of him. He placed it in a letter he had written for his mother. Stopping to add a note on the back.

This is Octavia, not the best drawing, but I hope you get the idea.

***

With a contented sigh, Stan leaned back on the bunk opposite Hal, the crinkled edges of Gladys, his fiancé's many letters rustling softly as he finished them. The letters had been written over a few months, having only just tracked their way to him. Stan placed them in date order and read them in sequence avidly. The first few letters were five to six pages long and filled with information about her life, full of tenderness and yearning to see him again. The last one contained just one page. It was concise, factual, and unemotional. Stan guessed it was down to the fact that he had not responded to any of her letters. He had time at last, and he resolved to write her a long letter, pouring his heart out on the page. He missed her so very much and wanted to let her know.

Stan took out the tiny black and white photograph of her from his wallet. She faced the camera side on, the wind, catching her hair, a towel wrapped around her shoulders. He admired the close-up snap he had taken of her from one of their dreamy days swimming and mucking about by the river. The photo had been taken on the day he had asked her to marry him before he left for this god-awful war. Childhood sweethearts separated by Hitler. His daydreaming was interrupted by Hal hovering above him, waiting for the right moment to intrude.

"That your girl Gladys?"

Stan ran a finger across Gladys's picture. "Yeah, that's my girl." Stan's voice was tinged with a softness he couldn't entirely hide.

"Must be good knowing you got someone to get back to," reflected Hal as he considered his next request before asking. "Can you do me a favour, mate?"

Hal dropped an envelope onto Stan's abdomen as he lay semi-recumbent on his bunk, Gladys' letters strewn around him, the last one still in his hand. Stan fumbled to find it amongst his own. He picked it up and read the name in Hal's scratchy writing. "Octavia Matanti," he read the name aloud.

"Could you drop by munitions and give it to her today?" Hal implored, talking over him to distract from the amusement he saw in Stan's expression.

"Yeah, sure," Stan sat up, his interest piqued. "Any message to go with it?"

Hal gave it a second thought and shook his head in a definite no.

Stan waved the envelope at him.

"Be careful. Getting messed up with Italian women. You're gonna get more than you bargained for."

"I bloody hope so Stan!" Taffy chuckled from across the room.

Taffy strutted towards them, peacock-like, from the far end of the hut. Before he added. "Who's coming to Naples with me tonight? I am ready for a night of beer and girls."

"Hey, I will just take the beers," Stan replied.

He was looking once more at the picture of his beloved Gladys. The reason that he had kept sane in this mad war.

"You've gone way too soppy with that Gladys of yours. C'mon, these Neapolitan women are beauties and cheaper than the beer. They'll be wanting a nice bit of a hungry Welsh man. They will virtually give it away." Taffy finished as he arrived at the foot of Stan's bunk, his grandiloquence reflected in his raised chin posture.

"Not if you pick up more than you bargained for, Taff. They ain't clean. You read the posters in the men's lav," Stan continued to tease. "Too stupid to read or too randy to care."

Taffy replied by humping the air at Stan.

"Taff, you're an arse. If they weren't so hungry, they wouldn't act so cheap," Hal contributed.

"You're all bleedin' high and mighty now you got an Itie bird on tap," Taffy rallied back.

Hal lunged at Taffy and pushed him against the wall, its flimsy panel wobbling with the force. Hal's anger had risen in response to Taffy's boorish ignorance. Taffy's words were sharp in his mouth, but Hal couldn't tell if the rage came from Taffy's ignorant teasing or from the hollow feeling in his chest. His temper flared so easily now, like the fuse of a bomb, and it scared him. The urge to hurt Taffy was overwhelming, a primal need that he couldn't explain.

"Next time any dirt comes out of your effin' gob, I will pummel you until you shut up." Hal pushed him away as he spat out his words.

"Easy fellas. We're all a bit cooped up in here. No harm meant."

Stan, his voice calm and measured, had stood up, ready to pull his two best friends apart.

"Hal, mate, no offence. C'mon," Taffy spoke as he picked himself up off the floor, putting a wary hand out towards him.

Hal took a breath, shaky but steadying. There was a rawness inside him, something dark that felt like it could slip out if he let it. Hal mirrored Taffy and raised his hand; they gave a tentative shake. Trembling, Hal remained on edge, his recent altercation being the real cause. It had taken him a mountainous effort not to punch Taffy with his stupid, gobby mouth. He knew he wasn't angry at Taffy anymore; it was the rage that never seemed to leave him now. He wasn't sure if he could ever stop feeling like this. He knew if he had started on Taffy, he wouldn't have been able to stop. That bothered him; he knew the signs.

Hal wiped the sweat off his face from the towel he had pulled from around Taffy's neck. Placing a playful pat on his cheek as he did so—an attempt to divert his fury and make light of the situation. Taffy watched him closely, relieved that it had blown over. He was aware of the triggers. Having spent enough years around Hal, he knew he had overstepped the mark, and silence was the best option.

22

Meeting Mary Magdalene

The Villa gates opened automatically, and the car pulled into the curved gravel drive, stopping at the front of the house. Fi was let out by the chauffeur. She felt the evening heat invade the air-conditioned car. A chorus of cicadas filled the air, mixed with a heady scent of the Mediterranean still held trapped under the nearby pine tree's daytime umbrage. The front door opened, casting a lighter tint across the evening's shadow. A butler stood at the door, dressed immaculately, right down to his white gloves. The slender, fair-haired young man addressed Sergio.

"Good evening, sir." The butler spoke with an English accent as he dutifully relieved the viscount of his scarf and jacket.

Fi declined to hand over her shawl, remembering Nonna Salerno's earlier disapproving look.

"I've moved dinner to the drawing room, being as you have company," the butler added with a hint of a Geordie tone.

"Excellent Clarence. Did you decant the Barola?"

"Most definitely, sir. Would you like me to serve it?"

"No, your presence this evening will not be required."

Clarence bowed his head in acknowledgement and departed from the drawing room. In daylight hours, the room afforded an impressive view through the French doors out onto the well-tended garden.

The doors were wide open, and voile curtains fluttered in the gentle evening breeze. The room was adorned with antique paintings dotted against the wood panelling. Marquetry furniture festooned with objet d'art complimented the pictures. A large table dominated the centre. The end of the table had been laid out for two diners. Sergio handed her a crystal glass containing red wine.

"I hope you don't mind," he said. "I tend to eat light in the evening. We have lobster, followed by formaggi e frutta."

"Sounds perfect," Fi replied, raising her glass.

They sat at the table, sharing stories and talking until late into the night. Fi delved into Sergio's background, discovering his noble lineage as a Viscount from the Falcone family, deeply rooted in Verona's history for generations. His tales enriched her understanding of his privileged upbringing. He was a lifelong bachelor and the sole surviving Falcone. Sergio, too, found her stories captivating, particularly the ones about her trip to Italy.

Eventually, they moved from the table to the high-backed, over-stuffed settee near the fireplace. Fi had declined more wine, feeling it affecting her. Clarence, at Sergio's request, brought her a chamomile tea. The straw scent filled Fi's nostrils as she carefully held the porcelain cup, its thinness apparent in her hands. The steam from the teacup curled in the air as Clarence, his task complete, paused at the door and asked Sergio if he needed anything else for the evening. With a slight shake of his head, Sergio confirmed that was all. Clarence hesitated, then asked if he should turn down the bed in the guest room. Sergio politely declined, waving his hand dismissively.

Fi thought she noticed an exchange of proverbial glances between them, the routine this evening not being an unusual one. When Clarence left, Fi felt a glimmer of unease. Sergio's hand touched her knee, with increasing frequency. She regretted removing her shawl. She looked down at her prominent nipples under the tight Lycra, folding her arm across her chest to cover them up. Fi's mind wandered for a moment while Sergio described the paintings in the room, obliging her interest in the artwork. It all began to make sense to her. She had the stark re-alisation that he had assumed she would stay the night. Fi shook her head. Why are you so naïve at times? No such thing as a free lunch, after all. It was easy to see how women were swept away by him. Not this girl, she declared to herself. Quin was the only man for her, even though he was far away. Sergio's voice trailed on in the background. She came to her senses.

"Finally, I give you my favourite," Sergio concluded as he waved his hand at the large oil painting above the fireplace. "The magnificent Mary Magdalene. This painting has been in my family since the early seventeenth century. It was painted by the artist when he stayed here as a guest."

Fi stood up to examine Mary Magdalene more closely. Spectre-like against a dark background, her head was thrown back, her face lifted towards the heavens, her sienna hair cascading onto her shoulders. Her garment draped low, partially revealing the pink areola of her breast. Her expression was finely captured with each brushstroke, her lips parted, her eyes half-open, a tear on her perfect pale cheek. The colours intricately painted captured her haunting beauty.

"She looks so sad and alone," Fi replied.

"You think so? Legend portrayed her as a hermit after Christ's death. Seven times each day, she heard the celestial choirs and was overcome by their harmonies."

"No wonder she is sad," confirmed Fi.

"That's interesting to see how you perceive that. Art experts have named the painting Mary Magdalene in ecstasy. Likening her expression to the moment of ecstasy a woman experiences at the point of orgasm." His words hung in the air, as he watched her for her reaction.

"You made that up to shock me!" Fi confronted him, her voice sharp.

Sergio leaned back into the settee, brushing a hand through his hair in a nonchalant gesture.

"I didn't make it up," he replied calmly.

"Anyway," Fi pressed on, "how would experts even know that, if your painting has been hidden away in your family home all this time?"

"I assure you, there are some exemplary copies circulating," Sergio said with a faint smile. "But this one is the original. My grandfather hid it during the war, along with many other family heirlooms. It was to protect them from Nazi plunder. Without his foresight, these pieces could have been lost forever."

"Still," Fi countered, her expression softening, "it's a shame she's been hidden away. Wouldn't you like people to enjoy it? You're the last in line to inherit all this. Who gets to see it?"

"I have a few cousins. It'll be shared among them. But as for the Falcone name and its titles—well, they end with me." He shrugged, then waved her words away with a flick of his hand. "Besides, Italy has more than enough artwork on display."

"It's not just about Italy," Fi said, undeterred. "This art belongs to the world. Falcone. What's in a name, anyway? That which we call a rose, by any other name, would smell as sweet."

"Ah, Shakespeare," Sergio mused, a glimmer of admiration in his eyes as he rose to stand beside her by the fireplace. "Juliet's lines, no less. Nicely done." He studied her for a moment, then added, "You have a quick, interesting mind, Fiamma. You're a woman of substance. Rare qualities in someone so beautiful."

His hand rose toward her hair, but Fi intercepted it, gripping his wrist and holding it firmly.

"It's late. Shall we go to bed?" Sergio's tone was matter-of-fact, implying the suggestion was inevitable.

Fi's gaze hardened.

"Sergio," she said, her voice cool and firm. "This may be a common occurrence for you, but it's not for me. I told you—I'm engaged and not available." She released his wrist, her eyes locking onto his. "I think it's time I went home."

"A shame," Sergio murmured. He closed the distance between them, his presence almost tangible, his stare unwavering. "You're alone," he said softly. "I can see it in your eyes. You may deny it but believe me

…I understand it."

The words landed like a challenge. Fi held her ground, though his intensity unnerved her. A lingering citrus scent, from his neroli-based aftershave, filled the space between them.

"No, Sergio," she replied evenly. "What you see is your own reflection." Her words were deliberate, unflinching.

She turned, gathering her bag and shawl.

"Please call for a taxi," she said, her tone final.

Sergio remained by the fireplace, watching her with a mix of admiration and frustration. He smiled graciously, accepting the novelty of being rebuffed by a woman. The evening had not gone as he'd intended, yet he couldn't help but admire her resolve.

"So be it," he said with a faint smile. "Clarence will arrange one. I hope you find what you're looking for and that you have a safe journey to your aunt's place."

"I'll see myself out," Fi replied curtly, heading for the door.

She paused with her hand on the handle, her fingers impotent around it. His words had stirred something—an uncomfortable blend of insult and intrigue. With a deep breath, she turned around and began to approach him but stopped midway. Redness crept into her cheeks, a tightness at her neck.

Her voice was softer now, hesitant. "If I ever..." She faltered, her mouth dry before she regrouped. "I think it's a shame you're the last of the Falcones. I've had a wonderful evening... despite everything." Her glance toward the sofa said more than her words. "You leave a legacy as remarkable as you are."

Sergio inclined his head, their eyes meeting with mutual respect. He said nothing as she walked away. In the corridor, Clarence waited, flustered and half-awake, brushing down his hair with gloveless hands, his jacket rumpled.

"Madam, your taxi is on its way," he said, his voice tinged with apology.

The headlights of the waiting car cast long shadows on the foyer walls. Clarence fumbled with the bolts and locks, to open the door for her.

"Thank you," Fi said as she stepped out.

Clarence escorted her to the taxi. He hesitated before closing the door. In a rare moment of candour, he gave her a sharp wink and a firm pat on the shoulder. His grip lingered for a moment before he spoke.

"He'll be in a right fettle tomorrow. It's a first for him, ye canny lass," Clarence declared, slipping effortlessly into his native Geordie dialect, his cheekiest grin lighting up his face.

The formality of his earlier manner was gone, replaced by a warmth that made her feel like a trusted confidante. Fi smiled, patting the hand he'd rested on her shoulder just before he removed it and closed the taxi door behind her. She caught one last glimpse of his mischievous grin in the glow of the porch light, and despite herself, she couldn't help but smile. Clarence watched the taxi's wheels spin away on the gravel path, the tail lights vanishing into the darkness.

With a slight shake of his head and an amused smile, he muttered to himself. "Wey, Falcone, hinny, ye're not gannin' te let this one drop, are ye?"

23

Good Day, Bad Day

She worked tirelessly; Ottie was adept at her job. She could virtually do it with her eyes shut these days. Annamaria silently worked beside her. They worked in sync, making light work of the monotonous chore. A new delivery had arrived that morning with more equipment to aid the war effort. This meant their workload had increased, requiring a faster pace than usual; the stock needed to be packed and moved on quickly. The boxes contained essential equipment headed for the Gustav line. Ottie was grateful there was no time for small talk with Annamaria. She wanted to engross herself in the mindless humdrum of her work. It gave her thinking time to fathom this shift in her emotions towards Hal. A change that made her feel more alive than she had been for a long time. It was not without consequences; she touched her sore temple from the altercation with her brothers. Alberto's image came to the front of her mind and stabbed at her conscience.

Alberto was everything she should want—a good man, from a respectable family, offering her security. But the thought of him felt cold, like a duty rather than a joy. With Hal, everything was different. His mere presence lit her up. Pushing away the heavy shadow of her old life, to hell with the ramifications, she thought. Ottie had seen enough suffering in her junior years in her own home without adding to the events of a war-torn world in which she found herself.

Ottie wondered where Hal was. She found it unusual that she hadn't seen him yet. Maybe his duties had changed; perhaps he would turn up at lunchtime. She knew she certainly wouldn't eat all the bread and tomatoes she had packed for lunch. It was raining, heavy and relentless, making sitting on the grassy bank nigh on impossible. Vesuvius had finally called it a day and ceased its rumbles and explosions to lie dormant again. The rain turned the ash-covered land into a slushy mess, sliding towards the sea.

The siren sounded for break time and interrupted her thoughts. Ottie made her way to the grassy bank, at least to look and see if Hal was there. The noise in the factory dipped as workers paused their activities, eager for their break. The rain pattered loudly on the tin roof. She raised her eyes at the noisy ceiling being pelted by the storm and grabbed her coat before heading outside. Ottie made her way towards the exit, anticipating getting soaked. She tightened her polka dot headscarf to avoid her hair getting wet and frizzy.

At the door, a soldier with bright strawberry-blond hair collided into her. They both stepped sideways together, awkwardly getting in each other's way. The soldier appeared distracted, peering over her head, attempting to see into the factory. He stepped back from the raised doorway to let Ottie pass, standing barely a head taller than her. He had a kind face, pale with pink undertones. She smiled at him, no longer wary of English soldiers.

"Sorry," Stan said to the cute-faced, smiley girl blocking his way. "Do you know Octavia Matanti?"

She looked surprised, her large brown eyes widening further. Ottie pointed at herself to clarify.

"Si, Octavia."

"Oh. I see you're her. Do you speak any English...English you speeeak?.... No. Ok, erm." Stan handed her the letter and continued. "It's from Hal. You know Hal," he repeated, tiptoeing while raising his hand above his head to indicate height. "The tall one."

"Hal. Grazie." Ottie answered as she took the letter from Stan.

"Tanka you." She attempted to speak in English, but the language felt strange on her tongue.

***

The door of the outhouse was partially ajar. Hal caught a shadow flicker across the muddy floor. Ottie's head cautiously peeked around the door. Her face lit up into a smile when she saw him.

"Ottie, my Ottie." Hal stood up as he spoke.

His head skimmed the ceiling of the cramped outhouse, overcrowded with potato sacks. A large bucket of peeled potatoes—the fruits of Hal's labour—stood between them. The fervour of their feelings for each other could not be contained, and the bucket of potatoes was a mere obstacle that they tumbled out of the way.

The siren hailed all too soon across the steely sky. Hal straightened her headscarf with one last lingering kiss at the outhouse door. He touched the bruise at her temple, his fingers brushing against her skin as though it might shatter.

"Be careful. We will sort this mess out," he said, his voice low and steady, he held her face in his hands, an earnest look in his eyes.

Ottie leaned into his touch, forgetting, just for an instant, the world outside, the factory, the whispers, Alberto. Here, in this cramped space, nothing else mattered.

"It's you that needs to be careful. I will find out who did this to you," she replied, her voice trembling with anger and something else—something that made her chest tighten.

The sight of the bruises on him sent a wave of horror through Ottie, and she was overcome with a deep disgust at the callousness of the men responsible. Hal exhaled sharply, his brow furrowing.

"Go quick. No point both of us getting in trouble."

Hal followed his words with a gentle shake of Ottie's shoulders and planted yet another final kiss on her forehead. He hesitated, his eyes glued to her, as if he wanted to etch the moment forever into his memory. There was something raw in his expression, a mix of longing and restraint. For a moment, it seemed he wanted to say more, but the words never came. Ottie ran back to the factory, waving one last time as she turned the corner. Her overalls were splattered up to the knees by the sodden, ash-filled earth. Breathless, she arrived at her workstation a few minutes behind Annamaria. Annamaria cast her eyes over Ottie, taking in the state of her.

"Where on earth have you been? You're covered in mud."

Ottie looked down at herself and chuckled into her words. "Oh, Annamaria. I am living life."

Annamaria shook her head, a faint smile pulling at her lips.

"Only you, Octavia."

Resuming her work, she couldn't help but steal another glance at Ottie a moment later, her expression inscrutable. The afternoon passed far quicker than the morning had. Ottie was surprised when home time came around so soon. She walked across the square with Annamaria to find her truck home. She caught Annamaria noticing her wave to Hal, who appeared at the corner of the square for a brief moment.

"You're very friendly with that soldier. You should be careful. You'll give him the wrong idea," Annamaria warned as she nudged Ottie into the truck.

"I don't know what you mean. There is no harm in being friendly, is there?"

Annamaria stepped closer, lowering her voice. "Maybe not in your eyes, but in this town? Being 'friendly' with a soldier could ruin everything for you. Don't forget, you're engaged. What would Alberto say if he found out? I'm familiar with the Orsini family; they have a good reputation. Alberto is a good catch."

Ottie sighed and turned away, her gaze fixed on the grey clouds outside.

"We will see how nice he really is after today," she said quietly

"What do you mean?" Annamaria probed.

Ottie placed her fingers on Annamaria's lips and motioned for her to be silent. The packed bus was unusually quiet, with pricked ears all around them. Annamaria pressed her lips together, clearly holding back a response.

She moved closer, her voice barely a whisper. "Don't do anything you'll regret. Your reputation—if it's ruined, there's no coming back from it."

***

Hal had stayed back in the shadows, watching Ottie against the truck's window, chatting with her friend. He observed the vehicle as it shuddered to a start and drove off. The square bustled with activity as trucks returned workers to their homes, and larger delivery lorries arrived, bringing critical supplies for the war effort. The battles at the Gustav line continued, and the bombardment had intensified. The British army and her allies, in their relentless attempt to punch through the German defences, demanded an endless stream of equipment to sustain the fight.

A large truck pulled up close to where Hal stood. The driver jumped down from his lorry, struggling as he did. His injured arm, encased in a heavy plaster cast, pulled him off-balance, making it difficult for him to walk steadily. Hal narrowed his eyes, a rage rising within him. The driver was short and stocky, with a cocksure air about him. He strode to the back of his lorry, shouting for help to unload the vehicle. Hal's mind flashed back to the orange grove, recalling the sound of bone crunching underfoot. This had to be the man.

Hal leapt into the square, his long strides closing the distance before the lorry driver had time to react. The sheer ferocity of Hal's attack knocked the man to the ground. Hal's fists rained down mercilessly as the driver screamed for help. The man raised his plastered arm in a futile attempt to shield his face, cowering beneath the blows.

"YOU bastard. I ain't no rapist. Where are your mates now!" Hal shouted, his voice filled with hatred as his punches landed relentlessly.

Soldiers came running from all directions, crossing the square to intervene. They were on Hal in no time, dragging him off the lorry driver. Stan was among them, shouting, his voice cutting through the chaos. Hal was shoved against the side of the lorry and pinned down by three soldiers. The red mist began to clear, and Hal's breathing slowed. Stan's voice finally reached him, the words beginning to make sense.

"Hal, this guy broke his arm here last week. He fell off the back of a lorry. He is not your man. It's not him. I tell you. Get the bloody medics. Someone, give Salvatore a hand!" Stan barked his orders.

Medics rushed in from the opposite end of the square, carrying a stretcher between them. Stan turned back to Hal, his pale complexion turned crimson with anger.

"For Christ's sake! You damn well buggered it up this time," Stan spat his words out at Hal, sharp and cutting.

Salvatore, the injured lorry driver, shouted profanities in his own vernacular as he was carted away.

"I guess it wasn't the best move for the Anglo-Italian conciliations," Hal muttered with a rueful smile.

Stan bent forward, his hands on his hips, shaking his head in frustration. He idly kicked a stone, trying to channel his fury elsewhere. Hal noticed, to his relief, that Stan's shoulders soon began to shake—not with anger, but with laughter.

It wasn't long before Hal found himself standing in front of the Captain again. He braced himself, knowing what was coming. The Captain's outrage was palpable.

"The Italians are our allies!" He thundered, pacing the room. "This kind of behaviour does nothing to keep the peace. "The captain's voice was clipped and cutting as he continued, "I'm fully aware of your reckless behaviour."

Hal stood stiffly as the Captain laid out his punishment.

"You're heading to Cassino on the next consignment out of the base. No leave before you go. In the meantime, you'll continue your extra duties in the cookhouse. This is your last chance. One more stunt like this, and you'll face a court-martial."

Hal left the meeting with the Captain's last words ringing in his ears.

"Consider yourself having got off lightly."

Going to battle certainly didn't feel like getting off lightly.

24

Revelations

As Alberto entered the room, his chest swelled at the sight of Ottie, perched primly on the edge of the couch. Yet, something about her posture—too still, too distant—stirred unease in the back of his mind. He pushed the thought aside and stepped onto the fireside rug, stirring a faded memory in Ottie's mind. She could almost see Mamma, late at night, tying scraps of fabric together to make it. The memory hovered, fragile and bittersweet, before slipping away.

Alberto was still in his work attire, his clothes dirty from a day that had begun at five in the morning. The farm had been relentless, with few hands to share the workload. How times had changed, the luxury of casual workers was long gone. But even as exhaustion weighed on him, he had hurried to see Ottie, anticipation driving him forward. All day, between the clamour of work, she had been on his mind. Now, here she was, sitting primly, her hands resting neatly on her knees, her gaze drifting somewhere far away.

He spoke, recounting his arduous day, words tumbling out as he sought to close the silent gap between them. Then her eyes flicked up, and for a moment, the dreamy haze melted away. The twinkle returned to her chocolate-brown gaze, warm and vivid, and he realised with a pang that he had been rambling, oblivious to her quiet detachment.

"Well, listen to me going on. What about you? Fed up with your job yet?"

"Er yeah, erm it... it's fine. I like it," Ottie gave a distracted reply.

Alberto moved closer to Ottie, but his intentions were disrupted. Nari, a force of nature, burst into the room. She appeared from the kitchen, unable to keep away. In her hands was a tray of marzipan sweets, leftovers from the bakery, the stale—unsold remnants of the day.

To freshen them up, Fina had just sprinkled a little water on the sweets. She finished by playfully splashing water on her baby sister's face. Nari giggled at Fina's japery. She was defenceless with the tray held in her hands. Fina warned her not to be a nuisance or stay too long in the room. Nari would get more than just water thrown at her if she caught her snooping through the keyhole, she warned. Nari had acknowledged the threat with her protruding tongue. With outstretched arms, Nari held the tray towards Alberto and Ottie, proudly displaying the justification for her presence.

Ottie was relieved by her sister's timing and felt the air in the room lift. Alberto's expression, however, had not softened. His gaze remained fixed on the doorway where Nari stood,

"Sweets for you guys!" Nari boomed, throwing a sly wink in Alberto's direction.

Alberto, caught off guard, visibly adjusted himself and forced a smile at Nari, unimpressed by her intrusion.

"Oh, thank you. Nari, that's very thoughtful," he said with a stilted tone.

Nari bounced onto the couch, after placing the sweets on the side table nearby. She hung her legs over the arm of the sofa and grabbed a sweet, popping it into her mouth. Pink marzipan visible, as she spoke between chews.

"I like the pink ones best. How about you?"

"You can go now Nari," Ottie replied.

Nari sighed loudly, defiantly shrugged her shoulders, and stood up to leave the room.

"I was going already. Just being polite," she said over her dropped shoulder.

With Nari gone and the click of the door's latch, a moment's silence ensued before the remaining pair chuckled in unison.

"I heard you," Nari called through the door.

Fina appeared close at Nari's elbow, pulling her back to the kitchen.

"Will your sister ever grow up," laughed Alberto, having warmed to her spirit.

"I hope not," came Ottie's quick reply.

Alberto sat himself down next to Ottie. He reached across and cupped her hands between his.

"I have hardly seen you. I miss you, my beautiful fiancée." He leaned in to kiss her as he spoke.

Ottie offered her cheek. She felt the prickles from his stubble. His kiss was soft, pausing for a moment to savour her scent. As his breath warmed her skin, guilt tugged at her thoughts, pulling her mind to someone else entirely—Hal.

"I thought maybe we could go out for a ride on Sunday. I can borrow the horse and cart. Take you somewhere nice. Or we could go for a walk up by the vineyards. You know, where the Pardi's place is? It's nice and peaceful there. We could take a picnic." He continued to ramble on, unaware she had not answered.

"Talking of the Pardi's, that idiot Enzo seems to have disappeared, and his sidekick brother has moved into one of the worker's digs. I delivered some stuff up there this week. It's a strange atmosphere there. More so than usual. Signora Pardi is skulking about, as jumpy as ever. I saw Marco, too, out picking grapes. I asked after Elena, sent your best wishes with mine. He was shifty, not himself at all. He said it had all been sorted out, you know, the Elena thing. I wondered if they were involved in the lynching of that soldier.

Did you hear about it? In the orange grove, poor sod. Turns out he was beaten up for a rape he didn't do. I had to ask Marco. It's what everyone is saying. Marco was insistent that he had nothing to do with it. He was over the top, telling me the soldier was innocent. It struck me as odd how he could be so sure about it. You know it wouldn't surprise me if Enzo was behind all of this. Do you think that's possible?"

He looked at Ottie, alerted by her change of mood. Her pupils had doubled in size, and her chest was heaving.

"I know that soldier. He's lucky to be alive. He was really hurt."

"Yes, I guess you would know. Working in that place." Alberto's voice was sharp, the bitterness barely concealed.

"Marco is telling the truth. He's innocent. I know it because I know him, and he isn't capable of such a hideous crime. But Enzo? Yes, Enzo, I can see it in him," Ottie said, her voice trembling as she tried to contain her emotion.

Alberto narrowed his eyes.

"You seem very upset about it Octavia. I think those Brits have got to you. Don't place your trust in foreigners. If we ever see the end of this war, they'll disappear back to their own countries, leaving us to clean up the mess."

"He won't leave me behind."

The words slipped out before she could stop them, her voice trembling with conviction. She saw the confusion flicker across Alberto's face, quickly replaced by disbelief. Her chest tightened as she realised there was no turning back. Her feverish desire for Hal reverberated deep in her soul.

"Wha, wha, what are you talking about, Tavi?"

"I can't do this anymore," Ottie whispered, the weight of her words sinking in. "I'm so sorry, but I can't marry you, Alberto."

Alberto closed his eyes, screwing them shut as if trying to block out her words. His hands moved in rapid, agitated gestures, his thoughts racing too fast to contain.

"You! You and that soldier. Is that it?" His voice cracked, the anger was unmistakable.

Ottie couldn't bring herself to meet his gaze. She gave a small nod, her silence confirming what he already suspected.

"You! Why? How could you? You disgust me."

Alberto lashed out his words at Ottie. She kept her head bowed, not wanting to witness the pain she was causing him.

"Who else knows?" Alberto's tone shifted, calculating now, already considering the consequences.

"No one. Just you. It… it hasn't been long," Ottie replied, her voice faltering as she tried to soften the blow.

"Your father won't allow it. He will kill him… or you… or both," Alberto said, his tone filled with cold certainty.

"I never meant…"

Ottie's attempt to speak was trampled on by Alberto.

"Never meant? Enjoy the mess you're making, Octavia. It can only end in tears." His words were venomous now, his hatred building with each syllable. "Pray he takes you with him. You'll have no place here."

He left with an almighty slam of the front door, the vibration shuddering through the walls and shaking picture frames. Ottie ran to her room and fell onto the bed, biting her pillow to stifle the sobs threatening to escape. Her thoughts raced in turmoil—guilt, fear, and a flicker of hope tangled into a knot she couldn't unravel. Was this bravery or foolishness? The weight of her choice pressed heavily on her chest. Fina and Nari were soon at her side. Fina scooped Ottie into her arms, feeling the wetness of her tears soak through to her shoulder.

"It's alright. Cry. I know. This pain will heal," Fina soothed as she gently rocked Ottie.

Nari reappeared moments later, a tumbler of wine in hand at Fina's request. She handed it over, staring at her sister's distress with wide, concerned eyes. Fina placed the tumbler against Ottie's lips, encouraging her to take a sip to calm her nerves. Nari hovered close, her questions spilling out in rapid succession.

"What happened? Did you fight? Is it Alberto?"

Her voice grew frantic, her concern clashing with her curiosity. Her hands trembled as she wrung them, stealing a glance at Fina, whose face was like a mask of composure, betraying only the slightest tightening of her jaw. The heavy steps of Salvo ascending the stairs interrupted Nari's questioning.

"What have you done Tavi?" Salvo demanded, his voice sharp with suspicion. "I just nearly got mowed down by Alberto on my way in. He was furious. Have you had a row?"

Salvo leaned into the bedroom doorway, his head resting against the frame as he scanned the scene before him.

"No," Ottie whispered, her voice trembling. "I have ended it. I told him I cannot marry him."

She met Salvo's eyes through her tears, finding some measure of safety in Fina's arms. Her voice grew steadier.

"I love another man."

Nari squealed, clutching the edge of the bedpost as if bracing herself.

"What? No wonder he was so angry! Who?" Salvo's tone shifted to disbelief.

"His name is Hal Bennett."

"Hal Bennett?" Salvo repeated, his brow furrowing. "What kind of name is that? Who…? That's a foreign name. What the hell are you doing? …It's one of those soldiers from the base…Isn't it? … an Englishman?"

Ottie said nothing. She didn't need to. The truth was plain on her face.

"I knew it!" Salvo shouted, stepping further into the room. His shoulders tensed, fists clenching as though holding himself back. "You tramp!"

Fina's grip around Ottie tightened protectively.

"Don't you dare take one step closer," she warned, her voice low and dangerous.

Salvo rarely lost his temper, but when he did, the anger burned hot and fast. Nari clenched her fists, stepping between her brother and sisters, despite her diminutive frame. She was no match for Salvo physically, but her resolve was clear.

"I see them in the bar—drinking, gambling, taking women and tossing them aside when they're done. You disrespect yourself and our family. You stupid, selfish girl. Papa won't stand for this," he spat, turning his ire to Fina. "And you won't protect her from him."

Fina's eyes narrowed.

"You think you can speak for Papa? Maybe you should look in the mirror, Salvo. Hypocrisy runs in the family."

The tension in the room was suffocating, the siblings frozen in their standoff.

Throughout the night, Fina and Nari watched over Ottie, sleeping on each side of her in their spacious bed. To ward off any midnight confrontations, they had dragged the chest of drawers across the room to barricade the door. An angry Papa visiting in the middle of the night was something they wanted to avoid.

From below, Papa's raised voice raged up through the floorboards. Ottie curled closer to Fina, trembling as she felt her sister do the same. His temper always put the fear of God into them. The tirade ended with a loud slam of the front door, more vehement than Alberto's earlier departure. Papa had stormed out, no doubt to seek solace in places that only deepened his hypocrisy. Ottie's mind wandered, picturing Papa unleashing his fury at the bar, wondering if someone else would bear the brunt of his anger. Though his anger would erupt in a fiery outburst, leaving a trail of destruction in its wake, a quiet bitterness, the gnawing feeling of his resentment, always followed.

Ottie clung to Fina, her tears now spent but her heart still heavy. She knew she would have to face Papa soon enough. His anger was measured, precise—he would wait, biding his time.

25

For The Love Of Art

Late afternoon daylight seeped into the room, forming thin stripes through the closed wooden shutters. Fi narrowed her eyes as the sunlight infiltrated the room and blinded her. Her bones ached and her tongue felt dry enough to snap off. She rubbed the grit from her eyes. A light snore reached her ears, prompting her to remain mo-tionless as she pondered its origin. A faint movement at her heels drew her attention. Propping herself up on her elbows, she looked toward the foot of the bed. Ruffie sleepily raised himself, peering at her through his bushy grey eyebrows, before flopping back into his comfortable position.

Fi's mind wandered to the events of the previous evening. Her journey had certainly taken some unexpected turns. She needed to get to Zia Nari—a place where people truly knew her. A pang of longing pierced her chest. She missed her family deeply, and her yearning for Quin grew sharper. Would he have been happy with what she did? She believed so, even though last night's events were something she could never share with him. Guilt crept in at the thought of Sergio's charm; she was certain he'd dazzled countless women before her. She pulled on her jeans and a T-shirt and headed downstairs.

Nonna Salerno sat at the table in her small, rectangular kitchen, her back resting against the wall. The hum of the television filled the room. Her lunch, half-eaten, sat forgotten on the table. Nonna Salerno's sharp eyes caught Fi standing in the doorway. She rested her elbows on the colourful plastic tablecloth, propping her chin in one hand as she studied Fi. Shaking her head, her large hooped earrings swayed gently. With a sigh, she returned to her earlier position, leaving faint marks on the tablecloth where her elbows had been. Fi didn't miss the disapproval radiating from Nonna Salerno, likely because of last night's tardiness. Fi produced the shawl from behind her back and placed it on the table. "Thank you. Your shawl came in handy. The opera was lovely too," Fi added with a small smile.

To Fi's surprise, Nonna Salerno's face cracked into an unexpected grin.

"See? My handsome boy, Rocco, he is a good boy. He gets you the best tickets."

Fi bit back a response at the mention of Rocco. Last night hadn't been so bad, after all.

"I'll be going soon," she said, leaning her hip against the door frame.

Ruffie barked at her feet, and she bent down to make a fuss of him. "I'll miss you too, Ruffie. But maybe the next people who stay will find you just as cute."

"Nah, no more," Nonna Salerno said flatly. "He goes in the morning."

"Oh? Have you found a home for him?" Fi asked, her brow furrowing.

"No, he's going to the kennels. If they can't re home him in a week, they'll put him to sleep. The tenants don't want him wandering around. They've complained. He has to go."

Fi's heart sank.

"But that's awful! You can't..."

Nonna Salerno cut her off, shaking her head.

"You take him, then, if you care so much. Everyone cries, but no one ..."

"Hey, turn it up!" It was Fi's turn to interrupt.

Over Nonna Salerno's shoulder, something on the television caught her eye. A familiar figure appeared on the screen. Without waiting, Fi snatched the remote and raised the volume. Nonna Salerno complained that the news story had been on all day, but Fi simply ignored her.

Her attention was fixed on the screen. The camera shifted to the very painting she'd seen hours ago, and her mind raced to keep up with the presenter's words.

Images from Sergio's drawing room flickered on the screen. Clarence stood in the background, looking as stoic as ever. The presenter's voice narrated over the scene.

"As you can see, I'm standing before the missing Caravaggio painting of Mary Magdalene, protected by the Falcone family for generations. Its value is estimated in the millions. But let's not forget the other artworks in this room—an equally astonishing collection. This is the first time that Viscount Falcone has allowed the public to view his treasured collection."

The camera shifted to an older man—an art expert, evidently specialising in Caravaggio's work. He gestured passionately as he confirmed the painting's authenticity.

Nonna Salerno began speaking over the expert. "That Viscount—one of the richest men in Europe, I imagine. Been hiding like a hermit for years. Used to be a real playboy. Engaged to a famous French model, you know? Beautiful girl, back in the sixties—or was it the seventies? Anyway, she died falling overboard on his yacht. After that, he went wild—non-stop girls and parties. Surprised he has anything left. Ah, here he is now. Still a looker, eh?"

"Let me listen," Fi hushed her, her focus locked on the screen.

Nonna Salerno rolled her eyes and slumped back in her chair. The presenter continued to lavish praise on the artwork and Viscount Falcone. Finally, Sergio appeared on screen. He stood beside the presenter, his head humbly bowed as she spoke. At her final remarks, his brow quirked ever so slightly. Calm and self-assured, he lifted his focus to meet the camera, his enigmatic smile intact.

"It is my pleasure, Dina," Sergio said smoothly.

The presenter's tone grew probing. "You've been a man of mystery for many years, Viscount. This return to the public eye, and with such a flamboyant gesture—it's sparked just as much curiosity about you as the paintings themselves."

With a smug expression, she sent a glossy fuchsia lipstick smirk to her unseen audience behind the camera. Sergio's hazel eyes sharpened, their intensity unwavering, as though assessing the unseen audience through the lens. Sergio glanced away from the camera, meeting the presenter's gaze and nodding politely.

"These paintings will endure long after I'm gone. The collection is a legacy far greater than myself, and I hope it brings joy for generations to come," Sergio replied.

Fi's breath caught. The words echoed her own from the previous night.

The presenter pressed on. "So, the paintings will first be shown in Verona, correct?"

"Indeed. Close to my home—it's where it all begins," Sergio replied.

"And I understand there's a plan for an international exhibition?"

"Absolutely. I'm off to New York this afternoon to finalise arrangements. Art should be accessible to everyone, not just us lucky Italians." His stare flicked to the camera.

"And the collection will remain in your family?"

"Yes, of course. The public will see it annually, as part of the Fiamma Falcone collection."

The presenter tilted her head.

"An unusual choice of name."

Sergio's smile broadened. "What's in a name? It doesn't diminish the art. To all you Fiamma's out there"—he paused, his long lashes lowering, a subtle wink —"enjoy."

The camera zoomed in as his hazel eyes seemed to pierce through the screen. Fi felt her cheeks warm, as though his scrutiny had shifted from the television directly to her. An eagle focused on its prey.

"Hey," Nonna Salerno exclaimed. "He said your name! No, it can't be—were you out with the Viscount last night?"

"Seriously? Me? Don't be ridiculous."

Fi waved her off, but the grin spreading across her face was impossible to hide.

26

After The Storm

O ttie left the house late in the morning, the air already thick with the day's heat. Papa was still in bed, lost in his slumber. She walked along the uneven cobbles, choosing the shady side of the street a welcome respite from the sun's glare. The warm yeasty smell of freshly baked bread lingered in the air, mingling with the faint earthy tang of the cobblestone street. In her arms, she carried the rough, misshapen loaves of bread that Fina had sent for their sister-in-law—a rare gesture that Anna would reluctantly accept.

Anna lived in a compact, neat second-floor apartment in the centre of town. The small balcony overlooked the park and was adorned with pink geraniums in neatly arranged terracotta pots. At 6 a.m. that morning, as usual, Anna had been on her balcony. The time was important to her; it marked the moment she had last seen Marcello. She clung to the memory, replaying it like a film in her mind, desperate to keep every detail vivid. The way the morning light caught Marcello's dark blond hair, the confident tilt of his chin, the casual swing of his kitbag. She smiled back at him from the balcony, watching as he blew her a kiss, slung his kit bag off his shoulder, and climbed into the military vehicle bound for the port.

Their newlywed life in their apartment was cut short after only a week when Marcello had to return to the army, his wedding leave having come to an end. Anna had left the apartment exactly as it had been on the day Marcello departed. It was always spotlessly tidy, his shaving kit still resting by the sink. Every day, she prepared a table for two and sat across from his empty seat to eat. Today, however, Marcello's vacant place would be filled by his sister, Octavia.

"Octavia, the little woman with the heart of a lion."

Marcello's voice encircled Anna's mind, as vivid as if he were there. Marcello had liked to akin the women in his life to creatures. He had claimed that Nari had the wit of a monkey, Fina embodied the quiet wisdom of an owl, and Anna was his elegant swan.

The loud buzzing of the intercom jolted Anna from her thoughts. She headed to the front door to welcome Ottie, passing a succession of framed wedding photos along the wall. She paused briefly to straighten one. As she opened the door, the sound of Ottie's sandaled feet on the marble steps echoed upwards. A puffing Ottie entered, spreading bread-crumbs onto the polished hall floor, as she bumped against the opposing narrow walls, like a ball bearing in a pinball machine. Anna, trailed in her wake, correcting the skewed picture frames.

Ottie brought her trail of destruction to an end in the kitchen, her vision clouded by the bread she held. Anna relieved her of the loaves, noticing the imprint of flour left on Ottie's dress. Ottie took a seat at the table and brushed the dust off herself while Anna attempted to stack the tumbling loaves into a cupboard. The women exchanged pleasant-ries. Anna asked after the Matanti family and thanked them for their kindness, remarking that the bread was far too much for just her. She would share it with relatives, she said. A smile played on Ottie's lips for a moment before she grew serious, leaning forward to share her news. With a firm tone, she informed Anna that she would not be relaying Anna's gratitude to Papa the next time they met. Ottie poured out her heart to Anna, explaining her reasons and catching her up on the recent happenings.

"I've really done it this time," Ottie confessed, looking up at Anna after recounting her story.

Anna placed a steaming bowl of pasta e fasul in front of her, finishing it with a sprinkle of pepper. Ottie, who hadn't felt like eating that morning, now realised how hungry she was. She savoured the tender beans, the rich broth warming her as she eagerly devoured the dish. Anna watched Ottie consume the pasta, her spoon moving quickly. She sighed softly, swirling her spoon along the rim of her bowl and blowing gently on each bite.

"You hold your spoon like Marcello," Anna observed, her voice gentle.

Ottie froze, her spoon dropping back into the bowl as her attention shifted to Anna.

"Oh, Anna, here I am burdening you with my problems when you've lost so much more than I have."

Anna gave a small smile, her tone steady, filled with her indomitable bittersweet pragmatism.

"I haven't given up hope yet. I'll never give up. It's impossible to know for certain if he went down with that ship. I've written to the Pope again—maybe I'll get a reply this time. If not, I'll continue living each day with him in my heart."

The two women ate in silence for a while, maintaining a polite but unspoken distance. They looked out through the open balcony door, admiring the vista of trees leading up to the mountains.

The light swiftly darkened as charcoal clouds rolled in, swallowing the blue sky. A booming thunderclap echoed, followed by lightning that ripped through the sky in jagged, dazzling streaks. A downpour of rain fell from the dark swollen sky and hammered onto the balcony. Anna and Ottie hurried to shut the French doors as a gust of wind blew the panels inward, sending curtains flapping and rain splattering inside from the bouncing raindrops. Once secured, they stood together watching the chaos unfold. People on the street below scurried for shelter, newspapers held over their heads, children scooped up in arms, and instant puddles that flashed across the uneven road. The wind raged up into the branches of the trees, turning the leaves upside down and scattering them in the gale. Ottie laughed at the people below dissipating like played marbles.

"That could have almost been me," she gasped.

"Would it matter?" Anna asked quietly. "What would you have done if it had been?"

"Well, I'd find shelter, of course, until it passed," Ottie replied, her laughter fading at Anna's candour.

They stayed by the window, watching the storm take hold, forcing the town into submission. Soon, the street was empty.

"Do you think storms are an act of God?" Anna asked.

"Well, I suppose so. They're beyond man's control."

"Not that dissimilar to matters of the heart," Anna said, sending a sideways glance at Ottie. "If we could control our emotions and fall in love with those best suited to us, there would be no storms in life."

"Is that what you believe? How do you cope with the hand life has dealt you?" Ottie asked, her voice soft.

"Because I have to. The storm reminds me that we are mere humans. We are fallible, and that's okay."

"I see why my brother loved you," Ottie murmured. "You are both wise and beautiful."

Anna offered a subtle smile.

"Marcello loved your strength," she deflected before offering her advice. "You have a choice. Hide from the storm and wait for it to pass, or step into the rain and face it head-on. Whatever you decide, you're strong enough to ride it out."

Ottie stood before her, clearly troubled. Anna saw a flicker of Marcello in her expression, and grief clawed at her soul. The pain of a lifetime without him blindsided her. She reached out to Ottie in an uncharacteristic flood of emotion, seeking comfort in her own words.

"Sometimes, we are caught unprotected in the eye of the storm, helpless as it tries to destroy us. We hang on until we find safety and return to life, though our plans are forever changed. Caught up in the atmosphere. Nature stops humanity in its tracks, destroys, and then nourishes." Anna took a deep breath to steady her voice. "The storm leaves calmness in its wake, forgotten until it returns to remind us of our insignificance. It changes things— that is its purpose for better or worse, it clears the air."

As the rain subsided to a light patter, a distant rumble of thunder brushed down from the mountains. Moved by the depth of Anna's emotions, Ottie stayed silent, her own words failing her. Anna, lost in her thoughts, continued.

"The pull of your heart is strong. It will settle, and what remains will reveal the depths of your feelings. Hold on to what makes you happy, for it can be swept away in a single breath. Embrace it and be as brave as I know you are."

"Anna," Ottie said, her voice barely above a whisper. "Have I made a mistake? I can't change how I feel."

"Whatever happens, you'll have felt true love. You're only flesh and blood, Tavi... These things happen. That's the truth of the matter... The freedom to pursue it is why men are fighting and dying today."

27

Back Home

Dear Mother,

I hope you get this letter and the ones I wrote before and that you are well. It may be some time before you get any more, I am going to be a bit busy. I am being sent back out for another fight with Jerry. It will be different to when I was in Africa, but the terrain, I am told, is just as dreadful. I am sure you will get to hear about it all on the wireless. But to save the censor's pen, I can tell you no more. Touch wood, it will not be as sticky a time as before, and I will be back having a cup of char with the lads in no time. Don't worry, I have been lucky so far.

How is Bonnie? Give her a pat for me? I was thinking about the long winter walks across the sands to Broadstairs that I used to do with her. The sea rough and loud and the wind so hard it nearly blew me over. I miss the cold air of England. Write to me and tell me about home. I have enclosed a sketch of a local girl called Ottie. She is quite pretty, and I am fond of her. I think the nose isn't right, but it will give you an idea.

I had a bit of a spat recently with some of the local lads, which left me with a few scratches. It ended up being a case of mistaken identity on both sides. It didn't go down well back at camp though, and I have had to peel a lot of spuds to make amends.

Let's hope this damn war ends soon, and Adolf stops being a pest to us all.

Love

Harold x

***

Matilda Bennett folded Hal's letter neatly and placed it in the small drawer of the hall stand. In the bevelled mirror, she tutted at her reflection, adjusted her hat, and replaced an errant strand of hair. Matilda picked up her own letter, tucked between the antique's intricate carvings. She smoothed her coat and exited number 11 Warten Way, walking down the neat quarry-tiled path in the direction of the post office.

Away from the street, she faced the now-familiar sight of large piles of rubble where houses once stood. The only undamaged house had the baker's horse and cart parked in front of it. Matilda waved her hand at Mr Lillie as he mounted the bread-laden cart. She was relieved he was too occupied to exchange pleasantries. She had heard he had lost another son in battle, and she wasn't one who could easily find the right words in such situations.

Pretty much everyone on her street had lost someone, and it wasn't just young Tommys. Ramsgate endured its share of air raids, which unfortunately led to civilian losses. Luckily, the tunnels had provided a safe refuge. Matilda herself had lived in them for a good few months after her ceiling had caved in during the brutal raids two summers ago. The experience had knocked the wind out of her sails and forced her below ground.

She had endured a mole-like existence in the tunnels, a dull life of domesticity shrouded in damp gloominess. The worst part of being in the chalky depths of Thanet's cliffs was the smell of the communal rudimentary toilet. The old bedsheet partition for privacy wasn't very dignified in her eyes either. She considered herself fortunate that the blast hadn't destroyed her entire home. As soon as she could, Matilda moved back home. She was not one for the tunnel's camaraderie and preferred books to people.

Even now, Hal's letter weighed on her mind as she walked. He spoke of luck, but Matilda knew war turned luck into a fragile thread, liable to snap at any moment. Her fingers tightened around her handbag, almost as if she was trying to hold on to her son through it.

These days, when Matilda heard the familiar rising whine of the air-raid siren, she would seek refuge under her walnut table and listen out for the ominous drone of the Luftwaffe, followed by the hum of bombs and falling buildings. The worst sound was the banshee scream of diving Stukas mixed with the barking roar of guns. The aircraft left in its wake a dust that rose and morphed into an impalpable flour-like consistency, making it nigh on impossible to see.

Thankfully, nothing since had compared to that summer's raid. That day was the worst. She had picked up her skirts and run for the tunnel, Bonnie at her heels, shrapnel falling like rain. In the five minutes it had taken her to reach the entrance near the station, nearly five hundred bombs had been dropped.

Emerging from the tunnel, she had seen wardens with "ARP" boldly etched on their white saucer hats, gripping a large fire hose as they battled a raging sea of flames. Close by, a home had the unfortunate fate of being cut in two. It resembled a doll's house, décor and furniture visible in the rooms, coats hung up in the hallway. The road next to it had caved in and looked as fragile as a tapped pie crust.

Ramsgate had changed. People rallied together more these days, working closely with the foreigners in town—mostly Free French and Polish. Matilda didn't like change. She wanted things to be just as they were before Hal left. She wanted her only son back safe. It had just been her and Hal for years. It had been a long time since her husband passed away. Her nest felt empty, and she did not see an end to this godforsaken war. On certain days, she couldn't even make tea because of the sporadic gas supply from the bombed gasworks.

She maintained life's stability by adhering to a structured daily routine that started with breakfast and tuning in to Marguerite Patten's "Kitchen Front" on the radio to discover innovative ways to use dried eggs. Following that were chores that needed to be done outside the house. Afternoons were dedicated to the vegetable garden, followed by dinner and listening to the Home Service world news program in the early evening. Her day ended tucked up in bed with her cocoa before the curfew. When the tracer searchlights switched on and beamed across Ramsgate's night sky, casting dancing shadows over her curtains.

Matilda arrived at the post office and exchanged the expected polite dialogue with the postmistress, Mrs Mae Miggs. Not one for small talk, Matilda was polite, but brusque. She struggled to stop the corners of her mouth from curving into a smile when Mae's son, Billy, burst in, his tumbled bike outside with the wheel still revolving. One sock half-pulled down and muddy knees visible below his shorts, he was a cheeky, freckled, gap-toothed boy, full of the joys of street play: leapfrog, marbles, ball games, and swinging from lampposts.

"Mum! You never guess wha...."

Billy stopped in his tracks when he caught sight of Mrs Matilda Bennett at the other side of the counter. She lifted her eyebrows and focused her gaze on him. Billy flushed red between his freckles.

"At last, Master Miggs. I have the pleasure of your company. You have been very keen to see me these past few days, knocking on my door with your friends. But then, so very shy that you seem to run away. Would you care to enlighten me?"

Billy shook his head and stuttered, ready to deny her accusation. Matilda wagged her finger in his direction.

"Now be careful, young Billy. We don't want those pants to catch on fire. We both know it was you."

Billy hung his head in shame.

"For gawd shakes Bill. You can't just go around upsetting the old uns ... oh, begging yer pardon, Mrs Bennett. I mean, a lady of the finer years, so to speak."

Matilda brushed the comment away with a raised palm towards Mae. She bent down to Billy's eye level. Her face was so close to Billy that he noticed the powder layered over the downy hairs of her upper lip and the distinctive aroma of Pears soap.

"The secret to playing knock-down ginger is to tie a piece of cotton to the door knocker and hide around the corner. Not so far to run and not so easily seen from my bedroom window."

Matilda tapped the side of her nose as she straightened up.

Then, with a sharp nod, she turned to the exit and added. "Good day to you both."

Billy pulled the ugliest face he could muster and made his hands into talon shapes. Matilda, with her back still to Billy, pulled the door wide open. The shop's bell gave a frantic tinkle.

"I saw that young man. Gone are the days when children were seen and not heard!"

"Ouch, get off my ear!" Billy squealed.

"You little bleeder, that is the third time this week we've had customers coming in 'ere complaining about you and your antics. I've got chores for you to do!"

The conversation trailed behind Matilda as she walked away. She shook her head with laughter at the high spirits of young boys. She turned towards the seafront and scanned the row of buildings. The jaded Granville Hotel, now a military hospital, its gable end punched inwards by a lone bomb, a stark reminder of the war's impact. The crescent of regency cream houses curved around the coastline, an abrupt emptiness in the middle where homes had been blasted away. They stood like a row of teeth, sending a gappy, defiant smile across to France.

Matilda navigated around the side of the Granville Hotel towards her home. She caught sight of a soldier leaning against the wall near the tradesman's entrance. Kitchen sounds filtering out through the door. He lifted his head at her shadow, and she met his blank stare, a cigarette hanging idly from his mouth. A crutch propped under one arm, she noticed the flapping trouser leg, empty of a limb. She forced a smile that was reciprocated with vacantness.

The hill home felt steeper than usual, and her heart was heavy with thoughts of Hal. She prayed her son was safe and that his luck remained.

***

Dear Harold

I was so pleased to get your letter this morning and know that you are well. I am glad that my letters are getting through to you. I will send more before I get any back from you. I understand you are not in a position to write.

A bomb landed in the allotments yesterday and took Mrs Peat's scullery ceiling down. Luckily, she wasn't at home or working on the allotment. I heard aircraft overhead and that god awful silence just before it dropped. I knew it was close. It knocked Father's picture clean off the wall. Bonnie was shifty all evening afterwards.

I was pleased to not have a ruined plot at the allotment we are so fortunate in this house having the long gardens against the train track. I am surprised the station hasn't been targeted. I guess blowing the gas works to high heaven was enough. The garden is doing well. The runner beans are particularly good, and your chives have doubled. I haven't done potatoes this year. I find it quite back breaking. Besides, Mr Wilson trades with me. I find potatoes over the front wall for me quite often and return in kind with my extra produce. Do you remember his grandson, Edward? The one that became a pilot, well, he has gone missing overseas. It has been a while now, so doesn't sound too promising.

It is all so very different here from when you left. I do hope they will send you home soon. Tell me more about this Italian girl, Ottie. The only Italian I know here is Mr Morelli. I am glad to say he has not been interned. Sadly, his ice cream parlour has not been open for months now. I hope we will sit together soon on the seafront and have one of those ice creams. I must get back to the garden now and tackle the weeds. Bonnie sends a lick. Keep your chin up, son. One day, this will all be over.

Love

Mother x

PS I hope you get the chocolate with this letter. I have not bothered to add cigarettes, as you told me you did not receive them last time.

28

Monte Cassino

Highway six led up through the mountain range into the Liri Valley, heading towards Rome. The road passed through the town of Cassino, positioned close to the Gustav line. The Germans, the other side of the line, held onto a tight defensive position inside the Monte Cassino monastery. The monastery stood proudly lodged on a high rocky hill. It overshadowed the town below. For centuries, the majestic building's presence had been visible across the landscape, where it peacefully looked down over the valley. The structure now bore the scars of war; the monastery had been stripped back to its bare bones, now a pile of rubble barely recognisable. Nearby, Cassino had fared no better. Its buildings crushed into the ground, making it an uninhabitable abyss. The constant Allied air assaults finally stopped, allowing the dust to settle. The attacks for all the Allies' efforts had been fruitless. It enabled the Nazi army to assume a better position on the battlefield. Hiding out in the nooks and crannies provided by the tumbling buildings.

This marked the fourth attempt by the Allies to penetrate the formidable line. Hal had heard the talk among the men—this was their last chance. Failure here meant Rome might never fall, and the lives already lost would be for nothing. At least winter was over now. Conditions in the mountains had been brutal during those bleak months, frostbite gnawing at their feet and their morale, in equal measure. No frostbite

to contend with this time. As summer progressed, the heat would undoubtedly become more unbearable, but for now, the mountain air felt
pleasant, with the gentle warmth of a late spring breeze. Small mercies,
but ones the soldiers were grateful for.

The British Army, alongside Indian, Polish, and Canadian troops,
had one aim; to break the limping monastery's back and push through
to Rome. The simplicity of the plan to overthrow the Nazis was lost
on Hal as he witnessed the injured Polish soldiers, their faces pale and
drawn, their uniforms torn and bloodied, staggering back to camp. Red
Cross trucks, filled with the wounded, drove past his troop, heading in
the opposite direction. Entire battalions had been wiped out, but the
Poles' determination remained unbroken, a fierce resolve born of an
exiled nation.

At the camp, the Poles consoled themselves with local red wine,
singing anthems of their homeland late into the night. The Canadians,
positioned a day's march behind, were equally high-spirited, known for
their wild antics when given the chance. Alongside the Eighth were the
Indians, whom Hal had fought with before. He remembered them as a
tenacious and fearless force. But even with such allies, the monastery at
Monte Cassino loomed ahead—an obstacle unlike any they had faced.

Hal looked to the heavens, granting himself a quick prayer that he
would make it through again, that his nerves would hold steady, and
that he would remain on the right side of fate. His hand slipped into his
pocket, brushing against the edge of a photo Ottie had given him. He
could see it clearly in his mind: her heart-shaped face turned sideways
to the camera, her serene smile etched in his memory.

Now, his reasons for survival were stronger than ever before. Her
picture held the promise of a life beyond the war, its edges worn smooth
with the countless times he had touched it, a symbol of the hope he
clung to. He wondered where she kept the picture of him. She had insisted on a fair exchange, and for now, those photos were all they had to
bind them together. Each passing day deepened their connection, Hal
longed for a future where he could grow old beside her. He whispered

her name softly, a talisman against the evil that loomed before him.

That night, they bunked down near the ruined town, joining a tank division. Small Churchill tanks stood nearby, their battered bodywork bearing the scars of combat. Though slow, the tanks were durable and excelled in rocky landscapes. They stood little chance against the superior German Tiger tanks, but thankfully, the Tigers were scarce at Monte Cassino. The short range of the tanks meant the Germans were not considered a significant threat. Mules laden with packs roamed the area, their sturdy frames proving invaluable for carrying weapons and supplies across the rugged terrain. Stan, with a Bren gun slung across his shoulder, pushed past Hal.

"Let's get a quick brew in before the action starts," he said.

After setting up camp, they shared tea and corned beef sandwiches. Hungry from a long day of marching, they were thankful for anything to eat. Food was even more scarce on the battlefield, the rugged land hard to reach under fire. Air-dropped parcels often missed their intended target. Falling out of range and unhelpfully landing on German territory, feeding the Nazi's equally hungry bellies.

Hal's troop's orders were to advance under the cover of night towards the monastery. The difficult terrain meant large groups couldn't move easily, so small, stealthy units were essential for the ambush. The mission was clear, the task near impossible; root out the enemy hidden in the ruins and push upwards into Monte Cassino. The instructions left no room for hesitation; assume a do-or-die position until the line was broken.

As dusk fell, the air thickened with heavy mist. The Nebelwerfer rocket mortars, woken by the fading light, began their shrill assault, piercing the silence. The sky lit up in bursts, revealing soldiers scattering for cover. Stan and Taffy advanced, dodging bullets as they leapt through the rubble. Hal followed close behind.

The trio fell into a large crater, its depth providing just enough cover to set the Bren gun onto its AA tripod. Water pooled at the crater's base, soaking through into their leather boots. A grenade plopped into the water. Hal grabbed it, hurling it as far as he could. The explosion backfired rubble onto their backs. Taffy, acting as loader, handed ammunition to Stan, who fired the Bren gun in rhythmic bursts: *da da dom, da da dom.* They worked in quick succession, flawless, a slick team which came from a bonded comradeship—practised perfection born out of the need to survive.

Shells whistled overhead, debris crashed around them, and the screams of soldiers broke through between the minute reprieves in the chaos. The trio communicated through gestures—words were impossible over the battle's deafening noise. The synergy between the three infantrymen had kept them alive to date. The unspoken consensus between them was that they needed to push forward quickly, their position was vulnerable. Their chances were difficult under heavy machine gunfire. Paired with the sniper to their right, that was picking soldiers off as they tried to advance. A body side rolled into their crater. Hal recognised him instantly.

"Kamal!"

Hal helped Kamal to his feet. Between bursts of gunfire, they shouted brief exchanges close to each other's ears. Formalities, skipped, only brief direct sentences were possible.

"Bleedin' sniper!" Hal yelled between firing his gun.

"Cover me—I see his position," Kamal shouted back.

"You'll get yourself killed!" Hal protested.

"What! With you lads covering my back! Best chance I've got!" Kamal finished with a wink.

A wilful glint flickered a moment in his eyes. Steadfast brown, they met the silver of Hal's. Fear undetectable in his sharp features. Hal placed a comrade's slap onto Kamal's shoulder blade in silent agreement. The noise had escalated, and words were wasted. Hal hoped Kamal read his mind. Kamal gave a decisive blink as he went over the top. Rolling himself to safety, his figure disappeared upwards as he squatted behind a boulder to be seen again higher up, bullets breaking the ground around him.

Kamal climbed closer to the sniper. He could make him out stationed in a crevice heading up towards the monastery. Kamal had one chance only. He wanted to aim his grenade accurately. He needed to get closer and stand out in the open for a second to throw the grenade. Once the sniper saw him, Kamal knew he stood little chance of getting to safety before he was shot. He aimed the grenade to fall beyond the soldier's reach, but close enough to kill him. One of them was to die, and he wished it was quick for either of them. The grenade fell at exactly where he wanted it to. He caught the sniper barrel turn in his direction and jumped for cover. The grenade exploded, the sniper stopped. He scrambled upwards with a cursory look behind, he saw Hal's unit advancing. His bravery, without a doubt, had saved men and enabled the advancement.

Despite Kamal's valiant efforts and those of the other soldiers, the battle that night was halted. Under relentless shell and mortar fire, the men were forced to retreat. They stumbled over fallen comrades and the carcasses of mules as they made their way back to their lines, their bodies weary and broken. They barely had the strength to carry themselves, let alone bring the injured to safety.

The days that followed saw no respite. Exhaustion, hunger, and the oppressive smell of death weighed heavily on the troops. Supplies were scarce, brought in sporadically by the sturdy mules that navigated the treacherous terrain. The soldiers moved from ruin to ruin, often engaging in brutal hand-to-hand combat. The situation was grim, with casualties rising, morale faltered as the stalemate dragged on. In small dugouts, the men made preparations as best as possible for the forthcoming night's attack, alternating to take breaks.

In the pitch black of night, the troops forged ahead towards their desperate mission; the climb becoming steeper with each stride. The Gustav line felt impenetrable against such a stubborn defence. The troops marched in silence, unsure how close they were to the Germans. Soldiers slipped into darkness, losing their grip on the rocky mountainside. The tapes laid down to guide them proved useless, shot off and scattered by shells leading soldiers towards nowhere, adding to the confusion.

A flare soared into the night sky, casting an eerie glow. The moment revealed a swarm of soldiers advancing on the battlefield. Way ahead, unseen in the darkness, the Polish regiment scaled Monte Cassino's sides. The Germans, undeterred, unleashed a barrage of shells on the soldiers caught in the flares' glow. Another night of combat begun across the mountain range as the Allies launched a counterattack.

The long night bled into dawn. The sun's fingers folded over the top of the mountain, ready to pull itself up into the sky. The rays stretched slowly over the horizon, bathing the devastation in pale light. Hal's group trudged onward, their movements deliberate and cautious, knowing the enemy could be lying in wait just over the next ridge. A couple of British soldiers joined their group, marching in single file along a narrow path that twisted around the mountainside. German voices filtered through the air, carried across from a nearby ridge. The men quickened their steps, breaking off into smaller groups to find cover.

Hal took the rear, rifle in hand, ready to cover his comrades. Taffy led the group, with Stan close behind, the Bren gun ready to fire from his hip if he needed to. The tension mounted as they neared the ridge. Suddenly, shots rang out from above, posing a greater challenge to their defence.

Hal fired his rifle while running backwards, rounds shot out, his aim precise. With an abrupt jolt, his rifle jammed. He desperately scrambled to unlock the bolt, wrestling with the chamber as bullets tore through the air around him. In the semi-light, preoccupied and running backwards, he tripped, falling over a loose rock and fell, the ground slamming hard against his back.

An opportunistic hand grenade was thrown over the ridge. Landing dangerously close to Hal. He kicked at the ground, trying desperately to rise, but his boots slid helplessly against the loose stones. The panic surged through him, his pulse throbbing in his ears. The gap between him and his companions widened as they ran for cover, oblivious to his growing terror. Then everything stopped. Hal felt himself falling further and further, swooping down with the speed of an eagle aiming at its prey. A tunnel of white light opened up in the ground, and he fell through it into sudden darkness.

Taffy, just ahead, felt the shockwave ripple and the upturned land punch at his back as the grenade exploded. He turned briefly, catching sight of Hal's motionless form before ducking for cover. Taffy and Stan slid down the mountain. With heavy breath, they listened as the Germans marched by. They were lost in German territory and needed to get back to their side if they wanted to survive.

"Where's Hal?" Stan whispered as they slid further down the slope.

"Done like a kipper," Taffy replied, his voice grim.

With heavy hearts and no other way out, Taffy and Stan slipped further down the treacherous slope, their only chance of escaping.

***

Hal roused himself from the black abyss he had been sent into. Unable to move, he lay completely still as scrambled images flooded back to him. The daylight stung his eyes, he felt a weak numbness to his right side. German voices filled his ears. Hal shut his eyes and lay motionless, their footsteps trembled on the ground beneath him, the vibrations reaching up into his chest. He stayed still, taking shallow breaths, he played dead. Minutes passed, hours, perhaps. Hal eventually dared to open his eyes. He figured he must have looked as good as dead. Not one soldier had checked or fired at him. He found the strength to sit up. His right leg was soaked through with blood and had darkened the ground surrounding him. He could not feel his foot, but he could see that he was able to move it. Hal lifted his head to scan the landscape. Two German stretcher-bearers stood nearby, carrying a wounded soldier.

Desperation overtook him, and he called out, his voice hoarse. "Bitte... Hilfe!"

The stretcher-bearers turned, startled to see him alive. They spoke in hurried German before approaching cautiously. One of them gestured for Hal to remain still as they examined his leg. Using his own first aid kit, they applied a tourniquet and splinted the limb with practiced efficiency. Hal winced as the pain surged toward his groin, but their quick work made it bearable. They had no morphine to offer, but one handed him a chocolate bar and some water. The sweetness of the chocolate was almost overwhelming, its taste sharp against the metallic tang of blood in his mouth. Through broken English, Hal understood they would return once they had delivered the other soldier to safety. Hal expressed his gratitude, trying to speak German before watching them vanish, descending the hillside with the lifeless soldier on the stretcher.

As the stretcher-bearers disappeared, Hal was left alone once more. His mind raced with grim possibilities. Helplessness combined with frustration at his plight welled up inside him. The stretcher-bearers could be ages. He had no choice but to wait like a sitting duck. If he was confronted by a Nazi, he knew he wouldn't stand a chance. Hal believed he had two choices. He could wait for the stretcher-bearers to return and become a German prisoner, meanwhile possibly getting killed. Or he could try to make his way back to his army and probably get killed in the process. Hal forced himself upright, using a nearby boulder for support. His hands trembled as he surveyed the landscape, searching for a way out. He spotted a splintered tree nearby, its branches broken from the grenade blast. Limping forward, he snapped off a sturdy branch to use as a crutch. Hal, leaning heavily on his makeshift crutch, began his slow descent. Every step was agony, but he pushed forward, driven by the faint hope of survival. The distant sound of Allied voices spurred him on, a fragile lifeline in the chaos.

He wasn't ready to give up. Not yet.

***

Meanwhile, Taffy and Stan had reached the base of the hill. They stumbled upon a group of soldiers retreating from the front lines and learned that the Poles had finally seized Monte Cassino. A Canadian soldier offered his binoculars to Taffy, who scanned the horizon.

Through the lenses, he saw the aftermath of the battle. The Germans retreating toward Rome, their once-stronghold reduced to smouldering ruins. For now, the fighting had ceased, but the cost of victory weighed heavily on every man.

29

Lest We Forget

"Thank you. My grandmother knitted it for me a long time ago." Satisfied with Fi's answer, the woman of the couple, having admired the colours and enthused about the knitted craftsmanship to her politely interested husband, let the scarf fall back into Fi's lap. The train pulled out of Verona station. The couple had seated themselves opposite Fi, both too polite to mention she was sitting in one of their booked seats. They held onto brown paper bags containing fresh, doughy cornetto cremas, the sweet aroma wafted over to Fi. The smell, combined with their takeaway espressos, made her regret not bringing anything to eat on the train.

Fi re-wrapped her Doctor Who scarf around her neck a further three times to take up its slack. The scarf seemed out of place, ill-suited to the current weather, designed more for bitter winter days. The bright, hot sunshine streamed through the train's window, warming her face. Preoccupied, she threaded the scarf's tassels through her fingers.

Fi recalled the times she had worn it for winter walks to school, where she felt like the coolest kid in the playground, despite tripping over the scarf's trailing ends. She needed her scarf today regardless of the weather. It made her feel safe and reminded her of home and a Christmas Day years ago. It remained her most cherished gift, even surpassing the popular Rubik's cube present. The image of Hal's efforts to solve the cube, despite his failing eyesight, lingered warmly in her mind. He had worn a paper Christmas cracker hat tilted lopsided toward one eyebrow, his hands twisting the cube's-coloured squares in a determined grip.

Fi rubbed the wool scarf between her palms, admiring its bold colours as she did so. She still had most of the items that Ottie had knitted for her, from her own baby clothes to those of her daughters. Layettes, jumpers, hats, and bed socks were neatly folded and stored above her wardrobe. Fi pushed her neck down into the scarf, trying to catch Ottie's scent. She needed her strength today.

Her fingers tightened around the scarf's tassels. She hadn't called Zia Nari, she thought it would be better to arrive unannounced, starting with a nice surprise before delivering the bad news. Telling Nari would make it real. She clenched her jaw against the wave of emotion threatening to surface. A wet tongue nudged her nose. Ruffie licked the tears that slipped silently off the end. A gentle smile formed on her face in response to his comforting lick.

She whispered in Ruffie's ear. "What will Nari think about adopting you?"

He nestled into her lap while she playfully tickled the soft fur under his ear. Fi shifted her attention to the conversation between the couple, deducing that they had been married for a long time. A gentle discussion unfolded between them, their tones blending with the rhythm of the train. Looking out the window, she kept her gaze outside while her ears remained tuned to the couple's voices. The train passed through an olive grove, the trees arranged in neat rows across the countryside. A pang of envy washed over her as she observed the couple's easy comfort. She stole a covert sideways glance. Fi noticed the husband reach for his wife's hand as they watched the flat, sun-baked yellow and terracotta houses slip past the window. Though they had only been together for a short time, she had imagined a future with Quin—just like the couple's.

She had been so disappointed when Quin left for his travels. Fi had sent him off with sunflowers from Ottie's garden. It seemed fitting; after all, flowers had been how it all began. Ottie had wrapped the sunflower stalks in damp newspaper to keep them fresh before Fi brought them to him. Ottie had a fondness for Quin. They spent late nights playing cards together in the conservatory. Quin, overlooking the occasional cheat when Ottie didn't have good cards. They played for matchsticks, with a Morelli's gelato from the seafront as the coveted prize.

Fi thought of the times she had spent in Quin's flat, a few streets away from Morelli's. A modern and chic place with deep red walls contrasting with the white designer leather sofas. Artistic, oversized prints hung on the walls. A gleaming Fender guitar rested near his high-end sound system. She missed waking up next to him and trailing her fingers down his back. Slow Sunday mornings spent with coffee, biscuits, and long cuddles in bed. Her eyes stung at the memory. The train lurched, jolting her back into the present as they rounded a curve.

Quin had admired her grandfather's artwork on the walls and the pictures and sculptures placed throughout the house. More paintings were stored in the sheds at the end of the garden. Hal used anything he could find as a canvas, from old linen tea towels to the backs of wardrobes. The old potter's wheel and partially completed sculptures remained exactly as he had left them years ago. Ivy had overtaken the brick kiln. When his blindness prevented him from painting. Hal turned to sculpting, shaping red clay busts by tracing the features of his face, capturing emotions that stirred a hidden sadness. To Ottie, they were neither attractive nor useful.

Over time, the sheds were dismantled, and the vegetable plots were reduced. The garden transformed into a more conventional English country garden, though the potter's shed still stood. Ottie couldn't bring herself to take it down. The space now housed Ottie's mobility scooter. A half-finished sculpture, covered in cobwebs, lay untouched on the potter's bench.

Fi thought back to the wild, jumbled garden of her childhood — a chaotic paradise. The various sheds were cobbled together with half brick, half corrugated metal sheets. Their black cat, Gili, often basked in the sunniest spot on a shed roof. A rusty swing, a lopsided rocking horse with mangled springs, broken car parts, and patches of wilderness stood between the vegetable plots. The front garden was its opposite — festooned with roses, fuchsias, and pansies, neatly pruned and maintained. The front step was scrubbed daily, providing Ottie an opportunity to catch up on neighbourhood gossip.

Hal built fences from old doors, dividing the vegetable garden from the chicken coop. Each paint-worn door varied in size and design, with original letterboxes and house numbers still intact. The brick coal shed leaned clumsily against the house, with a small trapdoor at its base for coal collection. Called the "Fairy Door," it became another one of Hal's tales. Fi had watched the door for hours, hoping to catch a fairy. The coal man, in brown overalls and piercing blue eyes striking against his coal-darkened skin, always brought Fi a lemon sherbet. Their Jack Russell, Nipper, would latch onto his overalls, growling and shaking his trouser leg. The coal man would pass the time of day with Hal, both of them setting the world to rights, while Hal leaned on his spade, a pipe hanging from his lower lip.

The train's rhythmic roll unleashed Fi's memories further. She recalled the outside toilet near the coal shed, its yellowing porcelain, pull chain, and Bakelite seat. The musty smell, cobwebs, and gigantic spiders haunted her memory. A separate shed housed the ferrets and polecats. Hal let her feed them milk-soaked bread. Nets and hooks for fishing and rabbiting adorned the back wall of the shed, where a bucket of whelks from a morning forage often waited. Sitting together in the dilapidated conservatory, they would pluck the whelks from their shells for tea, looking down the garden toward the train tracks.

Her favourite place was the pantry, stocked with homemade wine, pickled goods, and drying herbs. In summer, the garden was covered in runner beans climbing high on a teepee structure, perfect for hiding. At that time of year, the garden resonated with Uncle Taffy's infectious laughter and his wife Aunty Wynne's, complete with her handbag full of humbugs.

Long, hot summers were followed by frosty winters. Longer nights meant gathering around the fire to share stories. Ottie knitted with Gili the cat at her side, entangled in the wool. Hal sat in his chair, a constant roll-up at his lips. Fi loved hearing their stories, imagining the people she knew only through their tales. A long-ago winter's eve surfaced in her memory, the rain lashing against the window.

Fi sat by the fire grate, legs tucked into her nightdress, watching shapes flicker in the flames. Hal shared stories about his time as a soldier in Africa.

"Did you kill any soldiers Grandad?" A young Fi asked.

"A soldier has a job to do," Hal replied gravely. "When face-to-face with an armed enemy, a choice has to be made."

His eyes held a trace of kindness in their silver depths, despite the weight of his words. He leaned in towards his roll up and took a slow drag, his gaze resolute.

"You must have been brave. You've got medals. I saw them in the drawer," Fi exclaimed.

"You! *Ragazza sfrontata,*" Ottie chastised from behind her knitting needles.

"Ah, those medals," Hal mused into the distance.

From his well-worn armchair, Hal leaned down toward Fi, the fire crackling softly behind her. He took a swig from his favourite chipped mug. Fi saw his Adam's apple jump as he swallowed. Clearing his throat, Hal studied his inquisitive granddaughter with one eye. With a slight tilt of his head, he took another drag on the tiny stub of his roll up, the burning end glowing faintly.

"You've been snooping again, my curious little Fi." His voice held a touch of sternness.

Fi held her breath, fearing she was in trouble.

"They were given to me for one reason and one reason only," he declared, shaking his finger in rhythm with his words. "For being able to run backwards the fastest."

A mischievous spark danced across his weathered face, landing at the silver in his eyes. Ottie's knitting needles paused momentarily, taking in Hal's jest. Fi giggled loudly, Ottie's laughter following close behind.

Fi's chuckle echoed in her ears. She coughed awkwardly to cover it up, noticing the couple across from her watching curiously. She turned to the window, taken aback to see the Leaning Tower of Pisa defying gravity. Her finger and thumb formed the Neapolitan gesture of affirmation. A profound sense of connection with her grandmother washed over her. Could this be the very view Ottie had gazed upon years past? The presence of her grandparents resonated within her.

The train entered southern Italy, mountains brushing against clouds. Random pillions appeared amongst little squat tumbling houses, tall apartments with busy balconies, the window's green shutters closed in the midday heat. Pointed cypress trees usually clumped in threes, lessening and making way for scant low-level foliage. Fi delved deeper into her memories as the train's trumpet sounded, declaring its presence along the curving track. She was getting closer to where it had all begun. She felt the train swing around and cut into a tunnel carved through the mountain, the blackness of the window showing up her reflection.

Fi delved into her memories to find her childhood and reminisced about her time in Italy. Every summer, she would come to Italy with Ottie. Ottie had been unable to see her family for the first eighteen years after she left. Aunt Nella talked about the initial visit as an emotional reunion that stopped Naples airport in its tracks.

Fi recalled the rare raucous occasions Ottie's sisters had skyped her in those last few years when Ottie could no longer make the journey—falling over each other to talk with a screen that would hold them suspended in unflattering poses before the signal regained—the excitement and animated gestures as they shouted over each other loudly in Italian.

Fi harked back to bygone summers in Vietri on the beaches, the picnics, the never-ending food. Her family always eating and laughing around a large chaotic table. At the head of the table was Zio Salvo, accompanied by his wife, Zia Valentina, who had a distinct aroma of warm biscuits and a habit of giving out painful pinches. Zia Valentina would kiss the pinch on her fingers from Fi's red skin before giving her a warm hug. Sitting on Zio Salvo's lap at the head of the table, Fi was made to feel special, being allowed to fork the fresh apricots from his tumbler of red wine.

Playing cards in the afternoon was a common activity for the grown-ups. Zio Geno usually winning. Geno enjoyed showing off his niece with the titian hair around Carva. Buying Fi bitter limone sorbet in a crunchy cornetto wrapped with a hard square of paper from the tiny, battered fiat van parked at the end of his aged apartment. The ice cream was taken out of the metal trap doors positioned along the van's spine. He often took her to his barber's shop, a busy den of male bonding. At one end was a pinball machine, where she would spend hours playing. A faded image of a cartoon bionic woman was displayed on the machine, with the light bulb faintly visible behind the chipping paint on the glass. Zio Geno, known for spending more time playing cards than working in his barbershop, would present her with multiple small bottles of liqueurs won from his games. He used the long nail on his little finger as a card player's aid. The reason behind his numerous wins.

While the family would gather to play cards after an endless feast, Fi passed her time sitting in the shade on the balcony reading her book. The balcony overlooked the mountains, offering a view of a small church with a prominent cross in the distance. During the night, the illuminated cross seemed to hover among the stars. She would hear her family's voices, a mix of laughter, arguments, and chaos. The love from the room would flow into her, filling her with pride for her family.

These memories were the reason she came to see Zia Nari. The last survivor of that generation. She returned to Italy to reconnect with her past. This was the place she had to be. Fi probed deeper into her own thoughts. The low-pitched horn of the train roused her as it wailed out its presence along the curving track. Fi was not sure how long she had been asleep for. The couple opposite had gone. Ruffie had slid off her lap onto the seat next to her. He lay with his head sliding downwards, falling off the seat.

The landscape had become familiar to her. Flashes of the sea peeked between the dip in the mountains. Vesuvius's magnificence outshone the scenery. Its giant form encroaching on the sky, the top cut off, as if sliced by a knife, left jagged like a boiled egg. The looming presence of the mountain felt symbolic — imposing yet familiar, much like her unresolved feelings. It wasn't long before the train slid into Salerno station, its brakes hissing in release. Fi grabbed her case and scooped Ruffie into her arms as the train slowed to a stop.

The salty air greeted her as she stepped down onto the platform, warmth rising from the sun-baked tiles. The familiar buzz of life in the streets beyond the station called to her—unmistakably Salerno. She entered the busy streets, a place pitted with scars from wars, earthquakes, and landslides. The tongue of the locals at her ears, speaking in the dialect of a nation as resilient as its land.

She strolled through the old, winding streets. Shops and cafes spilled their tables onto narrow cobbled lanes, friendly waiters trying to coax her in. Garages with mechanics in oil-stained overalls, trendy boutiques, old churches and office blocks stood side by side in uneven harmony. The buildings had grown from Salerno, higgledy-piggledy. Creating a labyrinth of narrow streets and alleyways sprawling between the sea and the surrounding mountains. The city a living ubiquitous octopus, its legs twisting, rambling and spreading, streets extending in unpredictable directions, never static, ever evolving.

Fi knew this place, she understood it. She felt the energy vibrating up from the streets into the soles of her feet. As she approached the heart of the old town, the aroma of roasting chestnuts mingled with the briny sea air. Market vendors called out their daily specials, their voices cutting through the city's steady hum. Laundry fluttered from wrought-iron balconies, vivid against the pastel walls scarred with time.

The sea sparkled in the distance, a constant reminder of Salerno's connection to the greater world. Fishing boats bobbed gently in the harbour, their paint chipped but still resilient. Fi watched them for a moment, their steady rhythm grounding her. She adjusted her bag, cast a look at Ruffie and turned down a narrow lane shaded by orange trees. The leaves rustled softly in the breeze. She knew the way instinctively, she could do it with her eyes shut guided by memory and something deeper—an unspoken pull drawing her toward Zia Nari's house.

30

Picture Perfect

Ottie traced her fingers along the bronze picture frame before adjusting it. She cast her mind back to the day she had placed Hal's photo on the mantelpiece next to Mamma and Marcello's, reflecting on how things had changed since that fateful day. Her behaviour had offended her brothers, and their disapproval was obvious. Papa, more composed in his feelings, expressed his anger differently. She had felt his hand strike hard across her face as she knelt before him.

"Let him come tell me his intentions. Let me see the man who disrespects me through my daughter. Let me see if he is what you say." Papa's words were as deliberate as his thinking.

Ottie spat the salty taste of blood from her mouth. She peered at her father through her fingers. *If Hal lives through this battle, I know he will return.* The thought remained locked within her. She returned to her room in silence and crawled onto the bed between the safety of her beloved sisters. They comforted her while she cried and treated her bruises with witch hazel.

The next morning, Nari replaced the upturned photograph of Hal back in its correct position on the mantelpiece. The strength of her defiance was equally matched by her brothers' anger. The sisters stood united the following day. Fina returned the photograph to its rightful place after their brothers knocked it over once more. On the day

Fina intervened, Papa also stepped in. He commanded the drama to stop. The atmosphere had become unbearable. The photograph was to stay where Ottie had placed it until the day he met Hal. On that day, he would decide the fate of the photograph—and of Ottie.

Papa kept his word despite his tendency to be capricious in mood. His decision stemmed from an intuitive wisdom honed by experience. Besides, he doubted Hal would survive the bloody war. Though his moods were prone to wild swings, his reasoning always held firm.

***

Hal struggled to lift his opioid-laden eyelids. He felt his focus tighten as the blurry lines around him began to make sense. The red cross stood out distinctly on the nurse's white uniform as she adjusted his bed linen. Startled, she gasped when he unexpectedly awake grasped her forearm to catch her attention. His mouth was so dry that he struggled to talk.

"Mamma mia, you have pain, si?"

With a weak shake of his head, Hal tried to raise himself. He leaned forward and clutched at the bandages as searing pain spread upward from his leg. As she tried to push him back down, the nurse shouted in Italian to her colleague for more medication. Hal shook his head fiercely.

He answered in her language. "No, please, I need pen, paper. I need...."

With his chest feeling tight, he took a deep breath in. He pushed aside the syrette of morphine she had poised to inject into him.

"No, no more. Get me a pen and paper."

Hal needed to clear his head. He wanted to get news to Ottie.

31

A Turn Of The Cards

My Darling Ottie

*I made it through the fight, despite Jerry doing their best to be rid of me.
I am safe. I am in hospital. The nurses hope to have me up and walking soon.
My darn leg took a hit. It is so long since I have seen you. I am determined
to be out of here soon and back to base. I hope you like my little sketch. I will
never tire of drawing your beautiful face. I am not so good at writing in Italian. I hope you can understand. I do know how to write Ti amo.*

Always yours

Hal x

Hal had used every grain of his strength to get himself out of the battlefield and back to safety. Weak and disoriented from blood loss, he looked a pitiful sight as he staggered into the military encampment. He was dispatched at once to Naples for surgery on his leg, which had been blasted back to the tendons.

A fellow soldier in the hospital bed next to Hal shared news about Stan and Taffy. Both had made it through and been assigned to the Hitler Line. Unaware of this, Hal didn't know they had signed up to return and aid in clearing the bodies from the battlefield before leaving. They spent two days helping to bury the dead and identifying the fallen men, their bodies decomposing in the elements. They returned to where they had last seen Hal and desperately searched for a sign of him before time ran out, just as they were posted onward to the Hitler Line to chase the Germans further up the boot of Italy. Hal hoped they would make it through this damn war and that one day all three of them would meet up in a pub back home to swap stories over a pint.

Hal no longer relied on a walking stick. Occasionally, he still had a slight limp, especially when he was tired. The purple scars on his leg were fading into patchy white keloid tissue. Unlike the others, he was desperate to get back to base and resume his post. For a few weeks, Hal had been placed on light duties. He wasted no time in visiting the Matanti household as soon as he could. He now had more reason than ever to see Ottie's father. He had resolved to marry Ottie. The timing seemed more urgent than he had imagined. First, however, he had to get through Ottie's father.

It looked like Italy was also experiencing a state of flux. Mussolini had been found by partisans and duly executed. Mussolini's lifeless body had been displayed like butchered meat for all to witness. He was hung upside down next to his mistress, his face badly beaten, his caved-in features unrecognisable—a macabre display of defiance from the public. With the fascist regime vanquished, Italy was on the path to independence as Allies pushed the Nazis northward, like a broom sweeping away debris.

Ottie always remembered the day Hal knocked on her door. She had just been out and posted yet another letter to him. Unsure when she was going to see him again, she was fearful of the news she had disclosed in her last letter. She cherished the letters he had been sending her from his sickbed. His words and sketches kept her going.

When she opened the door and found him standing there, she couldn't help but hug him tightly. She felt his thinned form through his uniform. Ottie, lost in the moment, had forgotten about his injuries, she released her grip. The pain for Hal was nothing compared to the joy of feeling her in his embrace again.

"Ottie, my Ottie." Hal smiled as he nuzzled into her hair. He cupped her face in his hand.

"I couldn't wait after the news you wrote to me. Are you feeling, okay? Mia Cara."

Her chin dipped a nod into his cupped hand. Ottie rubbed at the curve of her belly and felt the hard kick against her hand.

"I have come to see your father."

Ottie desperately tried to put Hal off until he was stronger, but he was adamant that it needed to be now. Holding Hal's hand discreetly behind her back, she guided him through the house to the kitchen, where Papa was playing cards with her brothers at the table. Fina was the first to see Hal at the door. His frame took up the entire door space, a flop of black brill-creamed hair across his forehead. He required no introduction. Fina dropped her jaw with surprise at the sight of him in her kitchen. Letting go of her tea towel that fluttered to the floor. Papa lifted his eyes from the cards splayed out in a fan shape in his hand.

"Papa, this is Hal. He has come to see you," Ottie spoke as she peered out from behind Hal.

Moving behind Hal, Fina escorted Ottie out of the room while Hal advanced into the kitchen. Papa carefully set his hand of cards face down on the table. Salvo and Geno had raised themselves up, kicking their chairs back behind them as they did. Papa motioned with his outstretched hands for his sons to return to their seats. Papa furrowed his brow, his eyes narrowed as he lifted his gaze to meet Hal's. He took in the sheer size of him. Hal was clearly a man weakened by war, but he still had the mass and strength greater than that deemed upon most men. He noticed Hal's heaving chest and recognised the rage that comes before a fight. The testosterone in the room was lifting to an uncontrollable level among the younger men.

"Hal, your face looks familiar to me. My daughter proudly displays your photograph. A stranger's face stares down at me in my own house." Papa sized him up carefully as he spoke.

Papa took in the uniform. Hal wore a thick khaki green wool shirt ill-suited to the current southern Italian heatwave. He noticed the full bag in Hal's hand and wondered what it contained.

"It looks like you had to get past a war to get here?"

Papa glanced down towards Hal's leg as Hal moved forward, his gait unsteady.

"Take a seat."

Hal positioned himself at the opposite end of the table from Papa, Geno, and Salvo, who were seated on either side of him. Their body language was unfriendly.

"Signore Matanti, thank you." Hal ingratiated as he sat down.

Papa remained silent, waiting for Hal to continue, his face pinched tightly into a scowl. Hal felt uneasy. He didn't want to mess this up, despite being aware how it must appear. The men at the table must harbour a strong hatred towards him. From their perspective, he had shown disrespect to the family and brought shame upon them. Hal intended to make things right. His love for Ottie outweighed the hate directed at him. They loved her too. He hoped that somewhere amongst the mess, a solution would be found.

Hal hesitated briefly, then blurted out his intentions across the table. "I want to marry your daughter."

Geno swore under his breath with a sarcastic laugh. Salvo pushed himself up to stand, placing his hands flat on the table. Papa leaned over and pushed Salvo back down. Papa stayed in a half-raised position, leaning towards Hal across the table for an extra second. His steely stare stayed on Hal as he slowly sat back down.

"You come straight to the point. I guess you have little time, given that she is pregnant." Papa was deliberate in his choice of words.

Surprise struck both brothers' faces in unison. Hal was also stunned. He found the words and answered. "You know."

Exasperated, Papa let out a puff of air from his cheeks.

"During our marriage, my wife had over fifteen pregnancies. Sometimes, I knew before she did. The broken dishes and tears, argh! Tavi is just like any other woman." Papa tapped his forehead. "I see."

Hal wondered how it all must look to Ottie's father. He hung his head, feeling a blush of shame. He recalled his purpose for being in the

Matanti kitchen, and his resolve renewed. Hal defiantly matched Papa's glare. The chocolate colour of Ottie's eyes reflected in her father's. They stared back at him, devoid of the warmth he felt in hers.

"I love your daughter, and I will marry her and take her back to England with me one day when we win this war," Hal spoke without faltering.

"You're very sure of yourself. You're sure you will win." With a sneer, Papa exposed his sharp incisor teeth and challenged. "You really think you can just steal her from me?"

"No, Signore Matanti. I am here today to ask for your blessing and seek her hand."

"And if I say no, then what?" Challenged Papa.

"I am going to marry your daughter. I want to be a part of your family, not take her away."

"But you are going to take her away to England," Papa rebuked.

"One day, yes," Hal replied with honesty.

"Are you catholic?" Questioned Papa.

"No."

"If you want to marry my daughter, you must become one. Our faith is important."

"I will do what it takes."

"Do you not care about your faith? Do you believe in God, Hal?" Papa pushed at Hal, looking for his weakness.

"I have just come back from the bloodiest fight. It was enough to question any man's faith."

Hal hung his head, the weight of recent events pressing down on him, shaking his faith. His eyes flickered to the bag in his lap before moving it onto the table. Wanting to change the topic, he redirected the conversation.

"I brought some cigarettes."

Packets of Pall Mall and Lucky Strikes spilled out of the bag, scattering across the table. Geno caught one before it fell off the side.

"Is that the price of my sister?" Salvo added, arms folded, swinging back on his chair.

Geno released a soft whistle while holding a squishy cigarette packet. The amount on the table could make him a tidy sum.

"No, this is a gift for her family, a family that matters to her. As she matters to me." Hal directed his answer at Salvo. While resting his eyes on each of the Matanti's at the table, he carried on speaking. "I never want to see her harmed by anyone. I will make certain that she isn't. If anyone were to lay a hand on her, I would repay them tenfold."

Hal rested his elbow on the table. He gently tightened his fist and raised it towards his chin, signalling his intentions. Unspoken words lingered in the air. Papa stretched across and pulled the bag's handle. He dragged the cigarettes closer and put them aside. In a theatrical gesture, he ran his arms along the bare tabletop.

"Can you play Scopa?" Papa inquired, tilting his head.

"Yes, I think so."

"Then, tonight, you may make me a rich man."

Papa almost smiled as he gathered the cards and began to shuffle.

32

Biscuits And Bombshells

Zia Nari lived in a two-story residence on the eastern side of Salerno, a short distance from the beach. In the night's tranquillity, after the busy day had settled, she could hear the sea outside her bedroom window. Nari's house was surrounded by typical, tall Neapolitan postwar apartment buildings, their concrete balconies jutting out in an Eastern Bloc style. On her street, the remaining prewar houses huddled together, their aging facades, whispering stories of a bygone era.

Nari watched the landscape change, regenerate, and grow over the postwar decades. Her small street, once neglected and dilapidated, had been modernised and improved. Nari had lived in the same house ever since marrying her late husband, Franco. Working together at the local general store, which they eventually bought, they saved enough for a down payment and mortgage on their house. Over time, they lovingly expanded it, cultivating grapevines, oranges, bougainvillea, and tomatoes in the backyard.

Fi leaned back on her heels. From Nari's front step, she looked along the well-cared-for street with its neat row of houses, tidy frontages, and gardens. A far cry from the broken concrete road she remembered as a child, playing ball with the children from the apartment blocks near the rubbish tip with giant black rats scurrying past in broad daylight. Fi noted that the area where she used to play as a child had been turned into a small, neatly kept park. The attendant caught her attention and gave her a nod while diligently watering the buffalo grass in the evening's shade.

Nari's street had fast become the premier area to live in her district. Working well into her eighties, she sold the shop on the seafront only a few years back. The shop had grown more successful with the arrival of tourists in the late seventies. Nari had enjoyed the social life the shop provided and was saddened when she could no longer manage it. While her body weakened, her brain stayed sharp, and she missed interacting with customers. Nari and Franco had one son, Luca. Luca worked in a law firm in Salerno. His parents' strong work ethic, love, and his own talent paved the way for his successful career.

Fi padded from one foot to another, impatiently waiting at the orange-panelled door. The brass plaque under the bell held the names of her aunt and uncle, its edges worn from years of polishing. Finally, after what seemed like an eternity, Fi could hear the pit-pat of open shoes on tiles echo from behind the door. Fi was met by the unexpected. A small square-shaped middle-aged woman with bleach-blonde hair and a heavy fringe opened the door. She clutched a broom in one hand, busy amid her daily chores.

"Tak ?" The woman spoke with a strong Eastern European accent.

Puzzled, Fi squinted at the woman, whose face was animated as she silently mouthed words before trying to speak them in broken Italian.

"I help you. How, please?"

Beaming with pride, the woman blinked twice at Fi, who looked puzzled and scratched her head.

"I have come to see my Zia," Fi explained. "My Zia Nari. I am her great-niece, Fiamma."

Fi smiled and nodded while pointing her hands to her chest to confirm who she was. Pulling back her head, the woman pouted, then shrugged, her face blank.

"No," she answered. "Give moment."

The door abruptly slammed in Fi's face.

"Hey! "

Fi pounded on the heavy panelled door, the thud resonating through the quiet hallway. The woman's voice filtered through the door.

"Moment!! I back!"

Fi flung her spine against the brick porch and folded her arms, gripping her forearms with frustration. She looked down at Ruffie, sitting patiently next to her, alternating his furry eyebrows, adding to his already naturally curious expression. Within a moment, the door burst open with a loud bang, flinging back on its hinges. With a sudden, sharp movement, the woman thrust her iPad into Fi's hand, the screen facing Fi.

"Ok, talk me."

Fi noticed the translation app was set to Ukrainian/Italian. Complying, Fi addressed the iPad in a slow voice, her eyes fixed on the woman's self-assured expression.

"I ..am ..here ..to see.. my aunt ...Nari. I am her... family."

Fi finished and handed it to the woman. The metallic voice, devoid of inflection, sharply pronounced the Ukrainian hard vowels. Confusion was etched on the woman's face. Bored with waiting, Ruffie darted between the woman's legs into the hallway, racing toward the light at the end of the passage.

"Ruffie!" Fi called after the determined dog.

She pushed past the woman in pursuit of Ruffie. The woman, shouting in Ukrainian, waddled behind. Ruffie dashed down the long, dark hallway, drawn to the kitchen light spilling into the hallway, and then toward the courtyard beyond.

Fi heard the familiar voice of Zia Nari as she made it to the kitchen door and descended the steps, bleached white from years of vigorous scrubbing, into the garden. She paused briefly, allowing her eyes to adapt to the sudden brightness. The garden's shadows dappled by the soft sunlight filtering through the grapevines on the trellis above came into focus. Nari was sitting in a large sun chair a short distance away, beneath the orange tree. A floppy pink faded sun hat pulled down too far on her head. Ruffie leaped onto her lap, wiggling and attempting to lick her vigorously while she laughed and tried to push him away from her face. Her laugh was so like Ottie's that it at once filled Fi with the comforting warmth that she was missing so much.

"Zia," Fi called out.

As Nari opened her arms to greet her niece, Ruffie jumped from her lap.

Nari's voice was full of care. "Fiamma. My Fiamma. I knew you would come."

Fi collapsed into her aunt's arms, breathing in the familiar scent of sun-warmed cotton and lemon, a comforting wave of long-forgotten memories washed over her. Using her palms, Fi's aunt wiped away the tears from Fi's face and gently pushed her hair back.

"Magda, it's alright; she is family," Nari advised over Fi's bent head.

Magda's square chin raised into a smile.

"Ahhh, family, Fiamma... English girl, your daughter Tak?"

"No, it's niece. She is my niece, not daughter," corrected Nari.

"Huh. I make coffee, no."

Magda carried on without stopping for a reply. She tottered off to percolate the espresso and decided to hunt for the sweet biscuits Nari had been reserving for a special guest in the sideboard.

"Where did she come from?" Fi laughed, keeping her head on her aunt's lap. Finding comfort in the familiar warmth and rhythm of Nari's breathing.

"She is my housekeeper and carer. She comes five days a week, it was Luca's idea. She lives nearby with her daughter." Nari responded while gently stroking her niece's hair.

"How do you manage to understand each other? Couldn't you get someone that you can at least talk to?"

"I had another woman before her. Luca, employed from a care agency. I got rid of her after one day. She wouldn't shut up, talking rubbish all the time, and she wouldn't clean either! It wasn't what she was paid for she told me! In my own home! She even tried to wash me!"

"Oh, Zia. What did Luca say?"

"He wasn't thrilled with me. He threatened to get another one from an agency. So, I found my own. She lives in the flats up there," Nari pointed at the flats overlooking her garden through the branches of the orange tree. "She is a lot cheaper too, and she cleans." Nari paused a moment and smiled down at her niece. "And she doesn't talk a lot of rubbish to me!"

Fi laughed. "Zia, you are as naughty as ever. Sat out here on your big bum, lauding it up."

Fi jokingly used the dialect term *culo grande* to refer to her aunt's large backside, a long-standing joke between them. Her aunt playfully tickled her on the ribs. The two women laughed. Nari spluttered and struggled to catch her breath. Her lips were tinged blue, she began to wheeze. Magda appeared at her side with a blue plastic inhaler and helped Nari breathe in a couple of puffs. Nari's breathing steadied. Magda frowned at her and shook her head.

"You! Too much laugh!" Magda told her sternly. "Come. Coffee. Table," she added over her shoulder.

Coffee and M&S Christmas shortbread, contained in a cute, tartan Scottish terrier tin, were laid out on the garden table. Using her wheeled frame, Fi helped Nari get to the table. She was struck by how much weaker she was than a decade earlier. Through a combination of iPad, Italian, and a unique sign language they shared, Nari conveyed to Magda the need to buy Ruffie's essentials.

With a roll of her eyes, Magda did as asked, her displeasure at having a dog to care for was clear. Magda, her face a mask of stern disapproval, landed a sharp pinch on Fi's cheek as she swept past. She tapped the iPad screen, the faint glow illuminating her face as she tried to read the English words.

"Bootiful lady," she triumphantly informed Fi.

Nari took the biscuit tin and peeled off the cellophane. Ottie always sent M&S biscuits to Italy in her Christmas hampers. English tea bags, custard powder, and biscuits were her family's typical requests.

Ottie's request in return was for floor cloths and clothes pegs. Ottie's biscuits were probably Nari's last gift. Fi's heart felt heavy, a lead weight in her chest, as she knew she had to tell her aunt why she was really there. There was never a right time; it had to be now. With a deep breath, she steeled herself; it was time to confront the challenge, however difficult it might be. Selecting a biscuit, Nari took a bite before handing the tin to Fi.

"Zia, I need to tell you something." Fi wanted to go gently; she spoke softly.

Nari, unaware of the change in her tone, made the Neapolitan sign for "What do you mean?" by gesturing and bringing her fingers together. She added. "Eat my little mouse."

Fi smiled faintly, acknowledging her aunt's term of endearment. Nari slid the tin down the table, inviting Fi to take one. *Ottie's tin* thought Fi as she held the lid in her hand. Every year, she'd take Ottie Christmas shopping for the family. Back home, they wrapped presents while singing made up Christmas carols. As Ottie's spiced puddings bubbled on the stove, their fragrant steam, fogging up the kitchen window.

Fi watched as Nari habitually huffed at her fringe, the grey and black strands speckled with age, falling back to frame her round face. Nari's deep brown eyes shifted left as she carefully considered her words.

"When you have something serious to say. You lean forward, just like your grandmother used to."

"Zia, I need to tell...Hang on, what did you just say?"

"I said you lean forward like she used to."

A held silence occupied the space between the two women, lucid in its form. Fi hung onto her aunt's last words.

Nari popped the invisible bubble and continued. "Fiamma, I know why you have come here. Ottie told me you would... She told me... after Quin and the accident... when it was her time ... she said you would block it out just like you have."

"No, no, NO! You can't know about Ottie."

Fi buried her head in her hands.

Nari persisted, her voice firm. "We sent flowers to her funeral. Remember? Your daughters sent pictures of the flowers to Luca. I have them here in the draw."

Nari reached out to stroke her niece's arm. A sob caught in Fi's throat, her voice cracking under the weight of her feelings. "I, I just, I felt, I should come. I needed...."

Overwhelmed by grief, Fi choked back silent tears, unable to find the words to express the depth of her sorrow.

"It's ok you don't have to explain."

Fi glanced at Nari through her fringe before she spoke. "You look so alike, you know? I always tell Quin how alike you both are. He can't wait to meet you. Once we...."

"Fiamma, enough!" Interrupting, Nari held up her open palms in frustration. "They are both dead! Ottie and ... Quin."

The finality of Nari's words was palpable. Exposed in the unforgiving light of reality, Fi's journey reached its final destination. She struggled to breathe as grief tightened its hold on her throat. The sound of her pounding pulse filled her ears. Fi felt time pause and spin backwards. Memories cascaded through her mind. Quin's face burned in her retina. The machine at his head dipping into a flatline of nothingness. Her trembling shoulder comforted by the nurse's reassuring squeeze. Fi dwelt on the nurse's words. "This isn't him; he is all the times you have had before this."

Quin and Ottie had not left her. They couldn't simply leave. They were at her side, their presence woven into her every day. Her sorrow was unbearable; tears of grief traced silent paths down her cheeks. Like a stone she could never set down, she carried her loss—time had not diminished the hurt. It had only strengthened her ability to bear it. Quin was no longer just a voice message on her phone. She had clung to his warm tones with fierce desperation. He embodied all the memories they had shared and the love she still held for him.

Ottie, her beloved Nonna, lingered in every room at Warten Way, each corner resonating with a lifetime of treasured moments.

Memories slowly faded, soft and fragile, slipping through her fingers like powdery dust. Exposed and vulnerable in the stark light of reality, she leaned into the pain. A chill threaded down her spine, tightening into a knot in her stomach. Suffering and gratitude surged through her, intertwined. The intensity of her pain reflected the depth of her love. Letting go was the hardest part; she had been so fortunate to have loved so deeply that losing them hurt beyond measure.

33

The Big Day

Chiesa di Santa Maria Assunta in Cielo e delle Anime Purgatorio. The little church with a big name, thought Hal as he waited alone outside. The crisp morning light cast a bright halo over the church's roof. He felt the lingering night chill that hung in the air. From its position on the church apse, the brightly coloured portrait of Maria Assunta seemed to follow his every move. Pointing skyward, her robes swirled around her, cherubs clinging tightly to her flowing garments. Hal acknowledged her with a nod. After weeks of passing beneath her gaze, he was officially recognised as a baptised Catholic by the church. He was ready to marry his bride.

The solid mahogany-panelled door swung open. With lauds complete, a small trickle of morning worshippers filtered out of the church. Hal stood with his back against the wall, extinguishing his cigarette as he attempted to fade into the shadows. He received discreet nods of recognition from a few familiar faces who had seen him at recent ceremonies. He spotted Elena among the crowd and felt grateful for the kindness she had shown Ottie. Hal couldn't always be there to protect Ottie from the hostility she faced for marrying a foreign soldier, which seemed to intensify whenever she ventured into town. Fair-weather friends had abandoned her, but Elena remained loyal, just as Ottie's family had supported Elena during her struggles. Only the previous week,

Ottie had been spat on and called cruel names by a passerby.

***

Elena had personally witnessed Ottie's struggle at the fish market a few weeks ago. She couldn't believe how quickly the narrow-minded townsfolk had turned against Ottie. Though she tried to ignore the comments, the whispered remarks about Elena continued, sharp and cutting, like an icy wind. Elena saw Ottie standing apart, near the white marble tables laden with the day's catch—fish atop each other, their vacant eyes staring. The air in the hall bustled with the lively clamour of trade echoing upwards. The pungent smell of the sea filled the market, its scent strong enough to raise the roof. Ottie remained composed, though Elena could tell she was being deliberately made to wait. Their eyes met, and Elena subtly beckoned her over.

"Tell me what you want, and I will get it," whispered Elena close to Ottie's ear.

With the purchase made, they left the bustling market, finally able to hear each other speak.

"Thank you. I thought I was invisible until I saw you. I'm not sure what's worse, being ignored or being ridiculed," Ottie said.

Elena handed over the fish, wrapped in brown paper, in exchange for payment. The sunlight caught the green in her eyes as she draped an arm over Ottie's shoulders. A spark of her usual spirit returned.

"Hey, we're fallen women together," Elena said with a reassuring squeeze.

Arm in arm, they headed home.

***

With the crowd dispersed, the priest stood in the doorway, flickering candlelight casting shifting shadows behind him. Dressed in a cassock and gold-embroidered stoles, he was ready for the ceremony. The padre watched as Hal stepped away from the shadows, his breath steadying as he prepared himself for what lay ahead. Hal moved back into the darkness. He needed a moment of solitude to compose himself. The padre motioned for him to enter. Hal stepped into the church to await his bride's arrival.

Ottie arrived in her favourite sky-blue dress, holding a bouquet of wild mountain flowers—pink, yellow, and blue—bound with a bright yellow raffia bow. With Papa close at her elbow, she entered the cool, dim little stone church, the hushed reverence palpable beneath the Gothic dome. The moment he saw her, Hal's nerves melted away.

Few people filled the pews, mostly Ottie's siblings. Elena lingered at the back with Anna, mirroring supportive nods as Ottie approached the altar. The powerful form of Hal silhouetted against the kaleidoscope of stained glass beamed into the church as the morning sun broke open. She caught Hal's eye as he glanced over the edge of his shoulder. His uniform was pristine, save for a rogue strand of hair escaping onto his brow. She heeded the wink he sent and felt a warmth flush down to her toes, momentarily captivated by his boyish charm.

A gentle squeeze from Papa's elbow jolted her back into the church. They exchanged glances, Papa nodded sharply, glancing briefly at Hal before focusing back to Ottie. She affirmed his silent encouragement with a slight dip of her chin. She was ready. A flicker of warmth melted in the rich chocolate of her father's eyes. Stepping back, he directed her forward and joined her brothers in the front row. Ottie felt the weight of the moment, her history resting just behind her.

Stepping into the unknown, she joined Hal, looking back one last time for reassurance. Overwhelmed by emotion despite the formality of the event, Hal impulsively reached out and clasped her hand. Ottie felt the comforting warmth, his fingers gently closing around hers. She held on tightly as she crossed the threshold from spinster to wife. The quiet ceremony concluded with a single staccato toll from the church bell.

Hal and Ottie kept the celebration intimate, dining that evening at a seafront restaurant in Vietri. After their meal, they strolled along the coast's edge. Where houses tumbled down towards the sea from the mountains in a tangle of yellow, cream and terracotta hues. The setting sun cast its final burst of fiery orange rays across the mountain's back. Amidst the sea's ink blue hue cast by the mountains' shade, small fishing boats were scattered, having anchored for the day.

Hal walked Ottie home along the steep, winding mountain trail, the earth's scent lingering beneath the trees. At her door, he kissed her gently, resting his hand on the curve of her growing belly as she guided him. For the first time, he felt the kick of their unborn child. Joy ignited in his soul.

Yet another last goodbye, filled with the familiar ache of parting, before Ottie watched him walk backward, his hand waving, a scene she'd witnessed countless times. She waited until he disappeared around the corner. Only to reappear at the edge of the wall. Pretending someone had pulled him back by his collar. His pranks made her laugh. Hal could hear her laughter trailing behind him as he turned the corner. He walked away with a light hearted spring in his step, determined to always bring a smile to her face.

Married couples were not permitted to stay at the base, and there was no room for Hal in Ottie's family home. Italy soon mirrored Hal's joy, celebrating the long-awaited news that the war was finally over. The streets came alive with jubilant festivities.

34

Small Blessings

Hal wrote to his mother to tell her about his recent marriage. Within a matter of days, unable to wait for her reply, he wrote another letter with more news that was unexpectedly earlier than predicted.

Dear Mother,

I am guessing that you have barely had time to read my last letter. I hope my news of marriage was a pleasant surprise. I cannot wait for you to meet Ottie, my wife. I am still not used to calling her that. I am a husband and now I write to let you know that I am also a father!

It feels like I have a lot of news for you lately, and it must all seem so quick. This war has made so many of us grasp at any happiness we can find. Not knowing what tomorrow will bring has that effect. I am thankful that I have a future, a family, and a home to return to. Your granddaughter is wonderful. She has jet black hair and big blue eyes. We have called her Tilda after you.

I hope to be coming back home in the next few months. We have lots to finish up here. Taffy was fortunate enough to be demobbed already, and he managed to get on one of the few boats that sailed out last week from Naples. That man could sell coals to Newcastle. It was strange seeing him head back home after all these years. We are, after all, the last few left from our unit. I will never forget those men. I like to think that he is back in those green

valleys raising a pint to me as I write this.
I will let you know as soon as I am able to leave. Pat that Bonnie for me.
Love
Hal x

***

Ottie was caught off guard when her baby arrived unexpectedly. It may have been sped up by all the dancing and celebrating she had done, revelling in Italy's freedom. As Ottie was helping Nari in gathering beans from the vegetable garden, she felt a sharp pain in her lower abdomen, causing her to gasp. Despite the pain, she persisted in picking the beans until she experienced a pulling sensation down her thighs. Bending down to shift the basket beside the line of beans, Ottie felt a warm trickle starting down her inner thigh. When she raised herself from between the beans to call Nari, the trickle had increased and was now gushing from under her. Nari quickly skidded around the corner of the row of beans and looked down at the sodden ground. Confronted with dilemmas, Nari typically huffed her fringe upward. Her black hair reset itself and curled around her elfin features.

The spilled basket of beans lay forgotten as Nari helped her sister, doubled over with labour pain. They hurried, tripping in unison across the road. Nari held out her hand to stop a farm truck and gain passage across the road. The farmer recognised the daughters of Renzo Matanti. Assessing the situation, he stopped at Bar Tabbach, Papa's familiar drinking spot. Upon hearing the news, Papa quickly reacted and abandoned his drink at the bar. He shouted, promising to return with news and a drink for anyone still at the bar.

Nari aided Ottie into the house, bursting in through the door and calling for Fina to come. Fina had been Mina's doula during her childbirth, and now her midwifery expertise was needed again. She rushed to her sister's aid. Fina took one look at Ottie and ordered Nari to take her upstairs while she fetched towels and hot water. She kicked Salvo awake in his mid-siesta and gave him the task of bringing up more warm water that she had put on to boil. He jumped to the job, shaking the sleep off his shoulders. Salvo paced the kitchen floor, watching a pot that refused to boil, lost in the mystery of women and the natural wonder of birth.

Papa arrived, breathless from pacing quickly up the hill. He shouted up to Nari for news. She appeared at the top of the stairs, her face glowing, with no news yet. Geno appeared soon after, and Papa sent him with the horse and cart to get news to Hal at the army base. He then reached into the cupboard for his prize bottle of Lacryma Christi wine produced on the slopes of Mount Vesuvius. He set it in the centre of the kitchen table with enough tumblers for his family, folded his arms, and waited patiently for news. A flustered Salvo paced around him, heading back and forth from the upstairs landing and back to the kitchen, taking orders from Fina and following through her errands.

Then the frenzy gave way to a moment's silence. Papa raised his eyes in the direction of the girls' bedroom. Ottie had fallen silent. Her moans no longer echoed through the kitchen, the floorboards no longer creaked with activity. He held his breath, closed his eyes, and prayed. His eyes jerked open with the sound of a shrill infant cry that pumped into the house, music to his ears. Papa leaned forward and uncorked the wine.

It was not long before an eager Hal arrived and laid eyes on his little girl. She had thick black hair that continued down onto her back, soft and downy. Her wide blue eyes stared curiously at her father while she sucked hard on her fist. He gently tickled the small hairy feathers of hair on her tiny ears.

"Fina said her eyes might not stay blue, and her hair will probably fall out in the next few weeks," said Ottie.

"I hope so, my little monkey baby," Hal said, winking at Ottie in bed as he talked to his daughter. "Tilda, after your grandmother Matilda. I wonder what she will make of you my little one."

Ottie watched Hal at the window with his daughter. Tilda's tiny spine curved around into his entire hand as she stared up at her father.

"I think she is hungry," Hal noted.

Hal brought little Tilda to Ottie, the loud slapping noise of her sucking her fist had increased. He planted a kiss on his wife's forehead before carefully placing Tilda down.

"Fina says you need to rest now," Nari interrupted the scene from the bedroom door.

Ottie rolled her eyes for Hal's benefit, and he responded with a smirk.

"Bossy Matanti women," Hal mouthed back into her smile.

Leaving his new little family behind, he carried the picture of them in his mind as he made his way down the stairs to return to base. Salvo stood waiting at the bottom of the stairs, an awkwardness remained between the two men. Hal nodded an acknowledgement and headed towards the front door. He felt the light touch of Salvo's fingers along the inside of his forearm.

"Where do you think you're going?" Hal turned to reply. Salvo continued, not giving him the opportunity. "Come drink with me," Salvo beckoned towards the kitchen. "Come celebrate with your family."

35

Poker Face

So, you are finally going to do the decent thing," mocked Salvo. Geno jokingly smacked Salvo's back as he strolled past with a confident strut, his elbows flaring out like a proud cockerel.

"Well, big brother, we all have to settle down one day. I have had my fill of wild oats."

Geno lowered his head towards Salvo, biting his lower lip. He was at least a head taller.

"You haven't reached that stage. Perhaps priesthood is on the cards for you?" Geno's eyes twinkled mischievously as he spoke.

Salvo shook his head at his brother's teasing.

"At least you kept your promise. Geno, you must be in love." Salvo selected his words to poke at his brother.

Geno finished checking his hair in the hall mirror. He looked back once more, tilting his head to admire himself from a different angle. Satisfied with what he saw, he faced Salvo to answer him.

"Now the war is over, it is time to start rebuilding. It's time to grow families." Geno grabbed Salvo's groin. "Do you know how to use this, brother? Would you like some lessons from an expert?"

With a touch of lion cub spirit lingering in them, the two young men tumbled into each other, knocking the pictures in the hallway as they bounced from wall to wall.

"Hey! Grow up you two," Fina scolded as she descended the stairs with baby Tilda in her arms.

Tilda twisted her body to keep her uncles in sight while Fina curved around the bannister. Tilda, entertained by what she saw, stopped sucking her teddy bear's ear and emitted a gleeful squeal.

"Be careful—you're wrecking the place. One of you needs to take hold of Tilda. I have bread to take out of the oven."

Fina lifted Tilda in the air and directed her towards her uncles. Her chubby legs kicked with delight at her new source of amusement. They both stopped fighting to make a fuss of her. Salvo took her in his arms as Geno made to leave for his date.

Tilda waved a dimpled little hand at Geno, who blew vigorous, playful kisses at her from the door before closing it behind him.

Geno's departure caused Tilda to cry. In an attempt to calm his niece down, Salvo put her teddy bear on his head. He pulled funny faces and made silly noises, believing that being completely stupid was the only way to distract an eight-month-old baby. After a few minutes, his daft display had the desired effect. Tilda began with loud chuckles, tears still heavy at her lower lashes. The sillier he became, the more she laughed. Her chuckles grew harder. Salvo, typically more reserved, couldn't contain his laughter as his niece reached for the teddy bear on his head. He lifted her up and then pulled her close, making raspberry noises on her neck, slightly wet with her dribble. Laughing, she clung tightly to her teddy bear as her little body kicked against his chest.

A prickling feeling crept up the back of Salvo's neck. He sensed someone else's presence and felt a gentle breeze from the slightly open front door behind him.

"Hey, Uncle Geno's back," Salvo told Tilda while lifting her up in the air once more. "Second thoughts little brother?"

Salvo spun round to face Geno, bringing the giggling Tilda back into his arms.

"Hello," she said with a small smile, her sultry red lipstick showing off her white teeth.

Salvo felt the embarrassment rise into his cheeks, he hadn't expected a stranger. He stared at her, taking in the dark brown tresses hanging around her pretty face. He was momentarily speechless before collecting himself and regaining his composure.

"Sorry, erm, the door was ajar. I didn't want to interrupt the fun," she smiled and reached out to stroke Tilda's cheek. "Hello, Tilda."

"You know Tilda?" Salvo deflected, still feeling uncomfortable that she had witnessed a side that he kept within the closeness of his family.

"Well, yes, I know Octavia. She is friends with my sister, Annamaria. They work together at the factory. You're Salvo, aren't you?"

Her large eyes stared into his, turning away at just the point of uncomfortable.

"Yep," he gulped, adding in a firmer tone. "That's me."

"I have seen you; you go to the Tabbach bar. You like to sit by the window on your own. You're always so serious. Not usually like this." She smiled as she spoke, directing her words towards Tilda but glancing at Salvo in between.

"Well, I didn't know I had such an avid observer," Salvo defensively remarked.

"Sorry, I didn't mean to offend. It's just nice to see. Men don't always relate to babies. I just wanted to see Octavia and give her these baby clothes from Annamaria," she explained, holding the bag of clothes up as proof.

"She's at work," Salvo replied.

"Oh, okay, erm, well. I will just leave... put them here," she said, placing the bag on the hall table, turning to leave. She concluded with, "Tell her Valentina says hi."

Salvo watched her neat form in a fitted-waisted tweedy jacket and pencil skirt walk towards the door. She looked back at him.

"You know you're quite handsome when you smile."

Valentina's features wore a Mona Lisa expression as she stepped outside and closed the door.

The word "Wait!" unexpectedly escaped Salvo's lips.

Surprise washed over him as he saw her head appearing from around the door, her fingers curled around its edge. Her flawless pale skin highlighted by the natural light filtering in from outside.

"Would you like coffee? I am sure Fina has just brewed some." Salvo tried at being casual, it felt awkward on him.

Valentina responded curtly, "Thank you, but I sense that I have imposed on you enough."

"Look," Salvo sighed heavily. "I would like to have coffee with you. Besides, I need help with Tilda. Being funny is exhausting."

He noticed a smile at her eyes and a slight flicker across her full mouth. Encouraged, he continued.

"I mean, I should stick to being the moody guy. Unbeknown to me girls like it. Even the pretty ones."

He felt relieved as she stepped back into the hall, gently pushing the door closed with her hands behind her back, while her pelvis tipped to click it into the latch.

Valentina casually responded. "I suppose, I could free up some time."

Cool in her demeanour, she kept her internal pleasure hidden. She finally had the chance to spend time with Salvo, the man she had admired from afar for so long.

***

Geno crossed paths with Valentina as he headed to Carlotta's house. He had decided that the walk would be good for him. He liked Valentina; she was appealing with her girlish looks and steely calmness. They exchanged pleasantries in the middle of the street before going their separate ways. Geno bounced along the street, choosing the sunny side, his fedora hat perched on his head. Walking past the shops and bars, he encountered familiar faces and received the occasional honk of recognition from passing cars. Playful shouts from passing vehicles would prompt him to respond with equal enthusiasm, shouting and gesturing back.

With a love for his small town, he revelled in its freedom from war.

He had no intentions of being anywhere else in the world. His desire was to grow old here, surrounded with grandchildren at his knee. The time had come to make a good woman of Carlotta. He considered himself fortunate in life, love, and card games. He flicked the long nail on the little finger of his left hand before reaching into his pocket to check his winnings. He patted his pocket, finding reassurance in what was inside.

Geno stepped into the aging apartment where Carlotta and her mother, who had been a widow for many years, lived. He climbed the uneven stone stairs two at a time, he noticed the dampness present in the building's air, particularly on the caliginous stairwell. An ethereal light stretched out from the opening door. Carlotta in its midst, an angelic glow encircled her. He pulled her in and kissed her with intense passion on the mouth. Crushing the irises, he held onto in his spare hand. His hat was pushed back by the tender moment he shared with his beloved. He lifted his eyes to see his future mother-in-law standing with her arms folded.

Geno gently let Carlotta slide from his clutches. After straightening the folds of her skirt, she raised her hands shyly to cover her mouth. Giving the irises a light shake, he reset their blue and yellow petals.

"Mamma. Flowers for you!" Geno held out his peace offering as he spoke.

"Mmmm. What grave did you get those from."

Instead of refusing the gift, she quickly grabbed them from his outstretched arm. His charm did not soften Mamma's cruel behaviour towards him. Geno possessed a natural talent that allowed him to skilfully leverage life to his benefit, even in challenging situations. He knew today that he would have his work cut out.

"The world is good. Life is good," Geno said aimlessly.

He leaned in towards Carlotta's mother to give her a kiss. He hit an invisible shield of resentment he turned his head to deflect it and strode past her into the lounge, stepping onto the newly washed tiles. Mamma frowned at the marked floor.

"Carlotta, my darling beautiful Carlotta. Come here," beckoned Geno.

"Geno, what are you doing? You're being strange."Carlotta expressed her discomfort.

She entered the room from the hall, taking cautious little steps. Not sure of Geno's unpredictable behaviour.

"Mamma, aren't you busy?" Carlotta hinted.

Geno's dramatic display clearly irked Mamma, she tutted and headed towards the kitchen.

"Mamma can stay. I have something important to say."

Mamma shrugged her broad shoulders and continued to walk away. Geno knew without looking that she had raised her eyes to the heavens. He ignored her body language and persisted. As he bent his knee, he could feel the wetness of the mopped floor soaking into his trouser leg.

"Carlotta, will you be my wife?" Geno spoke, noting that Mamma in the corner of his right eye, had spun around. He continued, reaching for Carlotta's left hand. "Do me the honour and say you will."

With Carlotta's hand in his, Geno took the ring from his pocket and put it on her finger. The ring, a few sizes too large, rotated on her slender finger. Carlotta examined the silver fede ring closely, twisting it around to observe the customary clasped hands carved into the metal, a symbol of love and fidelity.

"Oh my, Geno. It's beautiful. I never believed..."she gasped, shocked by his proposal.

Geno excitedly talked over her, unable to control his enthusiasm. "It's the finest platinum—only the best for my girl. We can go to the jeweller and get it fitted properly. Carlotta, what do you say?"

Geno pushed, retaking her hand and looking into her owl-shaped hazel eyes, now wide with disbelief. Unable to control herself, Mamma grabbed the ring and examined it in the light streaming through the window, even biting it to check the metal for dramatic effect.

"Huh, typical, this is second-hand silver. Where did you get it from?" she scathed, handing the ring back with her wrist dropped as if disposing of rubbish.

"What does it matter?" Ignoring Mamma, Geno continued while

looking into Carlotta's eyes, her pupils blackened with excitement. "I bring you my hand, Carlotta. We can get a different ring." He jutted out his bottom lip to mimic a sad face, his voice affected by the pose.

"If you don't like it," he finished

As Carlotta's giggle faded, he returned to the serious task. He planted a kiss on her hand before clasping it tightly and gazing intensely into her eyes. Revealing a chink of insecurity, he revealed his soul's desire.

"Please, my heart is yours. You are the only one I can give it to."

Mamma, dignified in defeat, handed the ring back. Carlotta immediately placed it back on her finger. She twisted it to face the correct way and held it steady by pressing her other fingers against the ring, inspecting it at the end of her outstretched arm.

"I do like it, and I want to wear it."

Mamma raised her hands in the air and wailed.

"Oh, Mamma, don't be sad. We can live here together," Carlotta said brightly, stepping toward her mother with hopeful earnestness.

Geno was quick to reply. "Carlotta, my love. There is only one bedroom. I want you to be my wife. Do you not see?"

He opened his palms out to her with a dramatic sigh, as though appealing to the heavens.

"Of course. I know that my love."

A shy giggle escaped Carlotta as her fingertips brushed his wrist, the gentle pressure like a silent, handcuff. Upon seeing Mamma's arms fold like iron gates, she coughed softly before continuing her explanation.

"It's just... old Signora Maroni passed away in the flat above us a few weeks ago. It only has two rooms. No bathroom, just a toilet. It wouldn't be suitable for us... But Mamma... if we had this... you could live there. We would be together every day."

Geno felt a twist in his gut, sharp as a bad poker hand. He forced a grin.

"We'd be... so close," he said lightly, though his voice faltered.

Mamma huffed. "Huh, I won't manage the cost of that place on my own."

She sniffed sharply, tilting her chin as if daring him to object. Being close, she could keep an eye on Geno's antics. She toyed with the corner of her apron, her thumb rubbing circles against the worn fabric. Carlotta's hazel eyes sparkled with innocent determination.

"But Mamma, Geno and I can help. These apartments are so old. They are a lot cheaper than if we went somewhere else. Come on, Geno, what do you say?"

Her fingers spun the silver fede ring on her hand, twisting it like a lucky charm.

"You do want this, don't you?" she whispered, her smile softening.

With a weary sigh through his nose, Geno dragged a hand across his face, feeling as resigned as a gladiator thrown to the lions. He could hear the faint drip of water from the leaky sink in the kitchen — each drop an irritating tick in a game he couldn't win. Geno knew that bargaining for Carlotta's hand was going to be tough, but he didn't expect it to have a long-term consequence. Geno looked from mother to daughter and back again. A born gambler, he was figuring out the odds. It was time to fold. He clapped his hands together with sudden, false cheer.

"It's perfect, of course. If that makes you happy," he said, flashing his most dazzling, gambler's smile—the one that never reached his eyes.

For the first time, Mamma's mouth twitched—not quite a smile, but close. Her fingers stilled at the edge of her apron.

The deal for Geno had been a hard one to strike.

36

Friends Reunited

Hal swigged back the last of his cold beer, shaking his head in disbelief.

"Incredible, just incredible," he commented.

"Well, we thought we'd seen a ghost when you showed up," Stan replied, tipping his pint toward Hal.

"Lechyd Da to our not-so-dead friend," chipped in Taffy.

"Had we headed up to Trieste, we might never have known," added Stan.

"Well, you lucky bastards, your demobs are through! You're both heading back to Blighty, leaving me behind yet again!" Chuckled Hal.

"Arr ... yours will come. Man up, you sissy. Teach ya to get your leg blasted. Poor excuse. Who's for another?" Taffy raised his empty glass.

The drinking carried on through the early hours. The drunk and cheerful trio returned to camp to drink more requisitioned German beer with their troop. Most of the men were heading home soon. Train travel through war-torn Europe was slow and arduous, with damaged railways complicating the journey. A lucky few caught a direct sea route on one of the limited ships transporting war heroes back home.

Whichever path they took, soldiers eventually glimpsed the white cliffs of Dover, standing majestic across the English Channel, seagulls circling the skies above. Home at last, they returned to a weary Britain no longer in need of its worn-out armed forces. Each soldier was issued a demob suit, courtesy of Montague Burton. A suit and a stiff upper lip became the prerequisite for civilian life, though war's toll left many uncertain how to fit into the society they had fought to protect. Their lives shattered by war, they came back to Britain, weary and displaced.

After Rome's liberation and Mussolini's execution, the war in Italy seemed to fade, its violent crescendo reduced to a faint purr. The BBC General Forces Programme announced its end with terse finality—brief words that could never capture the brutal campaign's cost. The victory was eclipsed by other equally devastating events across Europe. For these forgotten soldiers, the job was done. Weary and battered, they yearned for home comforts.

The next morning, after a hearty breakfast, Stan and Taffy received departure notices. Returning to their bunks, they stopped to read long-awaited letters. Taffy flicked through his stack, eyes darting across familiar handwriting, absorbing village news from the Welsh valleys. He missed the green of his land, the tranquillity within its hills. With his chin resting in his hand, he read perched on the edge of his bunk. The words escaping under his breath, his lips gently moving. A one-sided conversation with the letter's author.

"Well, that's good news. Looks like me tad has got a job lined up down the pits when I get back," Taffy said, looking up from his letter.

Stan stood silent by the window, hands deep in his pockets. Hal, face full of shaving foam, and razor in his hand, watched through the broken mirror tied to his locker. He noted Stan's tight jaw. Taffy noticed a discarded letter on Stan's bunk.

"Alright there, boyo?" He called.

Hal, still watching, calmly through the mirror, finished his shave. Stan turned slowly, he gave Taffy, a haunting thousand-yard stare at the horizon above his head. In a few strides, he was out the door, letting it swing back on its flimsy hinges behind him.

Hal wiped the foam from his face and picked up the crumpled letter. Taffy joined him, unfolding the letter, the envelope postmarked Southampton, the date a few months ago. The letter's few lines left no room for misinterpretation. Taffy let out a low whistle. Hal reread the last lines, lost for words.

I have met someone else. We are to be married. Please try to understand, it's been so lonely. I never meant this to happen. My ship sails for America tomorrow. I did love you once. Gladys

Taffy bit his lip thoughtfully, eyeing Hal with raised eyebrows. Hal, at a loss for words, had no answers to offer. After all, they'd endured, this was uncharted territory. The door flapped against the outside wall, bending back against its hinges, refocusing their attention. Both men headed out in pursuit of Stan, jointly hesitant. They knew this problem could not be solved as in battle. Whatever the circumstances, they never left a man behind.

Stan hadn't gone far, his average frame deceptively taller due to the raised bank he stood upon. His silhouette crisp against the clear sky. His back turned, staring out towards the jagged outline of mountains in the distance. Taffy, who was pacing ahead, pulled a step back behind Hal at the sight of Stan. Hal pushed him forward with a large hand to the small of his back. Taffy shrugged his shoulders and shook his head to convey his reluctance. Inept in his counsel. Stan tilted his head, aware of the shuffle of feet on stony ground.

"That you, Taff?" Stan asked without turning.

"Yeah, it's me."

"And lofty?" Hal said.

"Who else's bloody, great, noisy feet?" Taffy replied.

Stan dropped his head down, he let it bounce back with a snort.

"I guess you both know?" Stan directed his voice out to the mountains.

"Yeah, well..." Hal began.

"No secrets in this place. What a bitch," backed Taffy.

"Yeah, my fiancée," Stan carried on, oblivious to their comments. "The one real thing, throughout this shitty war. Stringing me along. Huh, for months. Pitying me, I bet. I took it for granted throughout this that Gladys would be there waiting for me at the end of the line.

Now, what's there to go home to?"

"C'mon, mate, she ain't worth it. It's a right kick in the teeth. I can't deny that. Life doesn't come without pain. We got through this so we could start living." New adventures, eh?" Hal attempted to offer some optimism.

"Yeah, right. Now all I wanna do when I get back is shoot down every bleeding GI Joe that crosses my path." Stan spat out his final words, wanting to remove the unpleasant taste his thoughts left him with.

"Understandable," Taffy breathed.

I mean, what's left to go back to? Glorious England? A shattered town, no job, no girl... over half my twenties lost... for what? What did any of this achieve!" Stan bellowed into the darkening sky.

Silence met his cries. He let his tears fall. They stood with eyes fixed on his turned back, their feet rooted to the spot, tongues still. They were unable to comfort him, their actions felt clumsy and ineffectual. Stan's pain was raw, a fresh wound slashed across his soul. A strangled plea escaped Stan's lips, each word a painful effort, his body shaking as he begged to be left alone.

Later that day, Hal and Taffy approached the captain's desk with heavy steps and stood at ease upon his instructions. Without a word, he slid a folded note across to them allowing them to read it before adding.

"I believe this is intended for both of you. We found it next to the body."

Stan's familiar, precise handwriting etched in his final words: *So long, fellas. This world isn't worth fighting for anymore.*

37

Starry Night

From her spot on the terrace, nestled on the sloping terracotta-tiled roof, Fi had a 360-degree view of the night sky's stellar ceiling. Fi experienced a sense of complete unity with the sky, as if her being had become absorbed into its vastness. The stars were abundant that evening, each competing for its place in its liquid inkiness. Fi immersed herself in the euphoric calmness of the moment.

As a child, Hal had shown her the wonders of the skies. Memories of him flooded back, coursing through her veins and landing in her heart. The flask of cocoa on wintry school nights. Charting the stars together at the garden's far end, standing on the oblong of earth that Hal called the old carriage patch. The warmth of childhood reached into her bones, raising goosebumps on her skin.

Fi located the landmark she'd been searching for in the northern hemisphere. Ursa Major shone brightly above. Following the handle of the constellation's saucepan shape, she located the middle star. With a soft "There you are," she blew a kiss toward the heavens, aiming it at Ottie's star. Two stars along, she found Little Nanny's star—Hal's mother's—chosen by Hal and Fi after she passed.

Fi had been just four years old then. She clung to her few but vivid memories of Little Nanny. Arthritis had bent her nearly in half, reducing her average height. Her curled-up posture made her seem smaller than she really was. Before Fi was born, Hal had won the football pools—four hundred pounds, enough to buy the house next door. Number thirteen became Little Nanny's home, where she could have her privacy and independence. She was known for her passion for books and her calm yet firm personality. Fi looked forward to her daily visits with Ottie, who brought her lunch on a tray, the food mashed so she could eat with her two remaining front teeth.

Little Nanny's fall marked the end of those visits. Hal discovered her at the foot of the stairs. Fi remembered Hal's heart-wrenching screams over the fence, piercing into the back door. A missing fence panel between the two back gardens allowed quick entry. When Ottie heard Hal, she ran into Little Nanny's house. Nella held Fi back, stopping her from following. They stood by the back door, waiting for news.

They saw the ambulance. Fi refused to leave the doorway, unable to understand why she couldn't see Little Nanny. She wanted to sit on the rug in her front room and play with the ornamental dogs from the mantelpiece. Her legs ached, and she needed the loo. She focused on her blue velvet slippers, their plastic teddy bears fuzzing in her teary gaze. Warm urine escaped down her legs, a puddle formed beneath her. Nella's arms enveloped her, offering comfort in her warm embrace.

Nella coaxed Fi away with the promise of a sneaky ice cream from the chest freezer in the hall. A lace tablecloth draped over it, a futile attempt to disguise it as furniture. Nella cleaned up Fi and the dampened floor before slotting a rectangular block of yellow ice cream into a matching square cone. They sat together patiently, waiting on the back step. The arrival of the long black Batmobile fuelled Fi's hope that superheroes might intervene. She couldn't understand why it made Nella so sad.

***

Fi's eyes searched the sky. She quickly found the North Star, the brightest of them all—Hal's star. The moment had arrived. Fi fought to find another excuse, another reason to delay. She cast her mind back to earlier that day. Fi had held the locket close to Zia Nari's face, letting it swing gently from its fragile chain. Nari reached out, snatching it mid-swing.

"What have you here?" she enquired, searching for her spectacles.

"It's a locket. I think it must be yours. I found it when I was sorting through Nonna's things."

Zia Nari's shoulders tensed before she replied, "Surely not." Inspecting the locket's delicately scrolled casing, she glanced at her pensive niece.

"You inherited your grandmother's nosiness, you know that?" Nari tweaked Fi's nose. "Open it for me!"

Nari's cheeks flushed with excitement. Fi complied, watching Zia Nari scrutinise her younger self through her glasses perched on her nose.

"Well, well," she remarked, peering at Fi over her spectacles, a mischievous smile playing on her lips. "I was quite a looker back then."

"You sure were, Zia," Fi smiled, pushing harder with the burning question in her heart. "Could you tell me who that young man is?"

Zia Nari snapped the locket shut, her eyes drifting to the horizon before lowering them to caress the locket resting in her lap.

"He was my first love. I had to let him go... It was never easy. We had to keep it all so, oh, so under wraps. Papa would have beaten me to hell and back." Zia Nari observed the pity in Fi's expression before she continued. "Funnily enough, it turned out to be the right thing. I found out later I wasn't the only girl...At the time, it hurt. Love can be cruel."

She placed the locket in Fi's hand and clasped her fingers around it.

"Here, take it. You can have it. Tavi... I mean your Nonna... she would have wanted you to have it. I gave Tavi the locket to keep safe for me until I asked for it back. Well, I never asked, and here it is, so much time has passed since that day, my Fiamma."

"But Zia, what was his name?"

"His name? Ohhh, now .... that can stay in the past. That's the best place for him. Some things should be blown away. They are a part of us, but they don't define us. I have much more past now than I have future. So, let's just keep to today and what a day of surprises it has been. My English rose has come to see me. You, God willing, have so much time ahead of you. Look ahead and stop asking so many questions about the past! Now follow me. I have a surprise, especially for you!"

Zia Nari took Fi into her spare bedroom, now a study with a large computer screen. Pausing before opening the door, Zia Nari leaned on her walking frame to catch her breath. Her chin lifted as she gestured for Fi to enter.

"This is your reality. You must start to live again and not hide."

To Fi's surprise, Agatha and Edith's expectant faces appeared on the large computer screen as she entered the room. They yelled joyfully upon seeing their mother. Fi was speechless for a moment. Zia Nari gently closed the door behind them. They were too busy chatting and laughing to notice her. Fi promised to be home soon. She had arranged to cook them a roast, their favourite comfort food. The girls blew goodbye kisses, their faces frozen in animated expressions, until they vanished from the screen. Her heart sank; she missed the life they breathed into her world. She lingered for a moment, fingertips grazing the blank screen, wishing she could hold on just a little longer.

***

Fi could pontificate no longer. A sense of calm washed over her as she let go of the past and embraced the present. The middle star, Alnilam, blazed brightly in Orion's belt. She designated the star to Quin, its distant light a beacon in the vast, inky blackness. Tears welled as it was time to say goodbye, a lump forming in her throat. Under the night sky, she let him join the others, her soft farewell carried away on the breeze.

"I love you," she breathed to the heavens. She echoed his final words back to him.

"I thought I might find you up here." A familiar voice took her from her dreams.

Luca was standing nearby. He held his hand out towards her and stretched across the balcony railings. His gold watch caught in the moonlight against his hirsute arm.

"Come, cousin, it's been far too long," he said, his white teeth flashing against his olive skin.

Fi swung herself over the railing into her cousin's arms. Having not seen each other in years, their conversation was filled with excited chatter. They chopped and changed, catching up in chunks, forward and backward in time.

"Come, let's take a walk, like the old days, eh?" Luca offered, when they had exhausted their news.

"Will you pay for the gelatos like you used to?" Fi grinned.

Luca gave an affirmative, the answer coming from his near black, ever-changing, eyes. Arm in arm, they strolled along the seafront towards the beach, passing palm trees and parks filled with families enjoying their evening walk. They came away from the tourist stretch and headed onto the concrete squares that tumbled into the sea, gigantic wave breakers piled up against each other. Fi climbed downwards towards the edge of the water. She removed her shoes and dangled her feet into the sea. The salt dried on her calves with each wave that licked across her legs. Luca stood above her, his jumper tied casually across his shoulders. Its sleeves whipping upwards in the sea breeze.

"You know, your grandfather liked to come here."

Their gaze drifted across the bay to Salerno, its lights shimmering in the water's reflection. High-pitched giggles of children at play, carried on the gentle sea breeze, combined with the calming susurrus of waves harmonious symphony. Small, brightly painted fishing boats, their hulls gently rocking, danced with the waves.

"Yes," Luca continued, half to himself. "He told me it reminded him of his first sighting of Italy, when he landed on the beaches not far from here, not knowing what to expect."

Luca paused momentarily and kicked an imaginary stone with the edge of his shoe.

"During the war, he found himself a wife. I bet he never saw that coming!"

"I bet," laughed Fi. "I am so grateful that he found her."

"Well, you wouldn't be here, and I would have saved myself a fortune in ice cream over the years!"

Fi attempted to splash water at her cheeky cousin. She failed and instead, soaked herself, much to his entertainment. The years apart had dissolved, there was a comfort between them that could only be born over a lifetime. Fi clambered up the rocks, straightening herself up next to Luca. He remained steadfast and straight-backed, looking across at his town, his chest puffed out with pride. He was part of the land he scaled.

"Mamma told me how lonely she felt when Zia Octavia left for England. She cried every night at the extra space in the bed between her and Zia Fina. You would think she would have been grateful for the room. But no, she would have slept on the floor if it meant her return. In time, she understood why Zia Octavia went. She went to forge her own path, a path you now share with her." He turned, his stare focused directly on Fi's silver eyes. "We're shaped by both the past and the present—you and me. It's all part of who we become."

He moved closer and nodded in the direction of the shoreline.

"Come on, let's take a walk on the beach." Luca pointed across the bay. "The gelateria at the end has the best pistachio ice cream. Is that still your favourite?"

"You bet," Fi replied.

She took Luca's arm to steady herself over the jagged rocks. They strolled onto the beach, keeping their arms linked, heading to the lights radiating across from Salerno in the distance. The full moon hung low, half-dipped in the sea on the horizon's edge. They stopped to throw pebbles, skimming them across the moon's watery path. Walking barefoot along the water's edge, the cold water hit their ankles, making them squeal. Their footprints trailed behind them before they were washed away with each wave.

"Are you ready to go home?" Asked Luca.

"Yes, I think so," answered Fi. After a pause, she added, "No more trains, though."

Luca raised an eyebrow, then rolled his eyes. He placed his

palms together and shook them at her in a local questioning gesture, signifying why.

"Planes are easier, don't you think?" Fi replied, letting out a yelp as he poked at her ribs.

They walked further, each stride bringing them closer towards the gelateria. Salerno bustled with life, just a hair's breadth away from them.

38

Matchsticks

Hal let the soft bristles glide through her tresses, the brush sliding down towards her waist. The smooth strands shimmered like silk beneath his fingertips, warm and soft to the touch. As the light fell on Ottie's waves, her hair shimmered a deep indigo. Content with the completion of his nightly chore, Hal set the hairbrush down. He glanced into Tilda's cot, positioned close to the bed. As she slept soundly, he traced his finger across her cheek, captivated by the soft, peach-like feel.

"Careful, you'll wake her. I just put her down." Ottie scolded him softly, brandishing the hairbrush in his direction.

Hal watched her move across the room, her white linen nightdress skimming across the floor, its material meeting with her curves as she moved. He stroked his hand along the length of her hair, letting his fingers rest at the ends.

"Are you sure you want to get it cut off? It is so long and lovely. Promise me you will keep it for me," he urged.

"When you let me know, you are back in England, I will post it to you," she promised.

"Are you going to come over to England in pieces?" Hal ribbed.

They both chuckled, pausing with the murmur coming from Tilda's cot, a gentle rock, as she rolled over. Hal embraced Ottie tightly, his chin resting on her head.

"I can't wait to start our life together back home," he whispered into her hair.

"Tell me what it's like," Ottie asked.

"What again?" As he spoke, Hal held her at arm's length, then drew her in for a bear hug. "Don't you get fed up hearing about it?" He added with a smile.

"No, never. I can't imagine what it will be like—my new home. Tell me about where we will live. Please, Hal, tell me."

Hal feigned annoyance with a momentary frown. He guided her to the edge of the bed, where they sat side-by-side, the springs groaning under their weight. Ottie sat with clasped hands, waiting patiently.

"Well, it's er... nice, we are quite near the harbour, number eleven is at the top end of our street. There's a pub on the corner called the Brown Bear. Lovely old pub with flint stone walls and a great big fire burning away in the winter. Landlady pulls a nice pint, too." Hal paused, looking into her dark eyes wide open with interest. "On the other side is a corner shop. Old Mrs Wilson runs it. Funny ole gal. Never seen her without a hairnet and her blue pinny on. Her shop sells everything and anything. Cor, she must be hundred and two, if not a day."

Looking off into the distance, he thought back to England, a place that seemed worlds away, the home he had left long ago. He missed the sea breeze cutting through the harbour streets and the comforting glow of the pub's hearth on winter nights. Yet, a dull ache of uncertainty crept in—would the life he imagined still be waiting for him, or had time reshaped it into something unrecognisable? Would it be the same? He was no longer the same. How could it be? How could he be? His thoughts were broken by Ottie shoving his arm.

"The house, Hal. I want to hear about our house," she asked, impatience at the tip of her tongue.

Hal ran his hand over the back of his head, heaved a heavy sigh, and let the air slowly escape, weighed down by the uncertainty of the future. He longed for the comfort of familiar shores but feared how much might have changed—or worse, how much he might have.

"Huh, well, it's just a three up, two down kinda place."

Ottie continued to peer at him expectantly. Hal felt a swell of tenderness, mingled with guilt for the uncertain future he couldn't promise her. He wanted to be her sanctuary, but his words felt like paper boats tossed onto a stormy sea.

"Well ... I dunno. It's got a long garden down to the railroad. There's an old railway carriage at the bottom of our garden."

Hal took both Ottie's hands in one of his large hands and wrapped his fingers around them.

"We could always fix it up and live there if we don't want to stay with Mother in the house. I could fix some pipes around it and make a heating system." His voice grew with excitement.

"I really hope Mother likes me," Ottie said.

"Well, you're certainly different. She ain't come across many foreigners before."

"Could we grow vegetables and get some chickens? It will feel more like home then."

"Yeah, I guess. Sure, why not? Don't know what Bonnie will make of it. Chase the chickens all about the place she will."

Hal lolled his tongue and held his hands out as if begging, as he mimicked a mad dog. For a fleeting moment, their laughter filled the room, a bright contrast to the heavy shadow of his impending departure. She playfully slapped his arm, bursting into laughter as she flopped onto the bed. Hal adjusted his position to get a better look at her. Ottie lay with her arms stretched above her head, her inky hair contrasted against the white linen. His eyes travelled to the soft curve of her eyebrows, then to the tiny dimple in her chin. He sought to imprint the moment into his soul, keeping it safe until he saw her once more.

"My Ottie, *mia cara*," he let the words come out with gentle affection." I have to go back."

Hal observed a small frown appear on Ottie's face as she propped herself up on her elbows, one hand resting on the growing curve of her belly.

"You won't forget us, will you? As she spoke, she held his gaze and looked down at her stomach.

"Never." Came his quick reply, devoid of hesitation, as he leaned across and kissed her.

Hal shut the door softly as he left, the still air heavy with silence, broken only by the quiet creak of the old floorboards beneath his feet. In the semi-dark of the landing, he made out the shape of Fina and Nari huddled together on the top step. The pair had been waiting outside for Hal to leave so they could join Ottie in their big bed. Nari, fast asleep, had curled herself up and put her head in Fina's lap. Fina, also asleep, had slumped forward, her head resting against the wall. Holding onto the railing, Hal gingerly navigated the narrow stairway, trying not to wake the sleeping pair. Free from the human obstacles, he quietly took the next step and heard the loud creak under his foot.

"Hal."

The voice of Fina landed at his back. Hal turned his head towards her. Fina's face became visible as his eyes adjusted to the dim light, and she gave him a small, sad smile.

"Safe journey," she whispered.

Hal acknowledged with a quiet "thank you" and a dip of his head.

Nari stirred on Fina's lap.

"Look after her when she gets to you. She is precious, you know." Fina added.

"I promise. I will." Hal replied, his voice thick with emotion.

As Hal reached the bottom of the stairs, he noticed the kitchen light spilling its gentle luminescence into the hallway. The light on the floor flickered as a shadow passed by. With a push, he opened the door. Papa was sitting at the far end of the table, shuffling cards, a miniature glass nearby containing the thick yellow Strega liqueur. He lifted his glass and toasted Hal.

"Come drink with me," he bid.

Hal stepped into the kitchen, did as Papa requested, and helped himself to a drink before he joined him at the table. Papa continued to shuffle the cards methodically. Hal took a sip. He instinctively placed his hand at his throat as the sweet, strong taste of the Strega burned down into his stomach.

"Good, eh!" grinned papa. "Right then, let us play. Get the matches out of the draw."

Hal looked puzzled.

"Tonight, we play for matchsticks," Papa said. "I can't take money from my son-in-law."

Papa mocked with a shrug of his shoulders.

Hal scraped his chair back as he rose, arching an eyebrow. He looked at Papa sceptically before speaking.

"I see that you're convinced you will beat me."

"Do you feel lucky then boy?" Papa laughed, eyes twinkling.

"Yes, I do. I am far, far luckier than many."

Later that evening, Hal stepped over the small fence into the orange grove for the last time. A broad grin spread across his face as he reached into his pocket for the matchsticks. Moonlight filtered through the branches, illuminating his path, while the stars shone brightly overhead. He stopped to take in the canopy and wondered if his life was a course marked by the stars. His current life was a far cry from what he expected. He felt so alive. Stan entered his thoughts, how easily life could be broken. He had lost a brother in arms, needlessly gone, when they were so close to the finishing line.

39

Last Words

Fi placed her pen down and shifted back into her seat. She looked out the window, a layer of wispy clouds obscured her view. Her ears popped from the gentle descent of the plane. She folded the piece of paper neatly and placed it in her bag. Fi pictured Quin reading it. She conjured up his face in her mind. She struggled to recall his features sometimes.

My Darling Quin

Well, I made it to Italy. Not a far-flung traveller like you, I know, but a fair attempt, don't you think? I am sure you would have been amused by my adventures. I wish you had been there with me. It broke me seeing you fade away like that, and there was nothing I could do to change it. I believed you were returning, if anyone could have found a way back to me, it would be you. Nonna's death made things even harder. I'd sacrifice anything, even climb mountains, to have you both back. I wish I could. I just wanted you back, even if it was just for a moment. I believed my travels would make me closer to you and Nonna. I guess, in some ways, it did. Neither of you left my side the entire trip.

It's been quite a trip, covering so much ground and encountering so many different people. All an attempt to feel closer to you. It feels like a lot more than miles. I couldn't see a life without you. We had so many plans.

Everything we did was filled with your boundless love and enthusiasm. I guess I have a different life now, one where I carry you with me. We don't get to grow old together. You are with me in my soul.

I miss the feeling of your arms around me, your infectious laugh, and your upbeat attitude. Your unique approach to every problem. Thank you for the love we shared and the strength you still give me. I was without hope, and things needed to change. I embrace that change now. Just like Nonna did all those years ago when she arrived in England. It feels a bit scary, but that's good, right? You thrived on taking risks and achieving success. Sometimes making mistakes. It never seemed to phase you. I realise that without doing that, life is pretty mediocre. I am going to embrace things more and see where it all takes me. I'm considering a trip to New York. An art exhibition there has sparked my interest.

I love you always
Fi xxx

40

To England

The trip to the station with Ottie and her group had become a real expedition. Navigating crowds, managing luggage, and calming anxious chatter. She was surrounded by family and friends on the busy platform, Papa's absence painfully obvious. They had parted from each other with harsh words. Ottie had struggled to remain amiable as her father rebuked her with a coldness in his eyes that hit below freezing. She looked beyond the crowd with an incredulous hope that she might see his figure, a last-minute change of heart.

His words came back to strike her once more, his tongue much harsher than his hand. He had told her in no uncertain terms that she had chosen her path, caused discredit to her family and, no matter the circumstances she faced in England, her home was there now, and Italy was her past. She had stared defiantly at him, fuelled by the memory of every harsh dismissal and unmet expectation that had defined their strained relationship. Papa's countenance was unyielding at the terminus of their cachectic relationship. Indignation welled from within her. She held it together, using every fibre not to strike back at his words, and cordially gave him her blessings before she allowed herself to storm off.

Little Tilda was passed between the family gathering that encircled Ottie. Enjoying the attention, Tilda's chuckles echoed up to the station's high ceiling and joined the babble of background noise. Ottie watched with amusement as her daughter, perched on Geno's shoulders, giggled with delight as he galloped her around the platform.

"Father material," commented Salvo with a sideways glance towards Carlotta.

Geno appeared in earshot, florid and breathing hard from the exertion of entertaining his niece. He dipped down for Salvo to take Tilda from his shoulders.

"Well, let's see how Zio Salvo compares," Geno quipped.

Carlotta opened her arms, inviting Ottie in. They bid their goodbyes with multiple kisses on the cheeks. Statuesque Mina, with her fiery auburn hair piled up in an elegant chignon, planted a ruby-red kiss onto Ottie's forehead. Her husband Paolo, pint-sized in comparison, offered his handkerchief to wipe away his wife's lipstick. Their sons ran around on the platform chasing each other, knocking into passers-by, and being chastised by their parents. Excited by the atmosphere, their parent's discipline fell on deaf ears.

A piercing whistle announced the train's arrival as it pulled into the station. Tearful goodbyes became imminent. Fina, the first in line, was still fussing over her little sister, ensuring she had the food parcel and warm coat ready for when she arrived in England. Salvo stepped in and reminded Fina that she wasn't heading to Siberia. Ottie laughed at her brother's joke, their laughter ceased abruptly as their eyes met. Salvo hesitated before breaking the mood by embracing Ottie with full force.

He whispered close to her ear. "No matter what the distance, we are all here for you. We are family forever linked."

Salvo's usual sangfroid evaded him, his composure cracking just enough to reveal the depth of his care, laid bare in the tightness of his embrace and the faint tremor in his voice. Geno, more animated in his approach, deflected with humour. He commented on Ottie's short hairstyle; she would fit in already, like a local, he joked, as he tried to emulate his interpretation of a well-to-do English housewife. Finally, he took her hand to plant a kiss on it with a charismatic bow of his head. Nari squeezed in front of him, tears flowing, too distraught for words. She held tightly onto Ottie.

"Be good, little sister."

Ottie uttered with her head nestled on Nari's shoulder. Pulling back, Nari reached over Ottie's head and placed a locket around her neck.

"Look after this for me. Keep it safe. Please don't forget about me," Nari pleaded.

"How could I ever?" Ottie said, opening the locket.

She gazed upon her sister's picture and raised her eyebrows to see Marco Fragopane on the opposite side. Nari hushed Ottie with a finger on her lips, her wide, tear-filled eyes silently pleading for understanding while her trembling hand betrayed the depth of her emotion.

"Say nothing; we Matanti women cannot control our heart's desire."

They exchanged knowing glances.

"Oh Nari, be careful."

Ottie gave Nari a kiss on the head before letting her go. She moved her gaze and nodded an acknowledgement towards Anna, whom she had noticed standing a step back from the crowd. Her gratitude for Anna's solid advice could not be conveyed in a glance; she hoped she knew.

Ottie boarded the train, taking the luggage from her brothers as they passed the misshapen, twine-bound suitcases. With difficulty, she hauled them up onto the train. Fina held onto Tilda as long as she could, nuzzling into her neck to retain her scent. Ottie extended her arm to receive the last case being passed across the threshold. Her arm jolted as a firm grip clamped down on her forearm. The recognisable, solid square hand held on to her. She traced upwards along the hairy muscular arm, finishing at the strong jaw with a resting scowl, to find the face of Papa.

"Goodbye, my little lion heart." Papa said, his voice firm, like granite worn by time, revealing strength forged through hardship.

His vacuous vainglory absent, he pulled her from the train. She felt his physical strength as he placed her firmly into the nook of his arm. His feigned indifference lay wide open. He took her chin hard in his hand and focused on her eyes.

"Be as strong as I know you are," he said, his voice, thick with emotion.

Ottie felt the familiar ache of longing swell in her chest. A bittersweet recognition of the love he fought so hard to conceal yet could not suppress. She could no longer stem her tears. Ottie let them fall freely. "Thank you, Papa." Ottie forced the words past the lump in her throat. The train kicked into motion, she reached for Tilda. Papa firmly closed the door as it pulled away from the platform. Ottie watched her bundle of relatives' wave and shout as the train picked up speed. Papa stood prominently, his solid frame unyielding, arms folded, rooted to the spot. Nari, in her favourite scarlet dress, ran along the side of the train until she could no longer keep up with it, her outstretched arms reaching desperately as though willing the train to stop. Ottie pressed her hand to the window, overcome by a wave of loss as the distance grew, leaving only the fading blur of red against the grey platform. The bright material Nari wore was a beacon against the dullness of the station. Nari reached the end of the platform, jumping and waving, shouting words that Ottie could no longer hear. Ottie watched the red speck grow smaller until she disappeared. She focused on the empty space her sister had occupied. A lump formed in her throat once more.

She located her seat and was aided by fellow passengers to store her luggage. Heavily pregnant with a toddler in her arms on a rocking train, she was grateful not to have to lift the bulky cases overhead—a laborious task made harder by balancing a child on her hip and the constraints of her pregnancy. Ottie watched as the landscape of a territory she knew slipped away. Vesuvius's imposing form loomed on the horizon. She left its shadow and headed towards Rome—the furthest she had ever travelled.

Past Rome, the landscape felt different. The spaces between buildings and the countryside lengthened. The scars of war were evident throughout her journey. The land was damaged beyond recognition, like a cancerous growth that had been ripped out of the soil—its evidence seen in bomb craters, tumbling buildings, and the haunting faces of broken people. The cost of liberation had not come without pain. She was leaving Italy, an injured country, at the start of its rehabilitation.

The train halted, waiting for its cue to pass through to the next station. She caught sight of the Leaning Tower of Pisa. Excitedly, she pointed it out to a disinterested Tilda, who was now becoming bored and starting to grizzle. She gave her some of Fina's bread, still warm from the early morning bake, its smell bringing back images of home—the only place she had ever known.

With every revolution of the train's wheels, she moved closer to a house she had never seen before, leaving her known world behind. Panic washed over her, and her babies kicked, sensing the change in her heartbeat. Her hand caressed her swollen belly. Two heartbeats announced by the midwife were a secret she saved just for Hal. Hal was going to be in England waiting for her. He had to be.

The train was stifling, the seats were uncomfortable, and it was crowded with people. They headed into the mountains, the night sky seeping slowly down towards them. Tilda was asleep on her lap, and Ottie eventually drifted off too.

The trip across Europe was not a direct route. Zigzagging across the land, the train used the surviving tracks that hadn't been destroyed. Each time, she had to disembark, navigate herself, Tilda, and their cumbersome luggage. The persistent confusion and chaos had a negative impact on Tilda, turning her usual contentment into misery. They were forced to endure cramped spaces on stuffy, overcrowded carriages, often standing for hours in the oppressive heat generated by the packed human bodies. The unfamiliar routine made it hard to comfort Tilda. Ottie had no choice but to tolerate the arduous journey. She had put all her faith in the man she was heading towards.

Exhausted after two long nights and seemingly interminable days, she found herself at the Paris station, waiting for the train that would take her to Calais. She boarded the train, ready to take the ferry across to England. It was much quieter than the other trains, half-empty. No longer did she hear the tongues of her country folk, she felt alone for the first time. She sat opposite an English soldier, the uniform reminded her of Hal. He caught her looking at him, and his face broke into a smile.

Tilda reached out towards him. He took her hand and shook it playfully. "Hey, little un," he chirped.

He played peekaboo, much to Tilda's delight. Ottie and the soldier grew more intrigued by their fellow traveller as the journey progressed. They communicated through a blend of gestures and the few Italian phrases the soldier had picked up during his time in Italy. When she showed him Hal's picture, he studied it but didn't recognise him. He offered a warm smile, remarking that she had chosen a handsome Englishman with a twinkle in his blue eyes.

Ottie found the soldier's smile charming, particularly the gap in his front tooth. Through their fragmented conversation, she learned his name was Sid and discovered he was headed home to London. He chuckled when she struggled to pronounce his name with her accent. His amusement faded briefly as he mentioned that his family home had been obliterated during the Blitz, a quiet sorrow lingering behind his cheerful facade.

"Yeah, I got no ouse to go too. Even me dads barra got nicked. No work or ome. Thiefin gits bad as your bleedin' lot," the soldier remarked, slipping between black humour and bitterness.

Ottie smiled politely, having not understood a word he had said, a blank expression in her eyes.

As darkness descended, they reached Calais and sought refuge near the docks for the night. They snatched fragmented moments of sleep among their luggage in the drafty waiting room. Ottie felt grubby and worn down. It had been three days without a proper wash or change of clothes. Her dwindling food supply weighed heavily on her mind—she had given most of what remained to Tilda, leaving herself perpetually hungry and exhausted.

Sid, the soldier with the blue, twinkly eyed smile, had offered to share his chocolate with them. The sugar hit helped her fight off the fatigue that kept overcoming her in steady waves. She cradled Tilda in her arms. Gently, she removed the brown remnants of leftover chocolate from under the whites of her half-crescent fingernails. The sleeping, somewhat sticky, Tilda lay flopped across her lap, eventually giving in after twenty minutes of non-stop crying. Overtired and still hungry, she had suckled at her mother's breast between squirms and squeals before taking one last gasp, her head heavy with sleep falling backwards across the ridge of Ottie's forearm. A droplet of milk at the corner of her curled pink mouth. A layer of grime was visible in the chubby folds of her exposed neck. As Tilda drifted deeper into sleep, her head felt heavy against Ottie's arm. Ottie bore the discomfort, grateful that she had some peace at last.

Dawn broke, the sun's rays, soft and warm, seeped into the room, illuminating the floor and reaching out towards her. Ottie stepped outside the door to get some fresh air. The bundle of linen holding a sleeping Tilda in its midst, safely at the corner of her eye. She scanned the landscape. Tumbling remnants of coastal fortifications stretched across the beach of the war-torn French town. Nature was reclaiming the land, with concrete pillboxes covered in seagull droppings and abandoned machinery being swallowed by the golden sand. Out to sea, the grey sky moulded in with the silver tones of the sea. The only detection of where the sea and sky joined was the growing dot of a ship coming towards Calais on the horizon.

41

Seeking Hal

The ship carved through the soft mist of the morning as it gradually lifted off the sea. A fine drizzle held its ground, while a fleeting burst of sunshine briefly broke through the heavy clouds. Ottie felt a penetrating chill in the cold damp air, reminiscent of her mountain adventures with Papa. She took in the scene of England's magnificent white chalk cliffs, noting the earthy scalp at the top, layered with dark mud and topped with grass. The imposing cliffs descended dramatically towards the sea, where grey water swirled and crashed against their corrugated chalk formations. A natural world dichotomy of the seascape that she was familiar with. There was no familiarity. She saw no pastel-coloured houses tumbling down from the land towards the azure Mediterranean Sea.

Ottie felt a sharp jolt as the ship came to a halt in the harbour. She had observed the town getting closer. She could distinguish the letters on the shop signs, but the words remained a mystery. The harbour curved around the bay. A myriad of colourful boats dipped against the surge of the incoming ship. The crank of metal thundered through the vessel as its doors were opened. She tightened her coat around her, feeling the sharpness of the breeze, the coldness heightened by her body's need for warm food. Tilda huddled close in her arms, her little head raised upwards, frequently rotating from side to side, curious at the sights she could see around her. Sid came to Ottie's aid and helped her with her luggage as she stepped out onto English soil. The concrete felt hard against her lightly soled shoes. Ottie's gaze swept across the unfamiliar town, searching for any sign of Hal. A small family group had gathered to welcome their loved one home. There wasn't anyone else waiting. Panic started to rise inside of her. Hal's address was clutched tightly in her hand.

"You alright, love?" asked Sid, noticing the whites of her eyes increase as she began frantically searching for Hal.

Ottie shook her head, then passed the paper to Sid.

"Where is he?" she asked in her native language, frustrated by her lack of English.

Sid reviewed Hal's instructions, a smile spreading across his face as he noticed the figures drawn on the note's margins.

"You're on the wrong side. He wants you to meet him near the jetty by the clock house." Sid reiterated, gesturing toward the jetty. "Over there, the other side. C'mon, I will take ya."

He swung his kitbag over his shoulder and grabbed her bulky cases, lifting them with ease. He flicked his head towards the jetty to signal the way. Ottie followed in his footsteps past the brick archways at the harbour's edge. The docks were alive with activity, as sailors worked on their nets and hawked their morning catch. The salty air of the sea stung her nostrils. She walked along the road, half skipping to keep up with Sid's strides. The wintry wind rolling in from the coast nudged her inland with its strength. The sleepy town began to stir as shops opened for business. The words, spoken in a language she couldn't understand, drifted towards her from across the street.

Ottie's chest tightened as her gaze swept the bustling quay. An unsettling thought crept in—had something gone wrong? Was she too late?

They arrived at the clock house, a square slate-grey building with a four-sided clock tower at the centre of its roof. The bronze clock faces pointed both outward towards the world and inward towards Ramsgate, keeping time for the folk both on land and at sea. Sid placed the luggage in the arch of the building's door and rubbed his hands to bring the blood back into them. He blew his warm breath onto his palms.

"Bit parky, ain't it just. You gonna be alright, love?"

He stroked Tilda's head as he spoke. Ottie nodded, feeling a twinge of sadness that her aid was going.

"All the best in ya new life, darlin,"

Sid took hold of her hand, his grip firm. The sparkle in his eyes reminded her of Hal.

"E tu," Ottie paused. "Gooda bya, Sido," she finished with an embarrassed laugh.

Her attempt to speak English drew a smile from him. As he walked away, Tilda and Ottie waved and watched him vanish across the other side of the street.

Ottie swiftly surveyed the empty courtyard in front of the clock house, then proceeded to sweep her gaze up and down the street. The town was still relatively quiet, and the early morning activities were just beginning. Hal was nowhere to be seen. She felt the void left by her family and longed for their presence. She yearned for her past life.

For a moment, the weight of her journey pressed heavily on her. England wasn't home, but it was where Hal was—or should have been.

The mist clung to the sea's edge, advancing onto the shore. She kept losing visibility as it fell and rose in whirls. Gentle flakes of snow drifted down. Neither Ottie nor Tilda had ever encountered snow before. Tilda held out her hands to catch the snowflakes, letting them melt on her palms. Ottie brushed a flake from her round, velvety cheek. In a fit of hopeless hysteria, she threw back her head and laughed, letting the increasing snowflakes fall into her mouth. Tilda copied her mother, they chuckled as they hung onto each other.

A single chime from the clock above indicated it was half past the hour. Ottie wasn't certain how long she had been there. It felt as though she had wasted a lifetime waiting alone. It didn't matter. She had minutes, hours, months, and years ahead of her. England was her destination. Where she would start a life with her soulmate, the man she felt an unbreakable bond with. The pull was so strong she was destined to end up in this cold foreign land searching for him. Despite what happened now, she knew this moment would always be where she was meant to be.

Tilda screamed loudly, and Ottie followed suit. They screamed up towards the heavens to the snow that was now cascading down in a heavy flurry and covering them. Ottie spun Tilda around and held her warm body tight against her, seeking comfort in her daughter's giggles. She paused mid-swing, catching a brief flicker of a figure in the corner of her eye.

It was barely discernible through the patches of mist and falling snow. The person was steadily moving towards her. They possessed the same tall, broad-shouldered build and familiar gait as Hal. His thick hair was longer and fell onto his collar, the snow settling on him, the white snowflakes a stark contrast against his black hair. He wore a corded brown jacket, and a scarf knotted at his throat.

Hal paused for a brief second before he saw her. His pace picked up, soon breaking into a run. Ottie felt her legs move towards him before her mind had caught up. They collided at the courtyard's edge, folding arms tightly around each other, laughter combined with falling tears.

"Ottie, My Ottie." Hal kissed the tears from her face, feeling their saltiness upon his lips. "You're here; you made it."

"We made it, Hal."

Ottie took a step back, clutching her belly. Hal held Tilda, she looked so small in his large arms.

"All four of us made it."

Ottie saw the surprise flash in Hal's grey eyes. He scooped her up again into his arms, tightening Tilda between them, and swung her around. The three of them reunited, spinning together in the heavy snow. Hal came to a stop. He held her back from him and took in her beautiful face—a face he had visualised every day he had been without her.

"C'mon love, let's go home. We'll have a nice cuppa back at Warten Way."

Epilogue

Tilda absentmindedly picked at the worn nylon cushion's bobbly fluff. Her eyes lifted to Hal's artwork, which clashed with the brown and orange wallpaper. The logs crackled, drawing her attention back to the ornate mantelpiece surrounding the fire. Tilda stood up to tidy her beehive hairstyle in its mirror. She licked her finger and neatened the kohl smudges around her eyes before applying a slick of frosted lipstick, finishing with a smack of her lips. She felt presentable until she looked down at the bulge where her waist used to be. Her turquoise dress rippled with the movement of the babies inside.

After getting over the initial shock of being pregnant, Tilda became even more focused. Motherhood was never something she had wished for. She wanted to pursue a career and see more of the world. She believed there was more to life than the dull seaside town she lived in. Tilda planned to raise her children alone. It was the sixties, and she felt no need to marry, although she knew her parents would struggle with this modern concept. She was determined to pursue her career and not be tied down to a life of domesticity.

The shrill of the doorbell reverberated through the house. Tilda heard the slap of Ottie's slippered feet plod toward the front door.

"Nella! Turn that music down!" Ottie yelled up the stairs.

Tilda heard the Rolling Stones lower in Nella's room and the four-pawed scurry of Kelly coming down the stairs, giving a deep bark as she did.

"Shoo! Go lay down." Ordered Ottie, brushing Kelly aside.

Ottie flung the front door wide open.

"Oh, it's you." She feigned surprise.

A large bunch of flowers stood in front of her. Ed cautiously peered at her from amongst the foliage. He glanced down at Ottie's feet, noticing her fluffy pink slippers and American tan tights. He shifted his gaze to the straight navy skirt and powder blue turtleneck, finishing with the crimson lipstick. Ottie remained steely-eyed. The large Alsatian pushed its head through the gap at her waist and bared its teeth. Ed unwittingly felt his Adam's apple rise into the back of his throat—the dog he considered the friendlier of the two.

"Go lay down, Kelly." Ordered Ottie.

Kelly gave a small whine and reversed into the hallway. Her head bowed down, she cast a sorrowful glance through the front room's open door at Tilda before obediently retiring to her basket.

"In," Ottie motioned with an impatient flick of her hand at Ed, "and wipe your feet."

"For you, Mrs Bennett." Ed held out the flowers toward Ottie's scowl. "Oh, and this is for your husband." Ed produced a bottle of whisky from behind his back.

"Huh, like this is enough," came Ottie's sharp reply as she snatched the gifts from Ed.

"Mamma, let's try to be nice about this," Tilda implored as she leaned against the hall door frame with her arms folded.

Ottie pushed past her, eager to put the expensive flowers in water. She would show them off when the girls came around later to play cards. Ottie let out an irritated huff.

"Where's your father? ...Hal!" She called out toward the back of the house.

"Sorry, Mum doesn't hold back on her emotions. It's an Italian thing." Tilda gave an apologetic shrug of her shoulders in Ed's direction.

"Well, from what you told me about her, I feel I have got off quite lightly." Ed smiled, searching Tilda's eyes for feedback.

"It's not over yet. Come in and take a seat."

Tilda hesitated briefly, feeling a knot form in her stomach. Was this the closure she needed—or just another complication? Tilda waved her hand toward the front room.

They sat opposite each other on the low three-piece suite, leaning forward, with their knees touching the glass-topped coffee table between them. Ed nodded at Tilda's bulging stomach.

"How's things?"

"I am fine, Ed. You don't need to worry about me."

"Oh, I do. Tilda..." Ed's hand extended tentatively toward her; his words stuck at his throat.

Just then, Ottie burst into the room, balancing a tray of tea adorned with her finest mismatched Royal Doulton china. The clatter of the teacups echoed through the room as she positioned the tray between the couple, shooting Ed a disapproving look as he hastily retreated in his seat.

Ottie began pouring the tea. The creak of the floorboards resounded faintly as heavy deliberate steps approached, each one more distinct as they drew nearer. Ed couldn't help but notice the four cups on the tray, and his gaze shifted expectantly toward the door. Anxious anticipation bubbled within him as he heard the floorboards creak and caught a glimpse of a shadow through the crack of the slightly ajar door. Ottie leaned over to pour the tea, as she spoke through the gap under her arm

"You took those muddy boots off?"

"Of course I have, Cara."

The warm tones of Hal filtered around the door. The doorway darkened as Hal's broad frame filled it, silhouetted against the soft afternoon light spilling through the kitchen. Ed looked up as Hal towered over them, his frame filling the doorway. Ed noticed Hal's thick black hair devoid of any grey. Hal continued wiping his soiled hands on a rag, before extending it out towards Ed. Ed awkwardly raised himself taking Hal's hand, which completely engulfed his own. Ed felt the roughness of a labourer's hand against his skin. Hal had a weathered, handsome face with eyes that held a steel-grey calmness, a shade Ed had only ever seen before in Tilda's eyes.

"You must be Ed."

"Mr Bennett, good to meet you," Ed reciprocated.

Ottie paused, glancing at Tilda with something that almost resembled understanding, a flicker of softened emotion quickly masked by her usual briskness. Ottie began handing out the tea. Tilda shuffled up the sofa to make room for her father. Ed felt Ottie's hips nudge him, and the seat rise as she sat beside him. He moved clumsily, pulling out his jacket from under her, which gave Ottie another reason to frown in his direction. The four of them sat in silence, holding onto their cups and saucers. Ed turned his face into the teacup, wanting to hide. Hal tore back the hush in the room as he set down his tea.

"So, you come far, Ed?"

"Oh, no, no, just ten minutes away."

"Huh, for goodness' sake!" Ottie interrupted.

She swung her head around to Ed, her dark, neat curls falling across her face with the momentum. Her voice fierce.

"What are you going to do, Ed, huh?" She shook her hands, palms up in frustration at him as she spoke.

"Now then, Cara, let's be civil. This is not the first time something like this has happened, as we well know..."

Hal scratched his head, paused, leaned forward, and rubbed his hands together, thoughtfully surveying the three expectant faces.

"Let's just..."

Tilda softly pleaded, "Dad..."

"*Maronna Mia*," interrupted Ottie, flicking her hand under her chin in a gesture of disgust.

Hal's gaze lingered on Tilda, understanding her silent plea. He sighed, letting the weight of the moment settle. Heeding Tilda's appeal, Hal sighed again, this time even more deeply.

"I best go finish digging up the spuds," he announced, lifting his frame from the sofa.

"Ma! Useless, the lot of ya!" Shouted Ottie.

Ottie's fist made the *mano fico* gesture, and she stormed off in the same direction as her husband.

"Well, that went well." Ed whispered behind his teacup.

"I think you best go now, Ed."

Ed opened his mouth as if to speak but stopped. Something in Tilda's voice told him there was no space left for questions, only acceptance. Ed's voice softened, tinged with quiet desperation.

"Tilda, I can help. What do you need?"

"I need you to go. Her words landed with finality, steady but not unkind. For the first time, she felt free—not from Ed, but from the past. This—us—it's not... it would never be more than it is."

Ed nervously chewed at his bottom lip and ran a finger along the inside of his polo neck before standing up. He straightened his slim-fit jacket and pulled down on the cuffs to neaten himself, ending with a self-assured shrug. Tilda no longer saw the confident man she'd once admired. Her initial attraction had faded, replaced by something colder. Understanding. She saw the rejection take effect, and he responded in kind.

"Lucky escape for both of us, I guess." He muttered.

Ed left without saying another word. She could hear him muttering under his breath as he wrestled with the stubborn door. By the time she awkwardly rose from her low chair, he had already figured it out. The force of the slamming door sent a gust of air through the house. Ottie hurried eagerly toward the door, her curiosity outweighing her restraint.

"We won't see him again if that's what you want to know." Tilda answered Ottie's unspoken question, her voice low.

In an unusual turn, Ottie responded with silence, her sharp tongue momentarily stilled. Tilda's face lit up with a smile, and she couldn't contain her laughter at the pure madness of the moment. Ottie's brows furrowed in confusion as she watched her daughter dissolve into laughter. Her laughter was infectious, rippling through the room until Ottie, despite herself, joined in.

Tilda felt a rush of freedom. Tears filled her eyes as her laughter echoed through the air, mingling with Ottie's chuckles and Kelly's howls. The joyous noise spilled through the house, breaking the long-held tension, as if even the walls themselves exhaled. They sensed the imminent arrival of Hal and Nella, lured in by the commotion.

Bill

Ersilia

Printed in Dunstable, United Kingdom